The People of
the River

GREENHILL
FAMOUS
AUTHORS

Edgar Wallace, *Sanders of the River*
John Galsworthy, *Uncollected Forsyte*
Joseph Conrad, *The Rover*
Arthur Conan Doyle, *The Great Shadow*
Edgar Wallace, *The People of the River*

The "Sanders of the River" books

EDGAR WALLACE

The People of the River

A "Sanders of the River" book

GREENHILL
FAMOUS
AUTHORS

This edition of
The People of the River
first published 1987 by Greenhill Books,
Lionel Leventhal Limited, 3 Barham Avenue, Elstree,
Hertfordshire, WD6 3PW

British Library Cataloguing in Publication Data
Wallace, Edgar
The People of the River: A "Sanders of the River" book. –
(Greenhill Famous Authors)
I. Title 823'.912 [F] PR6045.A327

ISBN 0-947898-54-9

Publishing History
The People of the River was first published in 1912
and this edition is complete and unabridged.

For information about Edgar Wallace write to
The Edgar Wallace Society,
7 Devonshire Close, Amersham, Bucks HP6 5JG.

Greenhill Books
welcome readers' suggestions for books that might be added
to this Series. Please write to us if there are titles
which you would like to recommend.

Printed by Antony Rowe Limited,
Chippenham, Wiltshire.

CONTENTS

To
SIR SAMUEL SCOTT, BART., M.P.

I

A CERTAIN GAME

SANDERS had been away on a holiday.

The Commissioner, whose work lay for the main part in wandering through a malarial country in some discomfort and danger, spent his holiday in travelling through another malarial country in as great discomfort and at no less risk. The only perceptible difference, so far as could be seen, between his work and his holiday was that instead of considering his own worries he had to listen to the troubles of somebody else.

Mr. Commissioner Sanders derived no small amount of satisfaction from such a vacation, which is a sure sign that he was most human.

His holiday was a long one, for he went by way of St. Paul de Loanda overland to the Congo, shot an elephant or two in the French Congo, went by mission steamer to the Sangar River and made his way back to Stanley Pool.

At Matadi he found letters from his relief, a mild youth who had come from headquarters to take his place as a temporary measure, and was quite satisfied in his inside mind that he was eminently qualified to occupy the seat of the Commissioner.

The letter was a little discursive, but Sanders read it as eagerly as a girl reads her first love letter. For he was reading about a land which was very dear to him.

"Umfebi, the headman of Kulanga, has given me a little trouble. He wants sitting on badly, and if I had control . . ." Sanders grinned unpleasantly and said something about "impertinent swine," but did he not refer to the erring Umfebi? "I find M'laka, the chief of the Little River, a very pleasant man to deal with: he was most attentive to me when I visited his

7

village and trotted out all his dancing girls for my amusement." Sanders made a little grimace. He knew M'laka for a rascal and wondered. "A chief who has been most civil and courteous is Bosambo of the Ochori. I know this will interest you because Bosambo tells me that he is a special protégé of yours. He tells me how you had paid for his education as a child and had gone to a lot of trouble to teach him the English language. I did not know of this."

Sanders did not know of it either, and swore an oath to the brazen sky to take this same Bosambo, thief by nature, convict by the wise provision of the Liberian Government, and chief of the Ochori by sheer effrontery, and kick him from one end of the city to the other.

"He is certainly the most civilised of your men," the letter went on. "He has been most attentive to the astronomical mission which came out in your absence to observe the eclipse of the moon. They speak very highly of his attention and he has been most active in his attempt to recover some of their property which was either lost or stolen on their way down the river."

Sanders smiled, for he himself had lost property in Bosambo's territory.

"I think I will go home," said Sanders.

Home he went by the nearest and the quickest way and came to headquarters early one morning, to the annoyance of his relief, who had planned a great and fairly useless palaver to which all the chiefs of all the land had been invited.

"For," he explained to Sanders in a grieved tone, "it seems to me that the only way to ensure peace is to get at the minds of these people, and the only method by which one can get at their minds is to bring them all together."

Sanders stretched his legs contemptuously and sniffed. They sat at chop on the broad stoep before the Commissioner's house, and Mr. Franks—so the deputy

Commissioner was named—was in every sense a guest. Sanders checked the vitriolic appreciation of the native mind which came readily to his lips, and inquired:

"When is this prec—when is this palaver?"

"This evening," said Franks.

Sanders shrugged his shoulders.

"Since you have gathered all these chiefs together," he said, "and they are present in my Houssa lines, with their wives and servants, eating my 'special expense' vote out of existence, you had better go through with it."

That evening the chiefs assembled before the residency, squatting in a semi-circle about the chair on which sat Mr. Franks—an enthusiastic young man with a very pink face and gold-mounted spectacles.

Sanders sat a little behind and said nothing, scrutinising the assembly with an unfriendly eye. He observed without emotion that Bosambo of the Ochori occupied the place of honour in the centre, wearing a leopard skin and loop after loop of glittering glass beads. He had ostrich feathers in his hair and bangles of polished brass about his arms and ankles and, chiefest abomination, suspended by a scarlet ribbon from that portion of the skin which covered his left shoulder, hung a large and elaborate decoration.

Beside him the kings and chiefs of other lands were mean, commonplace men. B'fari of the Larger Isisi, Kulala of the N'Gombi, Kandara of the Akasava, Etobi of the River-beyond-the-River, and a score of little kings and overlords might have been so many carriers.

It was M'laka of the Lesser Isisi who opened the palaver.

"Lord Franki," he began, "we are great chiefs who are as dogs before the brightness of your face, which is like the sun that sets through a cloud."

Mr. Franks, to whom this was interpreted, coughed and went pinker than ever.

"Now that you are our father," continued M'laka,

"and that Sandi has gone from us, though you have summoned him to this palaver to testify to your greatness, the land has grown fruitful, sickness has departed, and there is peace amongst us."

He avoided Sanders' cold eye whilst the speech was being translated.

"Now that Sandi has gone," M'laka went on with relish, "we are sorry, for he was a good man according to some, though he had not the great heart and the gentle spirit of our lord Franki."

This he said, and much more, especially with regard to the advisability of calling together the chiefs and headmen that they might know of the injustice of taxation, the hardship of life under certain heartless lords—here he looked at Sanders—and need for restoring the old powers of chiefs.

Other orations followed. It gave them great sorrow, they said, because Sandi, their lord, was going to leave them. Sandi observed that the blushing Mr. Franks was puzzled, and acquitted him of spreading the report of his retirement.

Then Bosambo, sometime of Monrovia, and now chief of the Ochori, from-the-border-of-the-river-to-the-mountains-by-the-forest.

"Lord Franki," he said, "I feel shame that I must say what I have to say, for you have been to me as a brother."

He said this much, and paused as one overcome by his feelings. Franks was doubly affected, but Sanders watched the man suspiciously.

"But Sandi was our father and our mother," said Bosambo; "in his arms he carried us across swift rivers, and with his beautiful body he shielded us from our enemies; his eyes were bright for our goodness and dim to our faults, and now that we must lose him my stomach is full of misery, and I wish I were dead."

He hung his head, shaking it slowly from side to side, and there were tears in his eyes when he lifted them. David lamenting Jonathan was no more woeful than Bosambo of Monrovia taking a mistaken farewell of his master.

"Franki is good," he went on, mastering himself with visible effort; "his face is very bright and pretty, and he is as innocent as a child; his heart is pure, and he has no cunning."

Franks shifted uneasily in his seat as the compliment was translated.

"And when M'laka speaks to him with a tongue of oil," said Bosambo, "lo! Franki believes him, though Sandi knows that M'laka is a liar and a breaker of laws, who poisoned his brother in Sandi's absence and is unpunished."

M'laka half rose from his seat and reached for his elephant sword.

"Down!" snarled Sanders; his hand went swiftly to his jacket pocket, and M'laka cowered.

"And when Kulala of the N'Gombi raids into Alamandy territory stealing girls, our lord is so gentle of spirit——"

"Liar and dog and eater of fish!"

The outraged Kulala was on his feet, his fat figure shaking with wrath.

But Sanders was up now, stiffly standing by his relief, and a gesture sent insulter and insulted squatting to earth.

All that followed was Greek to Mr. Franks, because nobody troubled to translate what was said.

"It seems to me," said Sanders, "that I may divide my chiefs into three parts, saying this part is made of rogues, this part of fools, and this, and the greater part, of people who are rogues in a foolish way. Now I know only one of you who is a pure rogue, and that is Bosambo of the Ochori, and for the rest you are like children.

"For when Bosambo spread the lie that I was leaving you, and when the master Franki called you together, you, being simpletons, who throw your faces to the shadows, thought, 'Now this is the time to speak evilly of Sandi and well of the new master.' But Bosambo, who is a rogue and a liar, has more wisdom than all of you, for the cunning one has said, 'I will speak well of Sandi, knowing that he will stay with us; and Sandi, hearing me, will love me for my kindness.'"

For one of the few times of his life Bosambo was embarrassed, and looked it.

"To-morrow," said Sanders, "when I come from my house, I wish to see no chief or headman, for the sight of you already makes me violently ill. Rather I would prefer to hear from my men that you are hurrying back with all speed to your various homes. Later, I will come and there will be palavers—especially in the matter of poisoning. The palaver is finished."

He walked into the house with Franks, who was not quite sure whether to be annoyed or apologetic.

"I am afraid my ideas do not exactly tally with yours," he said, a little ruefully.

Sanders smiled kindly.

"My dear chap," he said, "nobody's ideas really tally with anybody's! Native folk are weird folk—that is why I know them. I am a bit of a weird bird myself."

When he had settled his belongings in their various places the Commissioner sent for Bosambo, and that worthy came, stripped of his gaudy furnishings, and sat humbly on the stoep before Sanders.

"Bosambo," he said briefly, "you have the tongue of a monkey that chatters all the time."

"Master, it is good that monkeys chatter," said the crestfallen chief, "otherwise the hunter would never catch them."

"That may be," said Sanders; "but if their chattering attracts bigger game to stalk the hunter, then they are dangerous beasts. You shall tell me later about the poisoning of M'laka's brother; but first you shall say why you desire to stand well with me. You need not lie, for we are men talking together."

Bosambo met his master's eye fearlessly.

"Lord," he said, "I am a little chief of a little people. They are not of my race, yet I govern them wisely. I have made them a nation of fighters where they were a nation of women."

Sanders nodded.

"All this is true; if it were not so, I should have removed you long since. This you know. Also that I have reason to be grateful to you for certain happenings."

"Lord," said Bosambo, earnestly, "I am no beggar for favours, for I am, as you know, a Christian, being acquainted with the blessed Peter and the blessed Paul and other holy saints which I have forgotten. But I am a better man than all these chiefs and I desire to be a king."

"How much?" asked the astonished Sanders.

"A king, lord," said Bosambo, unashamed; "for I am fitted for kingship, and a witch doctor in the Kroo country, to whom I dashed a bottle of gin, predicted I should rule vast lands."

"Not this side of heaven," said Sanders decisively. He did not say "heaven," but let that pass.

Bosambo hesitated.

"Ochori is a little place and a little people," he said, half to himself; "and by my borders sits M'laka, who rules a large country three times as large and very rich——"

Sanders clicked his lips impatiently, then the humour of the thing took possession of him.

"Go you to M'laka," he said, with a little inward grin, "say to him all that you have said to me. If M'laka will deliver his kingdom into your hands I shall be content."

"Lord," said Bosambo, "this I will do, for I am a man of great attainments and have a winning way."

With the dignity of an emperor's son he stalked through the garden and disappeared.

The next morning Sanders said good-bye to Mr. Franks—a coasting steamer gave the Commissioner an excuse for hurrying him off. The chiefs had departed at sunrise, and by the evening life had resumed its normal course for Sanders.

It ran smoothly for two months, at the end of which time M'laka paid a visit to his brother-in-law, Kulala, a chief of N'Gombi, and a man of some importance, since he was lord of five hundred spears, and famous hunters.

They held a palaver which lasted the greater part of a week, and at the end there was a big dance.

It was more than a coincidence that on the last day of the palaver two shivering men of the Ochori were led into the village by their captors and promptly sacrificed.

The dance followed.

The next morning M'laka and his relative went out against the Ochori, capturing on their way a man whom M'laka denounced as a spy of Sandi's. Him they did to death in a conventional fashion, and he died uncomplainingly. Then they rested three days.

M'laka and his men came to the Ochori city at daybreak, and held a brief palaver in the forest.

"Now news of this will come to Sandi," he said; "and Sandi, who is a white devil, will come with his soldiers, and we will say that we were driven to do this because Bosambo invited us to a dance, and then endeavoured to destroy us."

"Bosambo would have destroyed us," chanted the assembly faithfully.

"Further, if we kill all the Ochori, we will say that it was not our people who did the killing, but the Akasava."

"Lord, the killing was done by the Akasava," they chanted again.

Having thus arranged both an excuse and an alibi, M'laka led his men to their quarry.

In the grey light of dawn the Ochori village lay defenceless. No fires spluttered in the long village street, no curl of smoke uprose to indicate activity.

M'laka's army in one long, irregular line went swiftly across the clearing which separated the city from the forest.

"Kill!" breathed M'laka; and along the ranks the order was taken up and repeated.

Nearer and nearer crept the attackers; then from a hut on the outskirts of the town stepped Bosambo, alone.

He walked slowly to the centre of the street, and M'laka saw:

In a thin-legged tripod something straight and shining and ominous.

Something that caught the first rays of the sun as they topped the trees of the forest, and sent them flashing and gleaming back again.

Six hundred fighting men of the N'Gombi checked and halted dead at the sight of it. Bosambo touched the big brass cylinder with his hand and turned it carelessly on its swivel until it pointed in the direction of M'laka, who was ahead of the others, and no more than thirty paces distant.

As if to make assurance doubly sure, he stooped and glanced along the polished surface, and M'laka dropped his short spear at his feet and raised his hands.

"Lord Bosambo," he said mildly, "we come in peace."

"In peace you shall go," said Bosambo, and whistled.

The city was suddenly alive with armed men. From every hut they came into the open.

"I love you as a man loves his goats," said M'laka fervently; "I saw you in a dream, and my heart led me to you."

"I, too, saw you in a dream," said Bosambo; "therefore I arose to meet you, for M'laka, the king of the Lesser Isisi, is like a brother to me."

M'laka, who never took his eyes from the brass-coated cylinder, had an inspiration.

"This much I beg of you, master and lord," he said; "this I ask, my brother, that my men may be allowed to come into your city and make joyful sacrifices, for that is the custom."

Bosambo scratched his chin reflectively.

"This I grant," he said; "yet every man shall leave his spear, stuck head downwards into earth—which is our custom before sacrifice."

M'laka shifted his feet awkwardly. He made the two little double-shuffle steps which native men make when they are embarrassed.

Bosambo's hand went slowly to the tripod.

"It shall be as you command," said M'laka hastily; and gave the order.

Six hundred dejected men, unarmed, filed through the village street, and on either side of them marched a line of Ochori warriors—who were not without weapons. Before Bosambo's hut M'laka, his brother-in-law, Kulala, his headmen, and the headmen of the Ochori, sat to conference which was half meal and half palaver.

"Tell me, Lord Bosambo," asked M'laka, "how does it come about that Sandi gives you the gun that says 'Ha-ha-ha'? For it is forbidden that the chiefs and people of this land should be armed with guns."

Bosambo nodded.

"Sandi loves me," he said simply, "for reasons which I should be a dog to speak of, for does not the same blood run in his veins that runs in mine?"

"That is foolish talk," said Kulala, the brother-in-law; "for he is white and you are black."

"None the less it is true," said the calm Bosambo; "for he is my cousin, his brother having married my mother, who was a chief's daughter. Sandi wished to marry her," he went on reminiscently; "but there are matters which it is shame to talk about. Also he gave me these."

From beneath the blanket which enveloped his shoulders he produced a leather wallet. From this he took a little package. It looked like a short, stumpy bato. Slowly he removed its wrapping of fine native cloth, till there were revealed three small cups of wood. In shape they favoured the tumbler of commerce, in size they were like very large thimbles.

Each had been cut from a solid piece of wood, and was of extreme thinness. They were fitted one inside the other when he removed them from the cloth, and now he separated them slowly and impressively.

At a word, a man brought a stool from the tent and placed it before him.

Over this he spread the wisp of cloth and placed the cups thereon upside down.

From the interior of one he took a small red ball of copal and camwood kneaded together.

Fascinated, the marauding chiefs watched him.

"These Sandi gave me," said Bosambo, "that I might pass the days of the rains pleasantly; with these I play with my headman."

"Lord Bosambo," said M'laka, "how do you play?"

Bosambo looked up to the warm sky and shook his head sadly.

"This is no game for you, M'laka," he said, addressing the heavens; "but for one whose eyes are very quick to see; moreover, it is a game played by Christians."

Now the Isisi folk pride themselves on their keenness of vision. Is it not a proverb of the River, "The N'Gombi to hear, the Bushman to smell, the Isisi to see, and the Ochori to run"?

"Let me see what I cannot see," said M'laka; and, with a reluctant air, Bosambo put the little red ball on the improvised table behind the cup.

2

"Watch then, M'laka! I put this ball under this cup: I move the cup——"

Very leisurely he shifted the cups.

"I have seen no game like this," said M'laka; and contempt was in his voice.

"Yet it is a game which pleased me and my men of bright eyes," said Bosambo; "for we wager so much rods against so much salt that no man can follow the red ball."

The chief of the Lesser Isisi knew where the red ball was, because there was a slight scratch on the cup which covered it.

"Lord Bosambo," he said, quoting a saying, "only the rat comes to dinner and stays to ravage—yet if I did not sit in the shadow of your hut, I would take every rod from you."

"The nukusa is a small animal, but he has a big voice," said Bosambo, giving saying for saying; "and I would wager you could not uncover the red ball."

M'laka leant forward.

"I will stake the spears of my warriors against the spears of the Ochori," he said.

Bosambo nodded.

"By my head," he said.

M'laka stretched forward his hand and lifted the cup, but the red ball was not there. Rather it was under the next cup, as Bosambo demonstrated.

M'laka stared.

"I am no blind man," he said roughly; "and your tongue is like the burning of dry sticks—clack, clack, clack!"

Bosambo accepted the insult without resentment.

"It is the eye," he said meditatively; "we Ochori folk see quickly."

M'laka swallowed an offensive saying.

"I have ten bags of salt in my house," he said shortly, "and it shall be my salt against the spears you have won."

"By my heart and life," said Bosambo, and put the ball under the cup.

Very lazily he moved the cup to and fro, changing their positions.

"My salt against your spears," said M'laka exultantly, for he saw now which was the cup. It had a little stain near the rim.

Bosambo nodded, and M'laka leant forward and lifted the cup. But the ball was not there.

M'laka drew a deep breath, and swore by Iwa—which is death—and by devils of kinds unknown; by sickness and by his father—who had been hanged, and was in consequence canonised.

"It is the eye," said Bosambo sadly; "as they say by the River, 'The Ochori to see——' "

"That is a lie!" hissed M'laka; "the Ochori see nothing but the way they run. Make this game again——"

And again Bosambo covered the red ball; but this time he bungled, for he placed the cup which covered the ball on an uneven place on the stool. And between the rim of the cup and the cloth there was a little space where a small ball showed redly—and M'laka was not blind.

"Bosambo," he said, holding himself, "I wager big things, for I am a chief of great possessions, and you are a little chief, yet this time I will wager my all."

"M'laka of the Isisi," responded Bosambo slowly, "I also am a great chief and a relative by marriage to Sandi. Also I am a God-man speaking white men's talk and knowing of Santa Antonio, Marki, Luki, the blessed Timothi, and similar magics. Now this shall be the wager; if you find a red ball you shall find a slave whose name is Bosambo of the Ochori, but if you lose the red one you shall lose your country."

"May the sickness *mongo* come to me if I do not speak the truth," swore M'laka, "but to all this I agree."

He stretched out his hand and touched the cup.

"It is here!" he shouted and lifted the cover.

There was no red ball.

M'laka was on his feet breathing quickly through his nose.

He opened his mouth to speak, but there was no need, for an Ochori runner came panting through the street with news; before he could reach the hut where his overlord sat and tell it, the head of Sanders' column emerged from the forest path.

It is said that "the smell of blood carries farther than a man can see." It had been a tactical error to kill one of Sanders' spies.

The Commissioner was stained and soiled and he was unshaven, for the call of war had brought him by forced marches through the worst forest path in the world.

Into the open strode the column, line after line of blue-coated Houssas, bare-legged, sandal-footed, scarlet-headed, spreading out as smoke spreads when it comes from a narrow barrel. Forming in two straggling lines, it felt its way cautiously forward, for the Ochori city might hold an enemy.

Bosambo guessed the meaning of the demonstration and hurried forward to meet the Commissioner. At a word from Sanders the lines halted, and midway between the city and the wood they met—Bosambo and his master.

"Lord," said Bosambo conventionally, "all that I have is yours."

"It seems that you have your life, which is more than I expected," said Sanders. "I know that M'laka, chief of the Lesser Isisi, is sheltering in your village. You shall deliver this man to me for judgment."

"M'laka, I know," said Bosambo, carefully, "and he shall be delivered; but when you speak of the chief of the Lesser Isisi you speak of me, for I won all his lands by a certain game."

"We will talk of that later," said Sanders.

He led his men to the city, posting them on its four sides, then he followed Bosambo to where M'laka and his headman awaited his coming—for the guest of a chief does not come out to welcome other guests.

"M'laka," said Sanders, "there are two ways with chiefs who kill the servants of Government. One is a high and short way, as you know."

M'laka's eyes sought a possible tree, and he shivered.

"The other way," said Sanders, "is long and tiresome, and that is the way for you. You shall sit down in the Village of Irons for my King's pleasure."

"Master, how long?" asked M'laka in a shaky voice.

"Whilst you live," said Sanders.

M'laka accepted what was tantamount to penal servitude for life philosophically—for there are worse things.

"Lord," he said, "you have always hated me. Also you have favoured other chiefs and oppressed me. Me, you deny all privilege; yet to Bosambo, your uncle——"

Sanders drew a long breath.

"——you give many favours, such as guns."

"If my word had not been given," said Sanders coldly, "I should hang you, M'laka, for you are the father of liars and the son of liars. What guns have I given Bosambo?"

"Lord, that is for you to see," said M'laka and jerked his head to the terrifying tripod.

Sanders walked towards the instrument.

"Bosambo," he said, with a catch in his voice, "I have in mind three white men who came to see the moon."

"Lord, that is so," said Bosambo cheerfully; "they were mad, and they looked at the moon through this thing; also at stars."

He pointed to the innocent telescope. "And this they lost?" said Sanders.

Bosambo nodded.

"It was lost by them and found by an Ochori man who brought it to me," said Bosambo. "Lord, I have not hidden it, but placed it here where all men can see it."

Sanders scanned the horizon. To the right of the forest was a broad strip of marshland, beyond, blurred blue in the morning sunlight rose the little hill that marks the city of the Lesser Isisi.

He stooped down to the telescope and focused it upon the hill. At its foot was a cluster of dark huts.

"Look," he said, and Bosambo took his place. "What do you see?" asked Sanders.

"The city of the Lesser Isisi," said Bosambo.

"Look well," said Sanders, "but that is the city you have won by a certain game."

Bosambo shifted uncomfortably.

"When I come to my new city——" he began.

"I also will come," said Sanders significantly. On the stool before the huts the three little wooden cups still stood, and Sanders had seen them, also the red ball. "To-morrow I shall appoint a new chief to the Lesser Isisi. When the moon is at full I shall come to see the new chief," he said, "and if he has lost his land by 'a certain game' I shall appoint two more chiefs, one for the Isisi and one for the Ochori, and there will be sorrow amongst the Ochori, for Bosambo of Monrovia will be gone from them."

"Lord," said Bosambo, making one final effort for Empire, "you said that if M'laka gave, Bosambo should keep."

Sanders picked up the red ball and slipped it under one cup. He changed their positions slightly.

"If your game is a fair game," he said, "show me the cup with the ball."

"Lord, it is the centre one," said Bosambo without hesitation.

Sanders raised the cup.

There was no ball.

"I see," said Bosambo slowly, "I see that my lord Sandi is also a Christian."

*　　*　　*　　*　　*

"It was a jest," explained Bosambo to his headmen when Sanders had departed; "thus my lord Sandi always jested even when I nursed him as a child. Menchimis, let the lokali sound and the people be brought together for a greater palaver and I will tell them the story of Sandi, who is my half-brother by another mother . . ."

II

THE ELOQUENT WOMAN

THERE was a woman of the N'Gombi people who had a suave tongue. When she spoke men listened eagerly, for she was of the kind peculiar to no race, being born with stirring words.

She stirred the people of her own village to such effect that they went one night and raided French territory, bringing great shame to her father; for Sanders came hurriedly north, and there were some summary whippings, and nearly a burying. Thereupon her father thought it wise to marry this woman to a man who could check her tongue.

So he married her to a chief, who was of the N'Gombi folk, and this chief liked her so much that he made her his principal wife, building a hut for her next to his. About her neck he had fixed a ring of brass, weighing some twenty-four pounds—a great distinction which his other wives envied.

This principal wife was nearly fifteen years old— which is approaching middle age on the River—and was, in consequence, very wise in the ways of men. Too wise, some thought, and certainly her lord had cause for complaint when, returning from a hunting expedition a day or two before he could possibly return, he found his wife more happy than was to his liking and none too lonely.

"M'fashimbi," he said, as she knelt before him with her arms folded meekly on her bare, brown bosom, "in the days of my father I should bend down a stripling tree and rope your neck to it, and when your head was struck from your body I should burn you and he that made me ashamed. But that is not the law of the white man, and I think you are too worthless a woman for me to risk my neck upon."

"Lord, I am of little good," she said.

For a whole day she lay on the ground surrounded by the whole of the village, to whom she talked whilst the workmen sawed away at the brass collar. At the end of that time the collar was removed from her neck, and the chief sent her back to the parent from whom he had most expensively bought her. He sent her back in the face of great opposition, for she had utilised her time profitably and the village was so moved by her eloquence that it was ripe for rebellion.

For no woman is put away from her man, whether she wears the feathers and silks of Paris or the camwood and oil of the N'Gombi, without harbouring for that man a most vengeful and hateful feeling, and no sooner had M'fashimbi paddled clear of her husband's village than she set herself the task of avenging herself upon him.

There accompanied her into exile the man with whom, and for whom, she had risked and lost so much. He was named Otapo, and he was a dull one.

As they paddled, she, kneeling in the canoe behind him, said:

"Otapo, my husband has done me a great wrong and put dust on my head, yet you say nothing."

"Why should I speak when you have spoken so much?" asked Otapo calmly. "I curse the day I ever saw you, M'fashimbi, for my error has cost me a fishing-net, which was the best in the village, also a new piece of cloth I bought from a trader; these our lord chief has taken."

"If you had the heart of a man you would have killed Namani, my husband," she said.

"I have killed myself and lost my net," said Otapo; "also my piece of cloth."

"You are like a woman," she jeered.

"I could wish that my mother had borne a girl when she bore me," said Otapo, "then I should not have been disgraced."

She paddled in silence for a while, and then she said of a sudden:

"Let us go to the bank, for I have hidden some treasures of my husband near this spot."

Otapo turned the head of the canoe to the shore with one long stroke.

As they neared the bank she reached behind her and found a short spear, such as you use for hunting animals where the grass is thick.

She held it in both hands, laying the point on a level with the second rib beneath his shoulder blade.

As the prow of the canoe grounded gently on the sandy shore she drove her spear forward with all her might.

Otapo half rose like a man who was in doubt whether he would rise or not, then he tumbled languidly into the shallow water.

M'fashimbi waded to the shore, first securing the canoe, then she guided the body to land, and exerting all her strength, drew it to a place beneath some trees.

"Otapo, you are dead," she said to the figure, "and you are better dead than living, for by your death you shall revenge me, as living you feared to do."

She took the spear and flung it a few yards farther off from where the body lay. Then she got into the canoe, washed away such bloodstains as appeared on its side, and paddled downstream.

In a day's time she came to her father's village, wailing.

She wailed so loud and so long that the village heard her before she reached the shore and came out to meet her. Her comely body she had smeared with ashes, about her waist hung long green leaves, which is a sign of sorrow; but her grief she proclaimed long and loud, and her father, who was the chief of the village, said to his elders, as with languid strokes—themselves eloquent of her sorrow—she brought her canoe to land:

"This woman is either mad or she has suffered some great wrong."

He was soon to learn, for she came running up to the bank towards him and fell before him, clasping his feet.

"Ewa! Death to my husband, Namani, who has lied about me and beaten me, O father of fathers!" she cried.

"Woman," said the father, "what is this?"

She told him a story—an outrageous story. Also, which was more serious, she told a story of the killing of Otapo.

"This man, protecting me, brought me away from my husband, who beat me," she sobbed, "and my husband followed, and as we sat at a meal by the bank of the river, behold my husband stabbed him from behind. Oe ai!"

And she rolled in the dust at her father's feet.

The chief was affected, for he was of superior rank to Namani and, moreover, held the peace of that district for my lord the Commissioner.

"This is blood and too great a palaver for me," he said, "and, moreover, you being my daughter, it may be thought that I do not deal justice fairly as between man and man."

So he embarked on his canoe and made for Isau, where Sanders was.

The Commissioner was recovering from an attack of malarial fever, and was not pleased to see the chief. Less pleased was he when he heard the story the "Eloquent Woman" had to tell.

"I will go to the place of killing and see what is to be seen." He went on board the *Zaire*, and with steam up the little stern-wheeler made post-haste for the spot indicated by the woman. He landed where the marks of the canoe's prow still showed on the soft sand, for hereabouts the river neither rises nor falls perceptibly in the course of a month.

He followed the woman into the wood, and here he saw all that was mortal of Otapo; and he saw the spear.

M'fashimbi watched him closely.

"Lord," she said with a whimper, "here it was that Namani slew the young man Otapo as we sat at food."

Sanders' keen eyes surveyed the spot.

"I see no sign of a fire," said Sanders suddenly.

"A fire, lord?" she faltered.

"Where people sit at food they build a fire," said Sanders shortly, "and here no fire has been since the beginning of the world."

He took her on board again and went steaming up-stream to the village of Namani.

"Go you," he said to the Houssa sergeant privately, "and if the chief does not come to meet me, arrest him, and if he does come you shall take charge of his huts and his women."

Namani was waiting to greet him and Sanders ordered him on board.

"Namani," said Sanders, "I know you as an honest man, and no word has been spoken against you. Now this woman, your wife, sayest you are a murderer, having killed Otapo."

"She is a liar!" said Namani calmly. "I know nothing of Otapo."

A diligent inquiry which lasted two days failed to incriminate the chief. It served rather to inflict some damage upon the character of M'fashimbi; but in a land where women have lovers in great numbers she suffered little.

At the end of the two days Sanders delivered judgment.

"I am satisfied Otapo is dead," he said; "for many reasons I am not satisfied that Namani killed him. I am in no doubt that M'fashimbi is a woman of evil acts and a great talker, so I shall banish her to a far country amongst strangers."

He took her on board his steamer, and the *Zaire* cast off.

In twenty-four hours he came to the "city of the forest," which is the Ochori city, and at the blast of his steamer's siren the population came running to the beach.

Bosambo, chief of the Ochori, was the last to arrive, for he came in procession under a scarlet umbrella, wearing a robe of tinselled cloth and having before him ten elder men bearing tinselled sticks.

Sanders watched the coming of the chief from the bridge of the steamer and his face betrayed no emotion. When Bosambo was come on board the Commissioner asked him:

"What childish folly is this, Bosambo?"

"Lord," said Bosambo, "thus do great kings come to greater kings, for I have seen certain pictures in a book which the god-woman gave me and by these I know the practice."

"Thus also do people dress themselves when they go out to make the foolish laugh," said Sanders unpleasantly. "Now I have brought you a woman who talks too much, and who has been put away by one man and has murdered another by my reckoning, and I desire that she shall live in your village."

"Lord, as you say," said the obedient Bosambo, and regarded the girl critically.

"Let her marry as she wishes," said Sanders; "but she shall be of your house, and you shall be responsible for her safe keeping until then."

"Lord, she shall be married this night," said Bosambo earnestly.

When Sanders had left and the smoke of the departing steamer had disappeared behind the trees, Bosambo summoned his headman and his captains to palaver.

"People," he said, "the Lord Sandi, who loves me dearly, has come bringing presents—behold this woman." He waved his hand to the sulky girl who stood by his side on the little knoll where the palaver house stood.

"She is the most beautiful of all the women of the N'Gombi," said Bosambo, "and her name is N'lami-n'safo, which means the Pearl, and Sandi paid a great price for her, for she dances like a leopard at play, and has many loving qualities."

The girl knew enough of the unfamiliar Ochori dialect to realise that her merits were being extolled, and she shifted her feet awkwardly.

"She is a wife of wives," said Bosambo impressively, "gentle and kind and tender, a great cooker of manioc, and a teller of stories—yet I may not marry her, for I have many wives and I am wax in their hands. So you shall take her, you who pay readily and fearlessly, for you buy that which is more precious than goats or salt."

For ten goats and a thousand rods this "gift" of Sandi's passed into the possession of his headman.

Talking to his chief wife of these matters, Bosambo said:

"Thus is Sandi obeyed; thus also am I satisfied; all things are according to God's will."

"If you had taken her Mahomet," said the wife, who was a Kano woman and a true believer, "you would have been sorry."

"Pearl of bright light," said Bosambo humbly, "you are the first in my life, as God knows; for you I have deserted all other gods, believing in the one beneficent and merciful; for you also I have taken an umbrella of state after the manner of the Kano kings."

The next day Bosambo went hunting in the forest and did not return till a week was past.

It is the practice of the Ochori people, as it is of other tribes, to go forth to meet their chief on his return from hunting, and it was strange that none came to greet him with the Song of the Elephant.

With his twenty men he came almost unnoticed to his own hut.

Half-way along the village street he came upon an elder man, who ran to him.

"Lord," he said, "go not near the hut of Fabadimo, your chief headman."

"Has he sickness?" asked Bosambo.

"Worse, lord," said the old cynic. "He has a wife, and for six days and the greater part of six nights all the city has sat at her feet listening."

"What talk does she make?" asked Bosambo.

"Lord, she talks so that all things are clear," said the old man; "and all her words have meanings; and she throws a light like the very sun upon dark brains, and they see with her."

Bosambo had twenty men with him, men he could trust. The darkness was coming on, and at the far end of the city he could see the big fire where the "Eloquent Woman" talked and talked and talked.

He went first to his hut. He found his Kano wife alone, for the other women of his house had fled.

"Lord, I did not expect to see you alive," she said, "so I waited for death when the time came."

"That shall be many years away," said Bosambo.

He sent her with two of his men to the woods to wait his coming, then the rest of the party, in twos and threes, made their way to the outskirt of the throng before his headman's hut.

It was admirably placed for a forum. It stood on the crest of a sharp rise, flanked on either side by other huts.

Half-way down the slope a big fire blazed, and the leaping flames lit the slim figure that stood with arms outstretched before the hut.

". . . Who made you the slaves of a slave—the slave of Bosambo? Who gave him power to say 'Go forth' or 'Remain'? None. For he is a man like you, no different in make, no keener of eye, and if you stab him with a spear, will he not die just as you will die?

"And Sandi, is he not a man, though white? Is he stronger than Efambi or Elaki or Yako? Now I say to you that you will not be a free people whilst Bosambo lives or Sandi lives."

Bosambo was a man with keen animal instincts. He felt the insurrection in the air; he received through every tingling nerve the knowledge that his people were out of hand. He did not hesitate.

A solid mass of people stood between him and the woman. He could not reach her.

Never taking his eyes from her, he put his hand beneath his shield and drew his throwing spear. He had space for the swing; balanced and quivering, it lay on his open palm, his arm extended to the fullest.

"Whew-w!"

The light lance flickered through the air quicker than eye could follow.

But she had seen the outstretched arm and recognised the thrower, and leapt on one side.

The spear struck the man who stood behind her—
and Fabadimo, the chief headman, died without
speaking.

"Bosambo!" screamed the girl, and pointed.
"Bosambo, kill—kill!"

He heard the rustle of disengaging spears, and fled
into the darkness.

*   *   *   *   *

Sanders, at headquarters, was lying in a hammock
swung between a pole of his verandah and a hook-
fastened to the wall of his bungalow. He was reading,
or trying to read, a long and offensive document from
headquarters. It had to do with a census return made
by Sanders, and apparently this return had fallen short
in some respects.

Exactly how, Sanders never discovered, for he fell
asleep three times in his attempt and the third time he
was awakened by his orderly, who carried a tired
pigeon in his hand.

"Master, here is a book,"* said the man.

Sanders was awake instantly and out of his hammock in a second.

Fastened about one red leg of the bird by a long
india-rubber band was a paper twice the size of a cigarette paper and of the same texture. He smoothed it out.

Written in copying pencil were a few words in
Arabic:

"From Abiboo, the servant of God, to Sandi, the
ever-wakeful father of his people.

"Peace be to you and on your house. Declaring that
there is but one God, the true and indivisible, I send
you news that the woman you gave to Bosambo is
causing great trouble. This has come to me by messengers, Bosambo having fled with twenty men to the
edge of the Isisi country.

"Written at a place on the Isisi River, where there

_____
* Any written thing—a letter, a note.

are three crocodile creeks meeting in the form of an arrow."

Now Abiboo had been left in the village from which M'fashimbi had been ejected. He had been left to clear up the mystery of Otapo's death and he was not a man easily alarmed.

Pulling on his mosquito boots, Sanders walked over to the house occupied by the officer of Houssa.

He found that gentleman sipping tea in solitary state.

"I shall want you," said Sanders; "there's a dust-up in the Ochori country."

The officer raised his eyebrows. He was a young man on the cynical side of twenty-five.

"Not the gentle Bosambo," he protested ironically; "not that mirror of chivalry?"

"Don't be comic, my man," snarled Sanders. "The Ochori are up, and there is a lady missionary somewhere on the border."

The Houssa captain sprang to his feet.

"Bless the woman, I forgot her!" he said in a worried tone. He took a whistle from his breast pocket and blew it, and a bare-legged bugler raced across the little parade ground from the guard hut.

"Ta-ta-ta!" said the Houssa captain, and the quavering note of the assembly sounded.

"What is the palaver?" demanded the officer, and briefly Sanders related the circumstances.

With a full head of steam the little *Zaire* pushed her way up-stream. Day and night she steamed till she came to the place "where three crocodile creeks meet in the form of an arrow," and here Sanders stopped to relieve Abiboo and his handful of Houssas.

Sanders learnt with relief that the fighting had not threatened the mission stations.

"What of Bosambo?" he asked.

"Living or dead, I do not know," said Abiboo philosophically; "and if he is dead he died a believer, for the Kano woman he took to wife is a believer in the one Allah and of Mahmut, his prophet."

"All this may be true," said Sanders patiently, "yet I am less concerned by his prospects of immortality than the present disposition of his body."

About this Abiboo could tell him nothing, save that ten miles farther on Bosambo had held an island in the middle of the river, and that up to two days before he was still holding it.

Hereabouts the river twists and turns, and there was no sight of the middle island till the *Zaire* came curving round a sharp bend.

"Stand by those maxims!" said Sanders sharply.

The Houssa captain sank on the saddle seat of one little brass-coated gun, and Abiboo took the other.

The water was alive with canoes.

The Ochori were attacking the island; the thunder of the *Zaire's* wheel drowned all sound.

"They're fighting all right," said the captain. "What do you say, Sanders?"

Sanders, with his hands on the wheel, waited, his eyes fixed ahead.

Now he saw clearly. A party had landed, and there was fierce hand-to-hand fighting.

"Let 'em go," he said, and two trembling pencils of flame leapt from the guns.

For answer the canoes formed like magic into first two, then three, then four lines, and down stream they came at a furious rate.

Then one of the maxims jammed and as it did there came a shower of spears, one of which just missed Sanders.

In an instant the little boat was surrounded—the magic of the maxim had failed for the first time on the big river. It was so unexpected, so inexplicable, that a man might be excused if he lost his head; but Sanders' hand did not tremble as he swung the wheel over, and the steamer turned in a full circle.

The Houssas were shooting point-blank with their carbines; the Houssa captain, bleeding from the head, was re-adjusting the breech-lock of the maxim without concern.

Down-stream at full speed went the *Zaire*. The canoes could not keep up with it save one that had fastened itself to the side; the Houssas bayoneted the occupants without asking or accepting explanation.

"I've got the gun fixed," said the Houssa officer as he slipped in a fresh belt of cartridges.

Sanders nodded. A word to the steersman and the *Zaire* turned. She came back towards the lines of canoes, her maxim firing steadily.

The second line wavered and broke; the third never formed. In the centre of the fleeing canoes was one larger than another. At the stern stood a woman, waving her arms and talking.

"Abiboo," said Sanders, and the Houssa turned his gun over to a comrade and came to his master. "Do you see that woman in the canoe?"

"Lord, I see her," said Abiboo.

"It seems to me," said Sanders gravely, "that this woman would be better dead."

He rang the telegraph to stop, and the grind of the engines ceased. The *Zaire* moved slowly forward without a tremble, and Abiboo, lying on the deck with the butt of his rifle pressed to his cheek, took careful aim.

*　　*　　*　　*　　*

They found Bosambo conscious beneath a heap of dead. He lay across the Kano woman, who was also alive, for Bosambo had taken the spear-thrusts meant for her.

He had, as Sanders counted, twenty-five wounds.

"Lord," he whispered as Sanders stood by his side, "did I not tell you the Ochoris could fight?"

"They have fought to some purpose, my child," said Sanders grimly.

Bosambo grinned faintly.

"Lord," he said softly, "when I go back to them they will be sorry."

And sorry indeed they were, as I will tell you.

III

THE AFFAIR OF THE LADY MISSIONARY

THE house of De Silva, Mackiney and Company is not so well known as, say, the Rockefeller or the house of Marshall Field; nor does it inspire the same confidence in circles of world-finance as, say, the house of Rothschild or Pierpoint Morgan. Yet on the coast De Silva and Mackiney (where they dug up the last ethnological abomination, I know not) held a position analogous to all the houses I have named in combination. They were the Rothschilds, the Marshall Fields, the Pierpoint Morgans, of that particular coast. It is said that they put up a proposition that they should coin their own money, but a conservative government—with a small "c"—politely declined to sanction the suggestion.

They had a finger in all the pies that were baked in that part of the world. They had interests in steamship companies, controlled banks, financed exploration and exploitation companies, helped in the creation of railways, floated gold mines, but before and above all, they sold things to the natives and received in exchange other things of infinitely greater value than they gave. The trading store and the trading caravan were the foundation of the house of De Silva and Mackiney—De Silva had long since retired from the business, and was the Marquis de Something-or-other of the Kingdom of Portugal—and even in the days of its greater prosperity native truck was its long suit.

A little steamer would come slowly to a sandy beach, where the only sign of civilisation was a tin-roofed shanty and a flagstaff. Great hogsheads bound together by rope would be cast overboard, and a steam pinnace would haul the consignment to land.

Then would follow lighter after lighter loaded with straw-packed cases, and these a solitary white man, sweating under a huge sun-helmet, would receive on behalf of Messrs. De Silva and Mackiney and carefully remove to the store of De Silva and Mackiney till the caravans which had been despatched by the same reputable firm had returned from the dark interior. Then would the carriers be paid their wages—in gin. Some there were who preferred rum, and for these the big hogsheads would be tapped; but in the main the favourite form of recompense was to be found in the lightly packed cases, where between straw lay the square-faced bottles of German spirit.

Emanuel Mackiney was worth, if rumour be true, something over a million and, like John Bright's visitor, that was all he was worth. He was immensely wealthy and immensely unscrupulous, so that while his cheques were honoured from French Dacca to Portuguese Benguela, he himself was not honoured anywhere.

Though his English was not perfect, though his origin was obvious, he invariably spoke of England as "home."

That is all it is necessary to tell about Emanuel Mackiney. His son is entitled to a distinct description.

Burney Mackiney had completed his education in England, having exploited it with less profit than his father had exploited the coast.

He was big and coarse and strong. He had lived long enough in England to elaborate the vices he had acquired on the coast—for he had grown up in the business, knew the language of a dozen peoples, and the habits of every nation from the borders of Dahomey to Angola. A tall man, with plump cheeks of bronze rosi-

ness, full of lip and plump of chin, he had all the
confidence in himself which unlimited possessions
beget.

And Burney was in love.

He made the girl's acquaintance before the ship
which was carrying him back to the handsome stucco
mansion at Sierra Leone had reached Teneriffe.

A slim girl, with a wise, sad face, delicately moulded.
This was Ruth Glandynne.

*   *   *   *   *

"Missionary, eh?" Burney's good-natured contempt,
like Burney's wealth, was obvious. "Africa isn't the
sort of place for a girl."

"I know worse," she said with a smile.

"And what part of the coast are you going to?" he
asked.

"I am going to open a mission on the Isisi River."

"Alone?"

"It isn't very unusual, you know," she said. "There
were two missionaries coming, but my companion fell
sick—she will come out later."

"H'm!" said Burney. "Isisi River, eh?"

"Do you know it?"

She was interested. The grey eyes which had regarded him with suspicion and hostility were now
alight with interest.

"Not exactly; we've never got in there, ye know.
My governor does all the trade of the coast, but they've
kept us out of the Isisi. There was a commissioner
man there, perfect dog of a man, named Sanders.
You'll hate him. He loathes missionaries and traders
and all that."

This was the beginning of an acquaintance which
led within two days to a proposal.

To Burney's intense amazement he was unhesitat-
ingly rejected.

"It is most flattering that you should think that

way," she said, meeting his eye without embarrassment; "but I have no wish to marry—anybody."

"One minute, Miss Glandynne," he said roughly; "don't make any mistake. You think my being rich and your being poor makes a difference. My father wouldn't mind——"

"I never gave your financial position a moment's thought," she said, rising; "and you really cannot be any judge of mine."

"I love you," he muttered. "I've never met a girl as stunning as you. Look here," he laid his hand on her arm, "I could have had the pick of women at home, on my word I could. Titled ladies, some of them; but there's something about you——"

They were alone on the promenade deck and it was dark and he had dined and was full of confidence.

"There's something about you"—he tightened his hold on her arm—"that gets into my blood—Ruth!"

In a second she was clasped in his strong arms, struggling.

"Let me go!" she cried.

For answer he bent and kissed her fiercely.

With a superhuman effort she freed herself and staggered back against the rail, pale and trembling.

"You blackguard!" she breathed.

The scorn in her steady grey eyes cowed him.

"I'm sorry," he muttered. "I'm a fool—I've had a little to drink——"

She walked swiftly along the deck and disappeared down the companion, and for three days he did not see her.

Another man would have been ashamed to meet her again, but Burney Mackiney was not of this kind. He had views on women, and had no other regret than that he had apologised. That was weak, he felt. The stronger, the more masterful you are with women, the better they like it. He waited his opportunity.

The night before the ship reached Sierra Leone he

found her sitting on the forepart of the promenade deck, alone.

"Miss Glandynne!" he greeted; and she looked up with a cold stare. "Look here, what's the good of being bad friends. I've made up my mind to marry you."

She would have risen, but she feared a repetition of the scene in which she had been an unwilling actress. So she sat in silence and he misinterpreted her attitude.

"I can't get you out of my mind," he went on. "It's damnable to think of you on the Isisi River with nothing but cannibals and native brutes about you."

"Any variety of brute is preferable to you," she said; and the insult went home.

For a moment he stood incoherent with rage, then he loosed upon her a flood of invective.

She took advantage of his humiliation to make her escape. He did not see her again, though she saw him, for she watched the boat that carried him to land at Sierra Leone with heartfelt gratitude.

*   *   *   *   *

Mr. Commissioner Sanders came down to the beach to meet her and he was in no amiable frame of mind.

She saw a man of medium height, dressed in spotless white, a big white helmet shading a face tanned to the colour of teak. His face was thin and clean-shaven, his eyes unwavering and questioning, his every movement conveying the impression of alert vitality.

"I suppose I ought to be glad to see you," he said, shaking his head reprovingly. "You're the first white woman I've seen for many rains—but you're a responsibility."

She laughed, and gave him a cool, soft hand to shake.

"You don't like missionaries, do you?" she smiled.

"I don't," said Sanders; "but I've had all sorts of orders to see that you're made comfortable; and really there is a lot of work on the river—medical work amongst the women. You're the doctor, I suppose?"

She shook her head.

"I'm the nurse," she said; "the doctor was taken ill before I sailed."

"Humph!" said Sanders.

He had had a hut prepared for her, and two native women trained to the ways of white folk to wait upon her. He gave her dinner that night at his bungalow, and invited the Houssa captain to share the meal. It was the nearest approach to a chaperon he could find.

"I've had a hut built for you," he said; "and the stores and furniture which came for you have been sent up. There are three or four missionaries in the country. You will find Father O'Leary at Cosinkusu—that's about a hundred miles from you. He's a decent sort of chap. There's a man named Boyton—he's a Baptist, or something, and is always on the rampage against the father for proselytising his flock. Boyton lives about one hundred and fifty miles from you. They're the principal missionaries."

He gave her a brief history of the district in which she was to live; indeed, he told her much more than he ever intended telling, but those grey eyes were very compelling and those lips were so ready to smile.

She stayed two days at headquarters and on the third morning her belongings were packed on the *Zaire*.

Before this she met Bosambo of Monrovia, specially summoned.

"This man is chief of the tribe which lies nearest to your station," said Sanders; "though you are practically in the Isisi country. I have sent for him to—to——"

"Tell him to look after me," she smiled, and Sanders smiled responsively.

"Something like that. As a matter of fact, I wanted you to see him here so that he might know that you go as my guest and my friend."

He stammered a little, for Sanders was not used to saying pretty things.

When he had seen her on board he sent for Bosambo.

"Bosambo," he said, in the vernacular, "this lady is of my race, and she will be alone amongst my people, who are wicked and cunning, seeking to deceive her, for she is a God-woman, though she is also a doctor. Now to you I say guard her till your last breath of life, and be in my place, as me, in all matters that touch her."

Bosambo stretched out his hands, palm upwards.

"Master," he said earnestly, "if I swore by the Blessed Virgin whom I worshipped in Liberia, behold I do not know who I swear by, for I have forgotten the holy things that the fathers taught me. But by my head and spirit, and by my life-ghost, I will do as you say."

He turned and walked majestically to the boat. Half-way down the beach he turned about and came back to Sanders.

"Lord, when I have been faithful to your honour's satisfaction, will you buy for me at Sierra Leone a piece of gold cloth, such as a chief might wear?"

"Go, you bargaining child!" said Sanders, without irritation.

He watched the little steamer until it swept round a bend of the river out of sight, and then walked slowly to the bungalow, with—it must be confessed—a sigh.

*　　*　　*　　*　　*

In Sierra Leone, about this time, Burney Mackiney was engaged with his father.

The elder Mackiney was not pleasant to look upon, being grossly stout, puckered and yellow of face, and affected with stertorous breathing.

"It's worth trying," he said, after there had been long silence; "the country's full of rubber, and there's no law preventing the importation of liquor—except the law which gives the commissioner the right to make his own laws. How would you get in?"

"Through the French territory," said his son; "it's dead easy."

There was another long pause.

"But why do you want to go?" asked the elder. "It's not like you to go to a lot of trouble."

"I want to see the country," said the other carelessly. He wanted something more than that. For days he had been hatching his black plot—the Arabs had done such things, and it would not be difficult. Clear of civilisation, he would become an Arab—he spoke coast Arabic perfectly.

He could buy his way through the tribes; a swift dash across the French frontier, he could reach the Isisi River—stay long enough to establish the fact that it was an Arab trader who was the guilty man. She would have to marry him then.

This, in brief, was his plan.

He chose his caravan carefully, and a month later left Sierra Leone in an "S. and M." steamer for an unknown destination.

*   *   *   *   *

Exactly three months after he had said good-bye to the missionary, Mr. Commissioner Sanders was serenely and leisurely making his way along a small river, which leads to a distant section of the Lesser Isisi, when he met a common man, named I'fambi M'Waka—or M'Wafamba as he was called.

Sanders, at the time, was using a little launch, for the *Zaire* was in "dock"—in other words, she was beached.

The Commissioner was proceeding up stream, M'Wafamba was floating down in his battered iron-wood canoe and looking over the side, Sanders regarded the man with idle curiosity.

As they came abreast, M'Wafamba sat upright and turned his face.

"Ho, Sandi!" he called boisterously.

"Ho, man!" called Sanders. "Take your canoe nearer the shore, for my swift boat will make the waters dance and you may suffer."

For answer came a peal of hoarse laughter.

"Ho, Sandi!" bawled M'Wafamba; "white man, pig eater, white monkey!"

Sanders' hand tightened on the steering wheel, and he sent the launch round in a circle until he came up with the canoe.

One Houssa caught the canoe with a boat hook, another reached over and gripped the insolent M'Wafamba by the arm.

A little dazed, and resisting awkwardly, he was pulled into the launch.

"Either one of two things you are," said Sanders; "mad with sickness *mongo* or a great rascal."

"You are a liar, and an eater of liars," said the reckless M'Wafamba; and when Sanders put out his hand to feel the neck of the man for tell-tale swellings, M'Wafamba tried to bite it.

Sanders drew back sharply, not from fear of the bite, but for another reason.

Whilst two of his men sat on the struggling prisoner's chest, he steered the boat for the bank.

"Get him ashore," said the commissioner; and the luckless captive was dragged to land without ceremony.

"Tie him to a tree and make ready for a flogging," said Sanders.

They strapped his hands above the trunk of a young gum tree and stripped his cloth from his shoulders, whilst Sanders walked up and down, his hands in his pockets, his head sunk on his breast, for of a sudden on that sunlit day there had risen a cloud which blotted out all brightness from his official life.

When his men had finished their work Sanders approached the prisoner, a little frightened now, though somewhat rambling of speech.

"How do they call you, my man?" asked the commissioner.

"I'fambi M'Waka," whimpered the man by the tree, "commonly M'Wafamba—of the village of the Pool of Devils."

"M'Wafamba," said Sanders, "being of the Isisi people, you know something of me and my way."

"Lord, I have seen you, and also your way," said the man.

"And if I say 'death' what do I mean?"

"Lord, you mean death, as all men on the river know," said M'Wafamba.

Sanders nodded.

"Now, I am going to flog you till you die," he said grimly, "if you do not tell me where you found drink in my land—for you are drunk with a certain evil poison, which is called ginni, and it is forbidden by law that ginni shall be bought or sold in this territory."

Then the man rolled his head drunkenly.

"Strike, pig eater," he said heroically, "for I have sworn an oath that I will tell no man."

"So be it," said Sanders; "it is your oath against my whipping."

Abiboo, the sergeant of the Houssa, tall and strong of arm, took a firm grip of his hide-whip, stepped a little to one side and sent it whistling round his head, then—

"Flack!"

M'Wafamba woke the forest with a yell.

"Enough!" he screamed. "I speak!"

They loosed him.

"Lord," he wept, "it was an Arabi man, who came across the Frenchi border; this he gave me for certain rubber I collected, saying it would put the spirit of white men into my heart and make me equal in courage to the bravest. And so it did, lord; but now it has gone out of me, and my heart is like water."

"What manner of Arabi was this?" asked Sanders.

"Lord, he was big and strong, and had a fat face like a pig and he wore a ring."

"When did you see him?"

"Two days' journey from here, lord; but he has gone, for he has great matters on hand—so a man, who is my cousin, told me—for he goes to the Ochori country to lift the white woman, who gives us certain beastly waters to drink when we are sick."

The trees seemed of a sudden to spin and the ground to heave up under the Commissioner's feet. He staggered a little, and Abiboo, suspecting fever, leapt to his side and put his strong arm on his shoulders. Only for a second he stood thus, white as death; then—

"Into the boat!" he said.

There was wood enough on board for six hours' steaming—the mission station was twelve hours at the least.

He swept down the little river swiftly and turned to breast the strong currents of the Isisi. Six hours, almost to the minute, the wood lasted. It brought him to a fishing village, where a store of government wood awaited him.

But the "Arabi" had two days' start.

Mackiney had bribed and fought his way through the Mishadombi tribe (those "people-who-are-not-all-alike," about which I must tell you), which serve as a buffer State between French and British territory; he had corrupted the Isisi, and now, with a guide—the cousin of that same M'Wafamba—was moving rapidly on the mission station.

It had been built at the junction of two rivers, in the very spot where, a year before, Sanders had established himself as "the Silent One."

Mackiney had with him fifty men, mainly of the Kroo coast.

His plan was to take to one of the smaller streams that feed the Isisi. It was navigable for eighty miles and would bring him to within a month's march of the regular caravan route to Lago—by then he hoped the girl would be compliant.

His party reached within striking distance of his objective late in the afternoon.

The mission house was half a mile from the village, and he sent out spies who brought him word that beyond two native women and a couple of men there was no opposition to be feared.

He sat apart from his men as they cooked their evening meal.

In his long white burnous, his head enveloped in a filleted hood, he was an Arab to the life.

When night came his headman approached him. "Master," he asked, "what of this Kaffir?"

He spoke of the guide.

"Him you will kill," said Mackiney in Arabic; "for I do not know how much he guesses."

"He guesses too much," said the headman; "for he says that you are no Arab, but a white man."

"You must lose no time," said Mackiney shortly.

He sat waiting by the fire they had kindled for him. Soon he heard a little scuffle and turning his head saw a knot of swaying men and a muffled bellowing like that of a man with a cloth upon his face.

The group went staggering into the forest, disappearing in the darkness of the night.

By and by they came back laughing amongst themselves. The cousin of M'Wafamba, who went with them, did not come back.

"It is time," said his headman. "In two hours the moon will be here."

Very quickly the fires were extinguished and the cooking-pots stacked in the forepart of the big canoe, and in silence, with paddles striking evenly, they crossed the river.

The canoe was beached two hundred yards from the mission house, near a clump of bush.

From here to the path was a few steps.

In single file, headed by the white-robed Arab, the party made its stealthy way along the twisting path. On either side the trees rose steeply, and save for the call of night birds there was no sound.

The forest ended abruptly. Ahead of them was a little clearing and in the centre the dark bulk of the mission hut.

"Now may Allah further our enterprise," breathed Mackiney, and took a step forward.

Out of the ground, almost at his feet, rose a dark figure.

"Who walks in the night?" asked a voice.

"Damn you!" grunted Mackiney in English.

The figure moved ever so slightly.

"Master," he said, "that is a white man's word, yet you have the dress of an Arabi."

Mackiney recovered himself.

"Man, whoever you are, stand on one side, for I have business with the God-woman."

"I also," was the calm reply, "for our Lord Sandi put me here; and I am as he; here have I stood every night save one."

Mackiney had a revolver in his hand, but he dare not fire for fear of alarming the occupants of the hut.

"Let me go on," he said. He knew, rather than saw, the long spear that was levelled at his breast in the darkness. "Let me be, and I will give you many bags of salt and rods more numerous than the trees of the forest."

He heard a little chuckle in the darkness.

"You give too much for too little," said the voice. "Oh, M'laka!"

Mackiney heard the pattering of feet; he was trapped, for somewhere ahead of him armed men were holding the path.

He raised his revolver and fired twice at the figure.

A spear whizzed past him, and he leapt forward and grappled with the man in his path.

He was strong as a young lion, but the man whose hand caught his throat was no weakling. For an instant they swayed, then fell, rolling over and over in the path.

Mackiney reached his hand for another revolver. It closed round the butt, when he felt a shock—something hit him smoothly in the left side—something that sent a thrill of pain through every nerve in his body.

"Oh, dear!" said Mackiney in English.

He never spoke again.

*   *   *   *   *

"Arabi, or white man, I do not know," said Bosambo of Monrovia; "and there is none to tell us, because my people were quick to kill, and only one of his followers is left alive and he knows nothing."

"What have you done with this Arabi?" asked Sanders.

They held their palaver in the mission house in the first hours of the dawn and the girl, pale and troubled, sat at the table looking from one man to the other, for she knew little of the language.

"Lord," said Bosambo, "him I buried according to my desire that no man should know of this raid, lest it put evil thoughts in their heads."

"You did wisely," said Sanders.

He went back to headquarters a little puzzled, for he knew none of the facts of the case.

And when, months after, urgent inquiries came to him respecting the whereabouts of one Burney Mackiney, he replied in all truth that he could give no information.

IV

THE SWIFT WALKER

THEY have a legend in the Akasava country of a green devil. He is taller than the trees, swifter than the leopard, more terrible than all other ghosts, for he is green—the fresh, young green of the trees in spring—and has a voice that is a strangled bark, like the hateful, rasping gr-r-r of a wounded crocodile.

This is M'shimba-m'shamba, the Swift Walker.

You sometimes find his erratic track showing clearly through the forest. For the space of twelve yards' width the trees are twisted, broken and uprooted, the thick undergrowth swept together in tangled heaps, as though by two huge clumsy hands.

This way and that goes the path of M'shimba-m'shamba, zig-zag through the forest—and woe to the hut or the village that stands in his way!

For he will leave this hut intact, from this hut he will cut the propped verandah of leaves; this he will catch up in his ruthless fingers and tear it away swiftly from piece to piece, strewing the wreckage along the village street.

He has lifted whole families and flung them broken and dying into the forest; he has wiped whole communities from the face of the earth.

Once, by the Big River, was a village called N'keman-'kema, and means literally, "monkey-monkey." It was a poor village, and the people lived by catching fish and smoking the same. This they sold to inland villages, profiting on occasions to the equivalent of twelve shillings a week. Generally it was less; but, more or less, some fifty souls lived in comfort on the proceeds.

Some there were in that village that believed in M'shimba-m'shamba, and some who scoffed at him.

And when the votaries of the green devil went out to

make sacrifices to him the others laughed. So acute did the division between the worshippers and the non-worshippers become, that the village divided itself into two, some building their dwellings on the farther side of the creek which ran near by, and the disbelievers remaining on the other bank.

For many months the sceptics gathered to revile the famous devil. Then one night M'shimba-m'shamba came. He came furiously, walking along the water of the creek—for he could do such miraculous things—stretching out his hairy arms to grab tree and bush and hut.

In the morning the worshippers were alone alive, and of the village of the faithless there was no sign save one tumbled roof, which heaved now and then very slightly, for under it was the chief of the village, who was still alive.

The worshippers held a palaver, and decided that it would be a sin to rescue him since their lord, M'shimba-m'shamba, had so evidently decreed his death. More than this, they decided that it would be a very holy thing and intensely gratifying to their green devil, if they put fire to the hut—the fallen roof of wood and plaited grass heaved pathetically at the suggestion—and completed the destruction.

At this moment there arrived a great chief of an alien tribe, Bosambo of the Ochori, who came up against the tide in his State canoe, with its fifty paddlers and his State drummer.

He was returning from a visit of ceremony and had been travelling before daylight, when he came upon the village and stopped to rest his paddlers and eat.

"Most wonderful chief," said the leader of the believers, "you have come at a moment of great holiness." And he explained the passing of M'shimba-m'shamba, and pointed to the fallen roof, which showed at long intervals a slight movement. "Him we will burn," said the headman simply; "for he has been a sinful reviler of our lord the devil, calling him by horrible names, such as 'snake eater' and 'sand drinker.' "

"Little man," said Bosambo magnificently, "I will sit down with my men and watch you lift that roof and bring the chief before me; and if he dies, then, by Damnyou—which is our Lord Sandi's own fetish—I will hang you up by your legs over a fire."

Bosambo did not sit down, but superintended the rescue of the unfortunate chief, accelerating the work —for the people of the village had no heart in it—by timely blows with the butt of his spear.

They lifted the roof and brought an old man to safety. There had been three others in the hut, but they were beyond help.

The old chief was uninjured, and had he been younger he would have required no assistance to free himself. They gave him water and a little corn to eat and he recovered sufficiently to express his contrition. For he had seen M'shimba-m'shamba, the green one.

"Higher than trees, he stood, lord," he said to the interested Bosambo; "and round about his head were little tearing clouds, that flew backwards and forwards to him and from him like birds."

He gave further anatomical particulars. He thought that one leg of the devil was longer than the other, and that he had five arms, one of which proceeded from his chest.

Bosambo left the village, having established the chief in his chieftainship and admonished his would-be murderers.

Now it need not be explained that Bosambo had no more right to establish chiefs or to admonish people of the Akasava than you and I have to vote in the Paris municipal elections. For Bosambo was a chief of the Ochori, which is a small, unimportant tribe, and himself was of no great consequence.

It was not to offer an apology that he directed his paddlers to make for the Akasava city. It lay nearly ten miles out of his way, and Bosambo would not carry politeness to such lengths.

When he beached his canoe before the wondering people of the city and marched his fifty paddlers (who became fifty spearmen by the simple expedient of leaving their paddles behind and taking their spears with them) through the main streets of the city, he walked importantly.

"Chief," he said to that worthy, hastily coming forth to meet him, "I come in peace, desiring a palaver on the high matter of M'shimba-m'shamba."

When the chief, whose name was Sekedimi, recognised him he was sorry that he had troubled to go out to greet him, for the Ochori were by all native reckoning very small fish indeed.

"I will summon the children," said Sekedimi sourly; "for they know best of ghosts and such stories."

"This is a palaver for men," said Bosambo, his wrath rising; "and though the Akasava, by my way of thinking, are no men, yet I am willing to descend from my highness, where Sandi's favour has put me, to talk with your people."

"Go to your canoe, little chief," snarled Sekedimi, "before I beat you with rods. For we Akasava folk are very jealous, and three chiefs of this city have been hanged for their pride. And if you meet M'shimba-m'shamba, behold you may take him with you."

Thus it came about that Bosambo, paramount chief of the Ochori, went stalking back to his canoe with as much dignity as he could summon, followed by the evil jests of the Akasava and the rude words of little boys.

Exactly what capital Bosambo could have made from his chance acquaintance with M'shimba-m'shamba need not be considered.

It is sufficient for the moment, at any rate, to record the fact that he returned to his capital, having lost something of prestige, for his paddlers, who took a most solemn oath not to tell one word of what had happened in the Akasava village, told none—save their several wives.

Bosambo was in many ways a model chief.

He dispensed a justice which was, on the whole, founded on the purest principles of equity. Somewhere, hundreds of miles away, sat Sanders of the River, and upon his method Bosambo, imitative as only a coast man can be, based his own. He punished quickly and obeyed the law himself as far as it lay within him to obey anything.

There was no chief as well disciplined as he, else it would have been a bad day's work for Sekedimi of the Akasava, for Bosambo was a man of high spirit and quick to resent affront to his dignity. And Sekedimi had wounded him deeply.

But Bosambo was a patient man; he had the gift which every native possesses of pigeon-holing his grievances. Therefore he waited, putting aside the matter and living down his people's disapproval.

He carried a pliant stick of hippo hide that helped him considerably in preserving their respect.

All things moved orderly till the rains had come and gone.

Then one day at sunset he came again to the Akasava City, this time with only ten paddlers. He walked through the street unattended, carrying only three light spears in his left hand and a wicker shield on the same arm. In his right hand he had nothing but his thin, pliant stick of hippo skin, curiously carved.

The chief of the Akasava had word of his coming and was puzzled, for Bosambo had arrived in an unaccustomed way—without ostentation.

"The dawn has come early," he said politely.

"I am the water that reflects the light of your face," replied Bosambo with conventional courtesy.

"You will find me in a kind mood," said Sekedimi, "and ready to listen to you."

He was fencing cautiously; for who knew what devilish lies Bosambo had told Sandi?

Bosambo seated himself before the chief.

"Sekedimi," said he, "though my skin is black, I am of white and paramount people, having been instructed in their magic, and knowing their gods intimately."

"So I have heard; though, for my part, I take no account of their gods, being, as they tell me, for women and gentle things."

"That is true," said Bosambo, "save one god, whose name was Petero, who was a great cutter off of ears."

Sekedimi was impressed.

"Him I have not heard about," he admitted.

"Knowing these," Bosambo went on, "I came before the rains to speak of M'shimba-m'shamba, the green one, who walks crookedly."

"This is the talk of children," said Sekedimi; "for M'shimba-m'shamba is the name our fathers gave to the whirlwind that comes through the forest—and it is no devil."

Sekedimi was the most enlightened chief that ever ruled the Akasava and his explanation of M'shimba-m'shamba was a perfectly true one.

"Lord chief," said Bosambo earnestly, "no man may speak with better authority on such high and holy matters as devils as I, Bosambo, for I have seen wonderful sights and know the world from one side to the other. For I have wandered far, even to the edge of the world which looks down into hell; and I have seen wild leopards so great that they have drunk up whole rivers and eaten trees of surprising height and thickness."

"Ko, ko," said the awe-stricken counsellors of the chief who stood about his person; and even Sekedimi was impressed.

"Now I come to you," said Bosambo, "with joyful

news, for my young men have captured M'shimba-
m'shamba, the green one, and have carried him to the
land of the Ochori."

This he said with fine dramatic effect, and was
pleased to observe the impression he had created.

"We bound the green one," he went on, "with
N'Gombi chains, and laid the trunk of a tree in his
mouth to silence his fearful roaring. We captured
him, digging an elephant pit so deep that only men of
strongest eyesight could see the bottom, so wide that
no man could shout across it and be heard. And we
took him to the land of the Ochori on a hundred
canoes."

Sekedimi sat with open mouth.

"The green one?" he asked incredulously.

"The green one," said Bosambo, nodding his head;
"and we fastened together four shields, like that which
I carry, and these we put over each of his eyes, that he
might not see the way we took him or find his way
back to the Akasava."

There was a long silence.

"It seems," said Sekedimi, after a while, "that you
have done a wonderful thing; for you have removed a
devil from our midst. Yet the Ochori people will be
sorry, for the curse which you have taken from us you
have given to your people, and surely they will rise
against you."

"E-wa!" murmured his counsellors, nodding their
heads wisely. "The Ochori will rise against their chief,
for he has loosened an evil one in their midst."

Bosambo rose, for night was falling and he desired
to begin the return stage of his journey.

"The Ochori are a very proud people," he said.
"Never have they had a great devil before; the Isisi,
the Akasava, the N'Gombi, the Bush folk, and the
Lesser Isisi, the Bomongo, the Boungendi—all these
tribes have devils in many variety, but the Ochori have
had none and they were very sad. Now their stomachs

are full of pride for M'shimba-m'shamba, the green one, is with them, roving the forest in which we have loosed him, in a most terrifying way."

He left the Akasava in a thoughtful mood, and set his State canoe for the juncture of the river.

That night the Akasava chief called together all his headmen, his elders, his chief fighting men and all men of consequence.

The staccato notes of the lokali called the little chiefs of outlying villages, and with them their elder men. From the fourth hour of night till the hour before dawn the palaver lasted.

"O chiefs and people," said Sekedimi, "I have called you together to tell you of a great happening. For M'shimba-m'shamba, who since the beginning of the world has been the own devil of the Akasava people, is now no longer ours. Bosambo, of the Ochori, has bound him and carried him away."

"This is certainly a shame," said one old man; "for M'shimba-m'shamba is our very own devil, and Bosambo is an evil man to steal that which is not his."

"That is as I think," said Sekedimi. "Let us go to Sandi, who holds court by the border of the N'Gombi country, and he shall give us a book."

Sanders was at that time settling a marriage dispute, the principal article of contention being: if a man pays six thousand matakos (brass rods) for a wife, and in the first twelve months of her married life she develop sleeping-sickness, was her husband entitled to recover his purchase price from her father? It was a long, long palaver, requiring the attendance of many witnesses; and Sanders was deciding it on the very common-sense line that any person selling a damaged article, well knowing the same to be damaged, was guilty of fraud. The evidence, however, exonerated the father from blame, and there only remained a question of equity. He was in the midst of the second half of the trial when the chief of the Akasava, with his headman, his chief slave, and a deputation of the little chiefs waited upon him.

"Lord," said Sekedimi, without preliminary, "we have covered many miles of country and traversed rivers of surprising swiftness; also we encountered terrible perils by the way."

"I will excuse you an account of your adventures," said the Commissioner, "for I am in no mood for long palavers. Say what is to be said and have done."

Thereupon Sekedimi told the story of the filched devil from the beginning, when he had, with a fine sarcasm, presented the Swift Walker to the Ochori.

Now Sanders knew all about M'shimba-m'shamba. Moreover, he knew that until very recently the chief himself was in no doubt as to what the "green one" really was.

It was characteristic of him that he made no attempt to turn the chief to a sense of his folly.

"If Bosambo has taken M'shimba-m'shamba," he said gravely, "then he has done no more than you told him to do."

"Now I spoke in jest," said Sekedimi, "for this devil is very dear to us, and since we can no more hear his loud voice in our forests we are sad for one who is gone."

"Wait!" said Sanders, "for is this the season when M'shimba-m'shamba walks? Is it not rather midway between the rains that he comes so swiftly? Wait and he will return to you."

But Sekedimi was in no mood for waiting.

"Master, if I go to Bosambo," he said, "and speak kindly to him, will he not return the green one?"

"Who knows?" said Sanders wearily. "I am no prophet."

"If my lord gave me a book——" suggested Sekedimi.

"This is no book palaver," said Sanders briefly; "but justice between man and man. For if I give you a book to Bosambo, what shall I say when Bosambo asks me also for a book to you?"

"Lord, that is just," said Sekedimi, and he went his way. With twelve of his principal chiefs he made the journey to the Ochori City, carrying with him gifts of goats and fat dogs, salt and heavy rings of brass.

Bosambo received him ceremoniously, accepted his gifts but declined to favour him.

"Sekedimi," he said, "I am wax in the hands of my people. I fear to anger them; for they love M'shimba-m'shamba better than they love their goats or their salt or their wives."

"But no one sees him till the middle time between the rains," said Sekedimi.

"Last night we heard him," persisted Bosambo steadily; "very terrible he was, and my people trembled and were proud."

For many hours the chief of the Akasava pleaded and argued, but without avail.

"I see that you have a heart of brass," said Sekedimi at length; "therefore, Bosambo, return me the presents I brought, and I will depart."

"As to the presents," said Bosambo, "they are dispersed, for swift messengers have carried them to the place where M'shimba-m'shamba sits and have put them where he may find them, that he may know the Akasava remember him with kindness."

Empty-handed the chief returned.

He sent courier after courier in the course of the next month, without effect. And as time wore on his people began to speak against him. The crops of two villages failed, and the people cursed him, saying that he had sold the ghost and the spirit of fortune.

At last, in desperation, he paid another visit to Bosambo.

"Chief," he said, when all ceremonies had been observed, "I tell you this: I will give you fifty bags of salt and as much corn as ten canoes can hold if you will return to me our green one. And if your pride resists me, then I will call my spears, though Sandi hang me for it."

Bosambo was a wise man. He knew the limit of human endurance. Also he knew who would suffer if war came, for Sanders had given him private warning.

"My heart is heavy," he said. "Yet since you are set upon this matter I will return you M'shimba-m'shamba, though I shall be shamed before my people. Send me the salt and the corn, and when the tide of the river is so high and the moon is nearly full I will find the green one and bring him back to your land."

Sekedimi went back to his city a happy man. In a week the salt and the corn were delivered and the canoes that brought them carried a message back. On such a day, at such an hour, the green one would be cut loose in the forest of the Akasava. Afterwards, Bosambo would come in state to announce the transfer.

At the appointed time the chief of the Akasava waited by the river beach, two great fires burning behind him to guide Bosambo's canoe through the night. And behind the fires the population of the city and the villages about stood awed and expectant, biting its knuckles.

Tom-tom! Tom-tom! Tom-tom! Over the water came the faint sound of Bosambo's drum and the deep-chested chant of his paddlers. In half an hour his canoe grounded and he waded ashore.

"Lord Sekedimi," he greeted the chief, "this night I have loosened M'shimba-m'shamba, the green one, the monster. And he howled fearfully because I left him. My heart is sore, and there is nothing in my poor land which gives me pleasure."

"Fifty sacks of my salt I sent you," said Sekedimi unpleasantly; "also corn."

"None the less, I am as an orphan who has lost his father and his mother," moaned Bosambo.

"Let the palaver finish, chief," said Sekedimi, "for my heart is also sore, having lost salt and corn."

"I see that you have no stomach for pity," said Bosambo, and re-embarked.

Clear of the Akasava city, Bosambo regained his spirits, though the night was stormy and great spots of rain fell at intervals.

The further he drew from the Akasava chief the more jovial he became, and he sang a song.

"There are fools in the forest," he bawled musically; "such as the ingonona who walks with his eyes shut; but he is not so great a fool as Sekedimi.

"He is like a white man who is newly come to this land.

"He is like a child that burns his fingers.

"He is simple and like a great worm."

He sang all this, and added libellous and picturesque particulars.

"Lord chief," said the headman suddenly, arresting his song, "I think we will make for the shore."

Over the trees on the right bank of the river lightning flickered with increasing brightness, and there was a long continuous rumble of thunder in the air.

"To the middle island," ordered Bosambo.

The headman shivered.

"Lord, the middle island is filled with spirits," he said.

"You are a fool," said Bosambo; but he ordered the canoe to the left bank.

Brighter and more vivid grew the lightning, louder and louder the crackle and crash of thunder. The big raindrops fell fitfully.

Then above the noise of thunder came a new sound —a weird howling that set the paddlers working with quicker strokes.

"Whow-w-w!"

A terrifying shriek deafened them.

The man nearest him dropped his paddle with a frightened whimper, and Bosambo caught it.

"Paddle, dogs!" he thundered.

They were within a dozen yards of the shore when, by the quick flashing lightning he saw a jagged path suddenly appear in the forest on the bank before him.

It was as though giant hands were plucking at trees. They twisted and reeled like drunken men—cracked, and fell over.

"Paddle!"

Then something caught Bosambo and lifted him from the canoe. Up, up he went; then as swiftly down to the water; up again, and down. He struck out for the shore, choked and half-conscious.

His fingers caught the branches of a stricken tree, and he drew himself to land. He stumbled forward on his hands and knees, panting heavily.

Overhead the storm raged, but Bosambo did not heed it. His forty paddlers, miraculously cast ashore by the whirlwind, lay around him laughing and moaning, according to their temperaments.

But these he forgot.

For he was engaged in the composition of a hurried and apologetic prayer to M'shimba-m'shamba, the green one, the Swift Walker.

V

BRETHREN OF THE ORDER

NATIVE men loved Sanders of the River well enough to die for him. Some hated him well enough to kill him. These things have a trick of balancing themselves, and the story of Tambeli the Strong, and a member of that sinister organisation, the Silent Ones of Nigeria, offers an object lesson on this point.

From the Big River which empties itself into the Atlantic Ocean somewhere between Dacca and Banana Point—this is a fairly vague location—run a number of smaller rivers, east, west, and northerly, more or less.

The Isisi, or "Little River," is one of these. It runs to the conjunction of the Baranga River, and it is a moot point among geographers whether the right confluence is the true Isisi and the left confluence the Baranga, or vice versâ.

Commissioner Sanders, in defiance of all cartographers, traces the Isisi to the right, because the left river runs through the land of lawless tribes, which are called in the native tongue Nushadombi, or literally, "the-Men-Who-Are-Not-All-Alike."

Beyond the deep forest through which for twenty miles the Baranga runs, beyond and northward of the swampland where the crocodiles breed, lies a lake with a score of outlets, none of which are navigable. Here, at one time, was a village, and to this village had drifted the outcast men of a hundred tribes. Men bloodguilty, survivors of unlawful feuds, evaders of taxes, the sinful and the persecuted of every tribe and people within a hundred miles came drifting into Nushadombi.

So that in course of time what had once been a village grew to a city, and that city the hub of a nation.

They dwelt apart, a sullen, hateful people, defiant of all laws save the laws of self-preservation. Successive expeditions were sent against them. They were near the border of the German territory, and took that which pleased them, contemptuous of border line or defined sphere.

Germany sent a native army through a swamp to destroy them—that army drifted back in twos and threes, bringing stories of defeat and the unpleasant consequences thereof.

France, from the south-east, dispatched an expedition with no better success.

Sanders neither sent armed forces nor peace mission.

He knew a great deal more about this strange nation than he ever put into the dispatches, the production of which, for the benefit of an Under-Secretary of Colonial Affairs, was a monthly nightmare.

The commissioner ignored the existence of the People-Who-Were-Not-All-Alike. He might have continued in this attitude of wilful ignorance but for the advent into his official orbit of one Tambeli.

Tambeli had three gods. One was a fierce god, who came into his life when the rains came and the great winds howled through the forest, lifting up and casting down trees; when vivid flashes of lightning lit the forest with incessant stabbings of white flame, and the heavens crashed and crackled. He had another god, burnt and carved from a certain hard wood which is found in the N'Gombi country, and he had yet another god, which was himself.

Tambeli was the handsomest man of all the Isisi.

He was very tall, his shoulders were broad, his arms were perfectly moulded, the muscles being gathered in cordlike pads, properly. His hair he loved to dress with clay so that it billowed on either side of his head.

Wearing the skin of a leopard, and leaning on the long elephant spear, he would stand for hours by the edge of the river, the admiration of women who came to the shallow places to fill their cooking-pots. This was as Tambeli desired, for he was a man of gallantry. More so than was to the liking of certain husbands, so it is said; and there was an evening when, as Tambeli went stalking through the village, one M'fabo, an outraged man, sprang upon him from a hiding-place, roaring hoarsely in his mad anger. But Tambeli was as lithe as a cat and as strong as the leopard whose skin he wore. He grasped M'fabo by the throat, lifted him clear of the ground, and, swinging him round and round, as a mischievous boy might swing a rat by the tail, flung him into the hut he had quitted.

Thereafter no man raised his hand openly against Tambeli, though there were some who sought to injure him by stealth. A foreigner—a Congolaise man—slipped into his hut one night with a sharpened razor.

It was the little square razor that the Congo folk wear tucked away in their hair, and his pleasure was to cut Tambeli's throat. This Congoman was never seen again—the river was very handy, and Tambeli was very strong—but his razor was found by the river's edge and it was stained with blood.

Tambeli was a rich man, having goats and brass rods and salt in sacks. He had six wives, who tended his gardens and cooked for him, and they were proud of their lord, and gloried in his discreditable exploits. For Tambeli was a trader, though few knew it, and it was his practice to absent himself three months in the year on business of his own.

One day the chief of the village died, and the women having decked their bodies with green leaves, danced the death dance locked arm in arm.

Tambeli, watching the reeling line making its slow progress through the village street, had a thought, and when they laid the body on the bottom of a canoe and paddled it up-river to the middle island, where the dead were buried, Tambeli was swept down-stream, four of his wives paddling till, after a long day and a night, he came to the Isisi city where the king lived. To that great man he went. And the king, who was drunk, was neither sorry nor glad to see him.

"Lord King," said he, "I am Tambeli of Isaukasu by the little river, and I have served you many times, as you well know."

The king blinked at him with dull eyes, and said nothing.

"We are a people without a chief," said Tambeli; "and the men of my village desire that I shall rule them in place of C'fari, who is dead."

The king scratched his neck thoughtfully, but said nothing for a while; then he asked:

"What do you bring?"

Tambeli detailed a magnificent list, which comprehended goats, salt, and rods to a fabulous amount. He added a gift which was beyond price.

"Go back to your people—chief," said the king, and Tambeli embraced the knees of his master, and called him his father and his mother.

That is how Tambeli came to be sitting on the stool of chieftainship when Mr. Commissioner Sanders arrived unexpectedly from the south in his tiny steamboat.

$$* \qquad * \qquad * \qquad * \qquad *$$

Now, Isaukasu lay on the very border line of the Ochori country, and was a village of some importance since the back country produced rubber and gum. It was the kind of village which became a city in the twinkling of an eye.

The steamer was tied up to the bank, a gangway was thrown ashore and Sanders, in shining white, came briskly to the beach.

Tambeli, a picturesque figure, awaited him.

"Lord Master," he said, "C'fari has died, and I am chief of this town by order of my father the king."

Sanders perked his head on one side, like a curious bird, and eyed the man with interest.

"Your father the king is king no more," he said softly, "being at this moment on my ship, very sick; and though he were well and on his throne, no man says who may be chief of town or village save I. And truly, Tambeli, you are no chief for me."

Tambeli stuck out his jaw a little, for he was a very determined man.

"I have paid for my honour with salt and rods," he said.

"And gin," said Sanders gently. "Now you shall tell me how gin comes into my country when I forbid it."

Tambeli faced the white man squarely.

"Master," said he, twiddling the brass-bound haft of his spear, "I have been in many countries, and know many customs; also, they tell me, the black people of the coast, that there is no law, white or black, which prevents a man from buying or selling square-faces if he so wishes."

"I am the law," said Sanders, and his voice was softer than ever. "If I say thus, it is thus. And gin you shall neither buy nor sell nor barter, though the black law-givers of the coast be as wise as gods."

"In this matter of chiefship——" said Tambeli.

"You are no chief for me," said Sanders, "neither now nor at any time, for you are an evil man and a robber of that which men prize dearly. I have spoken; the palaver's finished."

Tambeli hesitated.

Behind Sanders stood a sergeant and two men of the Houssas, and as Tambeli stood irresolutely, the sergeant stepped forward and grasped him by the shoulder.

"Aleki!" he said, which is an invitation to hurried movement.

As the sergeant's grip tightened, Tambeli, the strong one, caught him by the slack of his uniform jacket and sent him spinning—then he stood stiffly, for the warm muzzle of Sanders' revolver was pressing against his stomach, and Tambeli, who had, as he claimed, a knowledge of countries and customs, knew Sanders for a man with little or no regard for human life.

They handcuffed Tambeli and ironed his leg to a staple in the deck of the *Zaire*, for he had shamed the authority of the Crown, had unceremoniously flung a full sergeant of Houssas down the bank that leads to the river, and such things are not good for people to see.

The steamer went thrashing down the river towards

headquarters and Sanders gave himself over to the question of Tambeli.

There was, as he had boldly said, no law prohibiting the sale of strong drink in the territory under his care; but Sanders never consulted constitutions. He had kept his lands free of the gin curse, and he had no intention of adding to the list of his responsibilities, which was already too long.

There was drink in the country; this he had reason to know. Polambi of Isisi, Sakalana of the Akasava, Nindino of the N'Gombi, all chiefs of parts, had gone from the straight path. There had been certain indiscretions which had sent Sanders hurrying "all ways at once." There had been, too, some drastic readjustment of authority.

The gin problem was half solved by the arrest of Tambeli; there remained the problem of the man. This he settled for himself.

The *Zaire* was tied to a wooding, and Sanders had retired to his cabin and was sleeping when a noise on deck aroused him and he came out in a hurry to find Tambeli, the strong man, gone, and with him the chain that fastened him to the staple and the staple that fastened him to the deck. He left behind him a private of Houssas with a cracked head.

Sanders whistled a little tune to himself all the way to headquarters. He sat in a deck-chair under the striped awning, whistling tunefully and very softly for the greater part of two days and his men, who knew him well and understood his mood, were careful to keep out of his way.

He arrived at headquarters still whistling.

He was the only white man on the station and was thankful. He had put one of his guests, a somewhat frightened king of the Isisi, under escort, but that was no satisfaction to him, for Tambeli had set the law at defiance and had broken for the bush.

News came down from Nushadombi at fitful intervals, because there was good reason why no courier should come from that country; better reason why its inhabitants should be bad travellers. Sanders hated Nushadombi with all the fierce hatred which a law-giver extends to a lawless community. He hated it worse because there was always at the back of his mind the uneasy conviction that he was rightly responsible for its government.

This responsibility he had triumphantly repudiated on more occasions than one; but, none the less, there was a voice which spoke very softly to Sanders in his silent moments, and that voice said: "Nushadombi is British, if you've the courage."

It was as a sop to conscience that he spied upon the People-Who-Were-Not-All-Alike. His spies came and went. He lost a few men in the process, but that was the luck of the game. He learnt of little murders, of family feuds, and the like, but nothing of moment.

On a sultry afternoon in March Sanders was sitting on a rock overlooking the mouth of the big river, fish-ing for Cape salmon, and thinking, curiously enough, of the Nushadombi folk. Whilst so engaged Sergeant Abiboo, his Houssa orderly, ran towards him, picking a dainty way over the sharp stones, his long bayonet flapping his thigh with every wild leap he made.

Sanders looked up inquiringly.

"Lord," explained Abiboo, his hand steadfast at the salute, "there has come a listener from Nushadombi, having much to tell your honour."

"Let him come here," said Sanders.

"Lord, he cannot walk," said Abiboo simply; "for the Men-Who-Are-All-Not-Alike caught him, and he dies to-night by my way of thinking."

Sanders threw down his line and followed the Houssa back to the residency.

He found the spy lying on a rough stretcher in the shade of the stoep.

The man looked round with a twisted grin as Sanders came up the steps that led to the verandah.

"Ho, Bogora!" said Sanders quietly, "what bad talk they make of you?"

"There is no talk worth the talking after to-night," said the man painfully. "As for me, I will make my report and sleep; and, lord, if I did not love you I would have died three nights ago."

Sanders made a brief examination of the man's injuries. He did not turn sick, for that was not his way— he covered the tortured limbs with the blanket again.

"One Tambeli, a man of Isisi, now sits down with the people of Nushadombi!" gasped the spy, "and is regarded fearfully, being a chief; also it is said that he is a member of a great ju-ju, and has powerful friends among the chiefs. He knew me when other men would have passed me by, and by his orders they did what they did. Also, lord, they are for attacking different nations, such as the Isisi, the Ochori, and the N'Gombi."

"How soon?" asked Sanders.

"When the second moon comes after the rains."

"That we shall see," said Sanders. "As for Tambeli, I will settle with him, Bogoro, my brother, for I will carry your blood upon my hands and at my hands he shall die; all gods witness my words."

The wreck on the stretcher smiled.

"Sandi," he said slowly, "it is worth all to hear you call me brother."

And he closed his eyes as if to sleep, and died as Sanders watched him.

Bosambo came from his hut one morning just before the dawn. The city of the Ochori was very silent. There had been a dance the night before and in the very centre of the city a dull glow showed where the great fire had been.

Bosambo drew on his cloak of monkey skins, for the morning air was chill, and walked to the end of the

village street, past the gardens and through the little
jungle path that led to his own plantation. Here he
paused, listening.

There was no sound save the distant "hush, hush,"
of the small river as it swept over the rocks on its way
to the River Beyond.

He squatted down in the shadow of a gum-tree and
waited patiently. In an hour the sun would be up;
before then he expected things to happen.

He had not been sitting longer than five minutes
when he saw a figure moving towards him, coming
from an opposite direction. It moved cautiously, halting now and then as though not certain of its ground.

Bosambo rose without sound.

"Friend," he said, "you move in silence."

"That is the royal way," said the figure.

"Life is full of silences," said Bosambo.

"None are so silent as the dead," was the response.

They said these things glibly, as men repeating a
ritual, as, indeed, they were.

"Sit with me, my brother," said Bosambo, and the
other came to his side and sank down on his haunches.

"This I say to you, Bosambo," said the stranger,
"that oaths are oaths, and men who swear to blood
brotherhood do live and die one for the other."

"That is true," said Bosambo; "hence I have come;
for when yesterday a strange forest man brought me a
little water in a shell, and in that water a berry, I knew
that the Silent Ones had need of me."

The stranger nodded his head.

"Yes, it is many years since I swore the oath," mused
Bosambo; "and I was very young, and the Silent Ones
do not walk in the Ochori country, but in Nigeria,
which is a month of marches away."

The man by his side made a little clicking noise
with his mouth.

"I am here," he said importantly. "I, Tambeli, a
traveller, also, by some accounted king of the People-

Who-Are-Not All-Alike. Also a high man in the Order of the Silent Ones, ruthless avengers of slights and controllers of ju-jus."

"Lord, I gathered so much," said the humble Bosambo, "by your honour's summons. Now tell me how I may serve my brother, who is alone in this country?"

There was a note of careless interrogation in his voice, and the hand farthest from his visitor fingered the thin, long blade of a knife.

"Not alone, brother," said Tambeli, with decision, "for there are many brethren of our society who watch my coming and going."

"That is as well," said Bosambo truthfully, and quietly slipped the knife back into its wooden sheath.

"Now you can serve me thus," said Tambeli. "I am the king of a vengeful people who hate Sandi, and, behold, he is coming with soldiers to punish them. And in his coming he must pass through the Ochori country, sitting down with you for a day."

"All this is true," said Bosambo conventionally, and waited.

Tambeli put his hand beneath his robe and brought forth a short stick of bamboo.

"Bosambo," he said, "there is a spirit in this which will do little good to Sandi. For if you cut away the gum which seals one end you will find a powder such as the witch-doctors of my people make, and this can be emptied on the 'chop' of Sandi, and he will know nothing, yet he will die."

Bosambo took the stick without a word, and placed it in a little bag which hung at his waist.

"This you will do in fear of the Silent Ones, who are merciless."

"This I will do," said Bosambo gravely.

No more was said, the two men parting without further speech.

Bosambo returned to his hut as the eastern sky went

pearl-grey, as though a shutter of heaven had been suddenly opened. He was a silent man that morning, not even Fatima, his wife, evoked the response of speech.

In the afternoon he caught a dog straying in the forest, and, dragging it to a place where none could see, he gave it meat. It died very quickly, because Bosambo had sprinkled the food with the powder which Tambeli had brought.

Bosambo watched the unpleasant experiment without emotion. When he had hidden all evidence of his crime he returned to the village.

At night-time came Sanders, and Bosambo, warned of the urgency of his visit, alike by lokali message, and the evident fact that Sanders was travelling by night, had a great fire kindled on the beach to guide the *Zaire* to land.

The little stern wheeler came slowly into the light; naked men splashed overboard and waded ashore with hawsers at their shoulders, and the boat was safely moored.

Then Sanders came.

"I sit with you for one day," he said, "being on my way to do justice."

"Lord, my house is in the hollow of your hands, and my life also," replied Bosambo magnificently. "There is the new hut which I built for you in the shadow of my house."

"I sleep on board," said Sanders shortly. "To-morrow at dawn I am for the People-Who-Are-Not-All-Alike."

They walked together through the village, Sanders to stretch his legs; Bosambo, as his host, from courtesy. The chief knew that eyes were watching him, because he had received an intimation that the Silent Ones awaited his report at no great distance in the forest.

They reached the end of the village and turned to stroll back.

"Lord," said Bosambo, speaking earnestly, "if I say a thing to you which is of great moment, I beg your honour not to stand still in this place showing your anger."

"Speak on," said Sanders.

"If," continued Bosambo, "there came from your ship when you sleep to-night news that you were in pain and nigh to death, I would save you a long journey."

Sanders could not see his face, for the night was dark, and there was only a tangle of stars in the sky above to give light to the world.

"I know you to be a cunning man, Bosambo," he said quietly; "and I listen to you without doubt. Now you shall tell why this is, and after I will do that which is best."

"Lord," said Bosambo quietly, "I am your man, and by all things which men swear by I am ready to die for you, and it seems likely that I shall die one way or the other. For though I vex you, and you have cursed me many times, yet I desire that I and all my house should die before you suffered pain."

"That I believe," said Sanders shortly.

"Therefore, lord, trust me without the palaver."

"That I will do also," said Sanders.

* * * * *

At five o'clock in the morning—as we count time— Bosambo went swiftly to the forest, taking with him a long-handled native spade. He reeled a little in his walk; the farther he got the more unsteady became his gait.

There was a clearing less than a mile along the forest path, a notable rendezvous for lovers in the soft hours of the evening, and by night the feeding place of devils.

To this spot Bosambo made his way; for this was the place where the Silent Ones awaited report. He came staggering into the clearing, his spade on his shoulder, and five men watching him from the shadows knew that he was drunk.

He came to a halt by the tree of the Weaver Birds, and sat down heavily. From the fold of his cloak he produced a bottle, and this he raised to his lips.

"Bosambo," said Tambeli, coming noiselessly before him, "this is a good sight, for something tells me that you have done what should be done."

"He was my father," whined Bosambo, "and of my blood; he was a great lord, and now that he is dead the white people will come with the guns and say 'Ha-ha-ha!' and eat me up."

He rolled his drooping head in misery.

"None shall know," soothed Tambeli the strong one, "for here are we all, the five silent men of the good order, and no man knows but us—we say nothing." He paused, and then added carefully: "So long as you do that which we bid, and send us tributes of women and corn."

Bosambo heard this programme for his enslavement without visible sign of distress.

"Why have you brought the spade?" asked Tambeli suddenly; "you do not bury Sandi here?"

"Who knows?" said the listless Bosambo.

He took the bottle from his pocket. It was a small square bottle, in which liquor, such as gin, illicitly and secretly trafficked, comes to the backlands.

"This I will take," said Tambeli. He reached out his hand and wrenched the bottle from the reluctant grasp of the other. "Men who drink spirits talk boastfully, and you shall not talk, Bosambo, till there are many rivers between me and Sandi's soldiers."

He took the little wooden stopper from the neck.

"Also," he said, "it is a long time since ginni came to me."

He waved his hand to his four shadowy companions.

"These are my brethren," he said, "and yours;

therefore, in the way of the white people of the coast, let us drink for happiness."

He lifted the bottle and drank, then handed it to the man nearest him. One by one they took long draughts, then the bottle came to Bosambo.

"Tell me, did Sandi die in pain?" asked Tambeli.

"He died peacefully," said Bosambo.

Tambeli nodded.

"That is the proper way," he said, "for if he died with a great shouting there would come soldiers. Now none can say but that he died of the sickness Mongo.* There is no medicine like this, being prepared by a celebrated witch-doctor."

Bosambo said nothing for a while; then he spoke.

"Who is there to betray me?" he asked; "for if it comes to the ears of the High Lords at the Coast that I slew Sandi——"

"Have no fear," said Tambeli, with a little cough, "for there are none but these"—he waved his hand unsteadily—"and—they—speak—never."

Indeed he spoke the truth, for the men were lying comfortably as though composing themselves for sleep.

"Up—up!" muttered Tambeli.

He went to kick the nearest sleeper, but his legs gave way, and he fell on his knees.

Bosambo watched him, deeply interested.

"Dog!"

Tambeli half turned his body toward the Chief of the Ochori, and spat out the word. He gathered all the great strength that was within him and leapt to his feet, launching himself straight at the other's throat.

But Bosambo was prepared.

His left hand shot out, caught Tambeli's shoulder, and half twisted him till he fell.

The man tried to rise, went down again, and soon he, too, fell asleep, uneasily at first, then calmly like a man tired.

* Literally the True Sickness, *i.e.*, any sickness which ends life.

Bosambo sat patiently.

After a decent interval, he looked round for the spade he had brought.

"Tambeli," he said as he went about his business—a hard business, for the digging of a grave big enough for five men needs much muscular strength—"you were foolish, or you would know that no man of my faith slays his friend and patron. And no man of very high temperament sits in the shadow of death. Oh, Silent Ones, you are very silent now!"

He covered up his work and wiped his steaming forehead, standing irresolutely by the grave. Then he scratched his chin thoughtfully. He had an uneasy recollection of a mission-school a thousand miles away and of sad-eyed fathers who had taught him certain rituals.

He dropped the spade and knelt awkwardly.

"Blessed Marki and Luko and Johann," he prayed, closing his eyes conventionally, "I have slain five men by poison, though they themselves took it without my invitation. Therefore they are dead, which is a good thing for us all. Amen."

VI

THE VILLAGE OF IRONS

SANDERS was used to the child-like buttering of his people, and accepted their praise without conviction. It was part of the game. He expected to be termed "Protector of Persecuted People," "Lord of Wisdom," and the like, and would have been suspicious if these terms were omitted, because that was all part of the game, and meant no more than the prefix "dear" in the epistles of the civilised.

Just so long as flattery and sycophancy ran along conventional lines, just so long as politeness followed a normal course, Sanders was satisfied; if compliment fell short or slopped over, all his intellectual bristles stood on end, and he looked around with narrowed eyes and a growl in his throat for the danger which lay somewhere to hand.

He was overlord of a million black people, sub-divided by language, dialect, prejudice, custom, jealousy, and temperament into twenty-three distinct nations. The Bangeli, who lived close to the head-quarters and were a selfish, bastard people, made up by accidental unions between Krooman, Congolaise, Angola folk, and Coast peoples, he did not heed, for they were civilised up to a point, and were wise in the way of white men. Also they were fearful of punish-ment, and just as the fear of the Lord is the beginning of wisdom, so is the fear of the Law the beginning of civilisation.

But beyond this people lay the fighting tribes, un-touched by the trader, only slightly affected by the missionary. Warlike, unreasoning children, with a passion for litigation and a keen sense of justice. And it was Sanders' business and his pleasure to know these as they were—to study them as you study your own children, perhaps more carefully, for you take your children and their peculiarities for granted—and to adjust his attitude as he adjusted theirs, which re-arrangement was usually made once in every twenty-four hours.

Sanders differed from ready-made Empire-builders in this respect, that, whilst his pompous superiors treated native people as an aggregate problem, Sanders dealt with them as individuals.

A certain excellency once addressed him through a secretary's secretary, asking him to explain the prevalence of crime among the people of the Lesser Isisi, and Sanders answered naïvely (as it seemed to the superior folk of his excellency's entourage) that the increase in crime was due to the dreams of a certain man named M'dali.

Sanders did not believe in clairvoyance, and when an agent brought him news that M'dali of Tembolini, in the Isisi country, had dreamt a dream in which he saw the river rising so that it flooded the middle island, which lay immediately opposite the village, he paid no heed.

Because he knew that the rains had been very heavy and that all the lesser rivers were swollen, and would in course of time swell the big river, and because the village of Tembolini stood so far above the level of the river that there was no danger to the people.

When a week later he learnt that all that M'dali dreamt had come to pass, he was neither impressed nor greatly interested. He thought M'dali was a shrewd guesser, and let it go at that.

When later he was told that on such and such a night M'dali had dreamt that E'timgolo, his second wife, would die—as she did—Sanders was mildly puzzled till he remembered that he had seen the woman the last time he was in the village, and that then she was in an advanced state of sleeping sickness. He gathered that M'dali had sufficient data at hand to justify his imagining.

News of other dreams came down the river—some first hand, and these were fairly commonplace; some, more wonderful, from mouth to mouth—and these were obviously exaggerated.

Sanders was a busy man about this time, and had neither leisure nor inclination to bother himself about such matters.

But one morning at break of day a canoe came swiftly, bearing Ahmed, chief of Sanders' secret spies.

"Lord," he said, presenting himself at Sanders' bedside and squatting on the floor, "there is a dreamer in the Isisi country."

"So I have heard," said Sanders in Arabic, and wearily. "I, too, am a dreamer, and I should have dreamt for another hour if you had not disturbed me."

"God knows I would not destroy your gracious sleep," said Ahmed. "And I pray God every morning and every night that you may slumber kindly; but this M'dali sells his dreams, and has a great following. For he says to such an one, 'You shall give me a bag of salt or I will dream that you will die,' and, being afraid, the people pamper him in his desires."

"I see," said Sanders thoughtfully.

He dismissed his spy and rose.

In a little while he sent for his sergeant of police.

"Go you with three men, Abiboo," he said, "to the village of Tembolini, by the crocodile creek, and bring me M'dali, a dreamer of dreams."

"On my head and by my life," said Abiboo, and departed joyfully in a canoe.

He was ten days absent, and came back empty-handed.

"For the people threatened to kill me," he said, "M'dali having dreamt a dream that I was coming, and saying that if I took him every man of the village would be stricken blind. And, lord! knowing your disposition I did not desire a killing palaver, so came back without him, though, as you know, I am fearless of death."

"You did that which was right," said Sanders.

In an hour his steamboat was ready and had cast off, her sharp bows cleaving the black waters of the river, her little stern revolving rapidly.

In two days and a night the *Zaire* reached the village, and was met in mid-stream by the chief, one Kambori, an intelligent man.

"Lord," he said. "I tell you that if you take the dreamer the people will rise—not only the people of my village, but of the country round about—for he is regarded by all as a very holy man."

"I'll 'holy man' him," said Sanders in English, and continued his way to shore.

He entered the village with two Houssas at his elbow, and walked straight to the hut where M'dali sat in state.

Now M'dali had been a very ordinary man as Sanders knew him in the days before he began to dream.

He had been a spearer of fish, no more and no less well-to-do than hundreds of others.

Now he sat upon the carved stool that Lalinobi of Kusau had presented to him for dreaming that his wife would bear a male child, and he wore about his shoulders a robe of monkeys' tail which Tonda, chief of the Lulangu River, had presented when M'dali dreamt that he would outlive his brother.

He had various other gifts displayed—the carved stick in his hand, the string of iron beads about his neck, the worked copper bracelets about his arm, the little French mirror within reach, all testified mutely to the excellence of his clairvoyance.

He did not rise as Sanders came up.

Five hundred pairs of eyes were watching the Commissioner; all the countryside had assembled, for M'dali had dreamt of the Commissioner's coming.

"Hi, white man!" said M'dali loudly, "have you come for my dreams?"

Then he stood up quickly.

Twice Sanders landed at him with his pliant cane, and each blow got home.

Sanders heard the rustle of spears behind him, and turned—a heavy black automatic pistol in his hand.

"I had a dream," snarled Sanders, his pistol covering the nearest group. "I dreamt that a man raised his spear to me and died. And after he died his soul lived in a place filled with fishes, and every morning the fishes fed little by little upon it, and every night the soul grew again."

6

They dropped their spears. With their knuckles to their teeth—a sure sign of perturbation—they regarded him with horror and consternation.

"I dreamt," said Sanders, "that M'dali came with me to the Village of Irons, and when he left, all his property and all the rich presents of the foolish were divided amongst the people of this village."

There was a little murmur of approval, but some there were who regarded him sullenly, and Sanders judged these to be the country folk.

He turned to M'dali, a dazed man rubbing the growing weals on his shoulder with a shaking hand.

"Ih, dreamer!" said Sanders softly, "speak now, and tell these people how, when you leave them, all things shall be well."

The man hesitated, raised his sulky eyes to the level of the Commissioner's, and read the cold message they carried.

"People," he said shakily, "it is as our lord says."

"So you dreamt," suggested Sanders.

"So I dreamt," said M'dali, and there was a big sigh of relief.

"Take him to the boat," said Sanders. He spoke in Arabic to Abiboo. "Let none speak with him on your life."

He followed the Houssas with their crestfallen prisoner, and losing no time, cast off.

This ended the episode of the dreamer—for a while.

But though M'dali worked in the Village of Irons for the good of the Empire, his work went on, for he had been a busy man. There were unaccountable deaths. Men and women lay down in health and woke only to die. And none thought it remarkable or made report, for M'dali had dreamt thus, and thus it happened.

Yet rumour has feet to carry and mouth to tell; and in course of time Sanders went up country with a hastily-summoned doctor from headquarters, and there were people who were sorry to see him.

Men who had lost inconvenient wives, others who had buried rich relations, wives who found freedom by the fulfilment of M'dali—his dreams—sat down and waited for Sanders, gnawing their knuckles.

Sanders administered justice without any other evidence than his doctor could secure in unsavoury places; but it was effective, and M'dali, a chopper of wood in the Village of Irons, saw many familiar faces.

The Village of Irons stands on a tongue of land which thrusts the Isisi River to the left and the Bokaru River to the right. It is the cleanest village in Sanders' land, save only headquarters; but nobody appreciated its cleanliness except Sanders.

Here the streams run so swiftly that even strong swimmers dare not face them. At the base of the triangle a broad canal had been cut for five or six hundred yards connecting the two rivers, so that the little tongue of land was less a peninsula than an island, and a difficult island to leave—since a barbed-wire fence had been erected on both sides of the canal. Moreover, this canal was the abiding-place of three crocodiles—thoughtfully placed there by Mr. Commissioner Sanders—and their egress at either end of the canal was barred by stout stakes.

The village itself was divided into three parts, one for men, one for women, and a third—and this overlooking the only landing-place—for half a company of Houssas.

Though it was called the Village of Irons, none but shameless or hardened men wore the shackles of bondage, and life ran smoothly in this grim little village, save and except that the men were on one side of a tall wire and the women on the other.

M'dali arrived, and was given a number and a blanket. He was also told off to a hut with six other prisoners.

"I am M'dali of Isisi," he said, "and Sanders has sent me here because I dreamt."

"That is strange," said the headman of the hut, "for he sent me here because I beat one of his spies—I and my brother—till he died."

"I came here," said another man, "because I was a chief and made war—behold I am Tembeli of the Lesser Isisi."

One by one they introduced themselves and retailed him their discreditable exploits with simple pride.

"I am a dreamer of dreams," said M'dali in explanation. "When I dream a thing it happens, for I am gifted by devils and see strange things in my sleep."

"I see," said Tembeli wisely. "You are mad."

*　　*　　*　　*　　*

It is not difficult to explain how it came about that M'dali secured a hold upon the credulity and faith of his new companions.

There is a story that he predicted the death by drowning of one of the guards. Certainly such a fatality occurred. Every new prisoner from Tombolini was a fresh witness to his powers.

And in his most fluent manner M'dali dreamt for them. And this is one great dream he had:

It was that Sandi came to inspect the Village of Irons, and that when he reached a certain hut six men fell upon him and one cut his throat, and all the soldiers ran away terrified, and the prisoners released themselves, and there was no more bother.

He dreamt this three nights in succession.

When he retailed his first dream, Tembeli, to whom he related it, said thoughtfully:

"That is a good thought, yet we are without any weapon, so it cannot come true."

"In my dream to-night it will be revealed," said M'dali.

And on the next morning he told them how he had

seen in his vision a Congo man among the prisoners,
and how this Congo man carried a little razor stuck in
his hair.

And, truth to tell, there was such a Congo man who
carried such a razor.

"Who struck the blow?" asked Tembeli. "That is
a matter which requires great revelation."

Accordingly M'dali dreamt again, and discovered
that the man who killed Sanders was Korforo, a half-
witted prisoner from Akasava.

All things were now ready for the supreme moment.
There was a certain missionary lady, a Miss Ruth
Glandynne, who had come to the Great River to work
for humanity.

There were reasons why Sanders should not be on
excellent terms with her, not the least of these being
his ever-present fear for her safety, and the knowledge
that she did not know as much about native people as
she thought she knew—which was the gravest risk.

One day he received a letter from her asking per-
mission to visit the Village of Irons.

Sanders groaned.

He was not proud of the village—it advertised the
lawlessness of a section of his people, and he was
absurdly sensitive on this point. Moreover, he was, as
he knew, a gauche showman.

With some ill-grace, he replied that he would be
ready to show her the village at any time that was convenient, except—here followed a maddening list of
forbidden dates.

In the compilation of this list Sanders showed more
than usual guile. He racked his brain for exceptions.
On such a date she could not visit the village because
of "quarterly inspection," on another because of
"medical inspection"; yet another forbidden day was
the "inspection of equipment."

With great ingenuity he concocted thirty-five
periods in the year, varying from one to seven days,

when the convict establishment was not visible; and he hoped most earnestly that she would be sufficiently annoyed to give up the visit altogether.

To his despair, she replied immediately, choosing a day that was sandwiched between a spurious "appeal day" and a "mending week"—both of which occasions were the products of Sanders' fertile imagination.

She came down stream in her canoe, paddled by twenty men, and Sanders met her half-way and transferred her to his steamer.

Sanders in dazzling white, but a little stiff and very formal.

"If you don't mind my saying so," he said, "I'd much rather you hadn't attempted this little jaunt."

"It is hardly a jaunt, Mr. Sanders," she replied coldly. "I have a duty to these people—you admit that they are seldom seen by missionaries—and I should feel that I had failed in that duty if I did not take the opportunity which you so kindly offer me" (Sanders swore to himself at her brazen effrontery) "of visiting them."

From under the shade of his big helmet Sanders glanced at her.

"I shouldn't like you to go through life under the impression that I wanted you to come," he said bluntly —and Ruth Glandynne's nose rose ever so slightly, for if she was a missionary she was also a woman.

They reached the Village of Irons at eight o'clock one blazing morning.

"Now what the devil does this mean?" said Sanders. For there were only two Houssas on the beach—one of them on sentry duty and the other his relief.

"Lord!" said this man when Sanders stepped ashore. "The men of the company have journeyed down stream to a Place of Palms."

"By whose orders?" asked Sanders.

"It was revealed them, lord," said the man, "they being of the Sufi sect, that the blessed son of the

Prophet would appear to them in this place and show them many miracles."

A light dawned on the Commissioner, and he half smiled, though in his heart he raged.

"It seems that M'dali the Dreamer still dreams," he said. "There will be some whipping here to-morrow."

His first impulse was to send the girl straight back; he had no fear that the temporary withdrawal of the guard would lead to any serious consequence—that thought never for one moment entered his head—but he was a cautious man, and his instinct was against taking risk of any kind.

He was half-way back to the boat when he decided that, as the girl was here and had, moreover, come a long way, he had better get the thing over.

"You had best confine yourself to the women's quarters," he said. "I will send Abiboo with you—for myself, I have a little palaver with one M'dali."

He unlocked the steel gate that led to the women's compound, and stood watching the slim white figure of the girl as she moved up the tiny street—the straight, broad-shouldered Houssa at her elbow.

Then he crossed the lane which separated the men from the women, opened the gate, and entered, double-locking it behind him.

None came to speak to him, which was strange. Usually they clamoured to him for a hearing, good-naturedly calling him by his familiar name—which in English is "The-Little-Butcher-Bird-Who-Flies-by-Night."

Now they sat before their huts, chins on knees, watching him silently, fearfully.

"I don't like this," said Sanders.

He slipped his hand carelessly in his pocket and pushed down the safety catch of his Browning.

His second finger searched carefully for the butt of the pistol to feel if the magazine was pushed home.

He stood on a bare patch of well-swept roadway, and had an uninterrupted view of the street.

One quick glance he gave to the right. He could see Ruth talking to some native women—a group of three who squatted at her feet.

Behind her, clear of the group, was Abiboo, his Winchester carbine—a gift of Sanders—in the crook of his arm.

As the Commissioner looked he saw the Houssa furtively bring the lever back.

"Abiboo is loading," said something in Sanders' brain.

His eyes came back to the men's village. There was no move. The convicts sat before their huts, silent and expectant. A thrill of apprehension ran through his frame. He glanced again at Abiboo. He had unostentatiously withdrawn still further from the women and now he was holding the rifle with both hands —the right gripping the butt, the left supporting the barrel.

Then he turned his head slightly and nodded, and Sanders knew the signal was for him.

Sanders turned swiftly. Whatever danger there was lay in the women's village. He walked quickly back the way he came. Four men who had sat quietly rose and came out to meet him, showing no sign of haste.

"Lord, we have a petition," began one.

"Go back to your hut, Tembeli!" said Sanders steadily. "I will come again for your petition."

"Crack!"

Abiboo was firing into a hut, and the girl was flying along the street towards the gate.

All this Sanders saw as he turned his head, and then the four men were upon him.

A great hand covered his face, a cruel thumb fumbled for his eye. Tembeli went down shot through the heart, and Sanders tore himself free. He raced for the gate, taking out the key as he went.

He turned and shot at two of his pursuers, but they had no heart for the fight.

His steady hand unlocked the gate and closed it behind him. He saw Abiboo on the ground in the midst of a swaying tangle of men. The girl had disappeared. Then he saw her struggling with two of the women, and the half-witted Koforo slashing at her over the shoulders.

He reached the women as one grasped the girl by her hair and pulled back her head.

Koforo saw him coming, and dropped his hand.

"Ho, father!" he said, in his foolish, jocose way. "I am to kill you because you are a devil!"

The women shrank back, and Sanders caught the fainting girl by the waist and swung her out of reach.

Koforo came at him mouthing and grimacing, the little spade-shaped razor in his hand.

Sanders shot definitely because he had only five more cartridges, then he turned his attention to Abiboo.

He was lying on the ground insensible; his assailants had fled, for the sentry and his relief were firing through the wire-netting—and your trained Houssa is a tolerably good shot.

Together they bore the girl to the boat, and Abiboo was revived, stitched, and bandaged.

At four in the afternoon the crestfallen guard returned, and Sanders made an inspection of both camps.

"Lord," said one who had been but a passive conspirator, "it was the plan to take you in the women's quarters. Therefore certain men concealed themselves in the huts, thinking your lordship would not carry your little gun amongst women. All this was dreamt by M'dali, who has escaped."

"No man escapes from the Village of Irons," said Sanders. "Which way did M'dali go?"

The man pointed to the wire fence by the little canal.

Sanders made his way to the fence and looked down into the weed-grown stream.

"I saw him climb the first fence," said his informant; "but the second I did not see him climb."

The Commissioner stooped, and, picking up a handful of grass, threw it at a green log that lay on the water.

The log opened a baleful eye and growled hatefully, for he had fed well, and resented the interruption to his slumbers.

VII

THE THINKER AND THE GUM-TREE

THERE are three things which are beyond philosophy and logic.

Three things which turn mild men to rage and to the performance of heroic deeds. The one is love, the other is religion, and the third is land.

There was a man of the Isisi people who was a great thinker. He thought about things which were beyond thought, such as the stars and the storms and time, which began and ended nowhere.

Often he would go to the edge of the river and, sitting with his chin on his knees, ponder on great matters for days at a time. The people of the village—it was Akalavi by the creek—thought, not unnaturally, that he was mad, for this young man kept himself aloof from the joyous incidents of life, finding no pleasure in the society of maidens, absenting himself from the dances and the feasts that make up the brighter side of life on the river.

K'maka—such was this man's name—was the son of Yoko, the son of N'Kema, whose father was a fierce fighter in the days of the Great King. And on the dam side he went back to Pikisamoko, who was also a strong and bloody man, so that there was no hint of softness in his pedigree. "Therefore," said Yoko, his father, "he must be mad, and if the matter can be arranged without Sandi knowing, we will put out his eyes and take him a long way into the forest. There he will quickly die from hunger or wild beasts."

And all the relations who were bidden to the family palaver agreed, because a mad son is an abomination. He wanders about the village, and in his wanderings or in the course of his antics, he breaks things and does damage for which the family is legally responsible. They talked this matter over for the greater part of the night and came to no decision. The palaver was resumed the next day, and the elder of the family, a very old and a very wise chief from another village, gave his decision. "If he is mad," he said, "by all laws and customs he should be destroyed. Now I am a very clever man, as you all know, for I have lived for more years than any of you can remember. Let me, therefore, test K'maka, lest he be not mad at all, but only silly, as young men are when they come to the marrying age."

So they summoned K'maka to the council, and those who went in search of him found him lying on a soft bank in the forest. He was lying face downwards, his head in his hands, watching a flower.

"K'maka," said the man who sought him out, "what do you do?"

"I am learning," said K'maka simply; "for this weed teaches me many things that I did not know before."

The other looked down and laughed.

"It is a weed," he said, "bearing no fruit, so therefore it is nothing."

"It is alive," said K'maka, not removing his eyes from the thing of delicate petals; "and I think it is greater than I because it is obedient to the law."

"You are evidently mad," said his cousin, with an air of finality; "this is very certain."

He led him back to the family conference.

"I found him," he said importantly, "looking at weeds and saying that they were greater than he."

The family looked darkly upon K'maka and the old chief opened the attack.

"K'maka, it is said that you are mad; therefore, I, being the head of the family, have called the blood together that we may see whether the charge is true. Men say you have strange thoughts—such as the stars being land afar."

"That is true, my father," said the other.

"They also say that you think the sun is shining at night."

"That also I think," said K'maka; "meaning that it shines somewhere. For it is not wise to believe that the river is greater than the sun."

"I perceive that you are indeed mad," said the old man calmly; "for in what way do the sun and the river meet?"

"Lord," said the young man earnestly, "behold the river runs whether it is day or night, whether you walk or sleep, whether you see it or whether it is unseen. Yet the foolish think that if they do not see a thing, then that thing does not exist. And is the river greater than the sun? For if the river runs by night, being part of the Great Way, shall the sun, which is so much mightier and so much more needful to the lands, cease to shine?"

The old chief shook his head.

"None but a man who is very mad would say such a thing as this," he said; "for does not the sun become the moon by night, save on the night when it sleeps? And if men sleep and goats sleep, and even women sleep, shall not the sun sleep, creeping into a hole in the ground, as I myself have seen it?"

They dismissed K'maka then and there. It seemed useless to talk further.

He slept in a hut by himself. He was late in returning to his home that night, for he had been watching bats in the forest; but when he did he found six cousins waiting. They seized him; he offered no resistance.

They bound him hand and foot to a long pole and laid him in the bottom of a canoe. Then his six cousins got in with him and paddled swiftly down stream. They were making for the Forest of Devils, which is by the Silent River—a backwater into which only crocodiles go to lay their eggs, for there are sandy shoals which are proper for the purpose.

At dawn they stopped, and, lighting a fire, cooked their meal. They gave their prisoner some fish and manioc.

"There is a hungry time waiting you, brother," said one of the cousins; "for we go to make an end of you, you being mad."

"Not so mad am I," said K'maka calmly, "but that I cannot see your madness."

The cousin made no retort, knowing that of all forms of lunacy that which recognised madness in others was the most hopeless.

The sun was well up when the canoe continued its journey, K'maka lying in the bottom intensely interested in the frantic plight of two ants who had explored the canoe in a spirit of adventure.

Suddenly the paddles ceased.

Steaming up stream, her little hull dazzling white from a new coat of paint, her red and white deck awning plainly to be seen, came the *Zaire*, and the tiny blue ensign of Mr. Commissioner Sanders was hanging lazily from the one stub of a mast that the vessel boasted.

"Let us paddle nearer the shore," said the chief of the cousins, "for this is Sandi; and if he sees what we carry he will be unkind."

They moved warily to give the little steamer a wide berth.

But Sanders of the River, leaning pensively over the rail of the forebridge, his big helmet tilted back to keep the sun from his neck, had seen them. Also, he had detected concern in the sudden cessation of paddling, alarm in the energy with which it was resumed, and guilt confessed in the new course.

His fingers beckoned the steersman, and the helm went over to port. The *Zaire* swung across to intercept the canoe.

"This man," said the exasperated chief cousin, "has eyes like the okapi, which sees its enemies through trees."

He stopped paddling and awaited the palaver.

"What is this, Sambili?" asked Sanders, as the steamer came up and a boat hook captured the tiny craft. Sanders leant over the side rail and addressed the cousin by name.

"Lord," said Sambili, "I will not lie to you; this man is my cousin, and is mad; therefore we take him to a witch-doctor who is famous in such matters."

Sanders nodded, and flecked the white ash of his cheroot into the water.

"I know the river better than any man, yet I do not know of such a doctor," he said. "Also I have heard that many mad people have been taken to the Forest of Devils and have met a doctor whom they have not seen. And his name is Ewa, which means Death."

Two of his Houssas hauled the trussed man aboard.

"Release him," said Sanders.

"Lord," said the cousin, in agitation, "he is very mad and very fierce."

"I also am fierce," said Sanders; "and men say that I am mad, yet I am not bound to a pole."

Released from his bondage, K'maka stood up shakily, rubbing his numbed limbs.

"They tell me you are mad, K'maka," said Sanders.

K'maka smiled, which was a bad sign, for native men, far gone in sleeping sickness and touching the verge of madness, often smile in this way. Sanders watched him curiously.

"Master," said K'maka, "these cousins of mine think I am mad because I think."

"What manner of things do you think, K'maka?" asked Sanders gently.

The other hesitated. "Lord, I fear to say, lest you, too, should believe in my madness."

"Speak," said Sanders, "and have no fear; for I am as your father and your king, being placed here to rule you by a man who is very high in the council of kings."

K'maka drew a long breath.

"I think of life," he said, "and of the stars; of why men do certain acts. I think of rivers. Lord," he asked, "why does a stone thrown into still water make little ripples in true circles widening, widening until the waves reach beyond sight?"

Sanders looked at him narrowly. He had heard of this thinker.

"Go on," he said.

"Lord, this also I think," said K'maka, encouraged, "that I am nothing, that all is nothing"—he waved his hand to the white hot world—"that you, our lord, are nothing."

"This is a shameful thing to say," said the chief cousin, shocked, "and proves beyond doubt that he is mad."

"Why am I nothing, K'maka?" asked Sanders quietly.

"Lord," said the man gravely, "that-which-is-not-always is nothing."

"Hear him!" appealed Sambili in despair. "Hear

this madman. Oh ko ko! Now, K'maka, you have shown your madness to our lord beyond doubt."

He waited for Sanders to summon the Man of Irons to shackle K'maka to the deck. Instead, Sanders was leaning against the rail, his head sunk in thought.

"K'maka," he said at last, "it appears to me that you are a strange man; yet you are not mad, but wiser than any black man I have seen. Now you are so wise that if I leave you with your brethren they will surely kill you, for stupid men hate the learned, and it seems to me that you have too much learning."

He gave orders that K'maka should be housed with the crew.

As for the cousins, he turned them into their canoe.

"Go in peace," he said, "for you have rid yourself of your 'madman' and have saved yourself a hanging—I will have no putting out of eyes in this land."

Sanders had no man handy to whom he might speak of the thinker, for his two subordinates were down with fever and on leave at the coast. He was inclined towards experiments. Bosambo of Monrovia had been an experiment, and a most successful one. Just now Bosambo was being a nuisance, as witness this journey which Sanders was making.

Contiguous to the land of the Ochori was a narrow strip of territory, which acted as a tiny buffer state between the Ochori and the Isisi. It occupied a peculiar position, inasmuch as though completely unimportant, it was desired by both the Ochori and the Isisi, and had at various times been absorbed by both, only to be ruthlessly restored to its neutrality by the iron hand of Sanders. There was no reason in the world why both nations should not have free access and passage through the Lombobo—as it was called— and a wise chief would have so ordered things that whilst Ochori man and Isisi moved in and through it, neither nation should claim the right to lordship.

This chief Sanders had been long in finding.

He had appointed many.

Kombanava the N'Gombi, who sold his kingship to the Isisi for a thousand rods and twenty bags of salt; Olambo of Akasava, who had hardly been installed before he bartered away his rights to Bosambo of the Ochori; M'nabo, the coast man; Tibini, the Lesser Isisi man; a whole string of little chiefs of Lombobo had come and gone.

Sanders thought of these, sitting under the awning of the bridge, as the *Zaire* drove through the black-yellows waters of the Big River.

He was very patient, and his was the patience of years. He was not discouraged, though the bitterness of a recent failure still rankled. For he had placed one Sakadamo in the seat of chieftainship, and he had known Sakadamo for years.

Yet once Sanders was out of sight, the mild Saka-damo, stiff with pride, had gathered his fighting men, and had led them with fine impartiality against Ochori and Isisi, and in the end had sold the country to both.

For which offence Sakadamo was at the moment working out a sentence of two years' labour in the Village of Irons, and Lombobo was chiefless.

Sanders smoked two cigars over the matter, then he sent for K'maka the Thinker.

They brought him, a tall young man, inclined to thinness. Sanders took him in from the broad crown of his woolly head to the big feet which ended his thin legs. He had knobby knees, and the skin cloak which partially covered him revealed the same tendency to thinness.

Sanders put his age at nineteen, which was probably an accurate estimate.

"K'maka," he said, after his survey, "such a man as you it is not usual to meet, nor have I met your like. Now I know you to be a man above ambition, above hates, and understanding large matters of life."

"Lord, I am one who thinks, and I myself do not

7

know whether my thoughts be mad thoughts or whether they are high above the common thoughts of men."

"Take to yourself the pleasure of knowing that you are not mad," said Sanders drily. "Surely I believe this, and to give you a sign of my faith I am for making you chief of Lombobo, standing in my place, giving and taking justice, and laying over the fiery spirit of your people the waters of your wisdom."

"Lord, I will do as you wish," said K'maka.

And so it came about that at a great palaver at which the headmen and lesser directors of the people were assembled, Sanders made the Thinker paramount chief and lord of the Lombobo tribe, hanging about his neck the steel chain and medal of his rank and office. To a separate palaver Bosambo and the King of the Isisi were summoned, and plain words were spoken.

After the Isisi had departed Sanders took the young chief a journey to the very edge of his new domain, and with them went Bosambo.

In a clearing on the very border, and by the side of the path which connected the two little countries, grew a great gum-tree, and here the party halted.

"Bosambo and K'maka," said Sanders, "this tree shall mark which is Ochori and which is Lombobo. For all that is on one side belongs to one and all that is on the other belongs to the other."

They looked at the tree, the two chiefs; they regarded it long and attentively.

"Lord," said Bosambo at length, "your meaning is clear, yet in whose country does this tree stand?"

It was a question worthy of Bosambo.

"That half which faces the Ochori is in the Ochori country; that half which faces Lombobo is in the Lombobo country," said Sanders.

One last warning he gave to K'maka.

"To Ochori and to Isisi," he said, "you will give

communion and freedom of trade; you shall hinder none, nor help any at the expense of the other. You shall be wise and large."

"Lord, I will do this," said K'maka, nodding his head, "for the things that grow and perish are nothing and only the spirits of men endure."

With which wise saying in his ears Sanders took his departure, happy in the belief that Providence had sent him at last the solution of the buffer state problem.

It is placed on record that K'maka began his rule with wisdom. The Lombobo people, used by now to strange chiefs, did their best to help him to destruction. They brought forward litigation for his judgment—litigation which would have taxed the sagacity of a Supreme Court or the Judicial Committee of the Privy Council. As for instance:

"If a man buys a wife, paying for her with two bags of salt, and she be a vixen, and, moreover, undesirable from many points of view, how shall he recover the price he paid for her when the salt has been capsized out of his own canoe, rowed by two of his own paddlers and two of his father-in-law's paddlers?"

Also:

"A man has borrowed a neighbour's spear to go hunting, and has invariably paid for the loan by a proportion of the kill. One day he went hunting with a defective spear, and became lamed by a leopard. Can he claim compensation because the spear was a bad one if the lender can prove that its defective condition is due to the carelessness of a mutual cousin?"

These were two of the problems they propounded, sitting in a solemn circle at palaver, and the Thinker judged at length. He was four days delivering his judgment in the first case. His people sat spellbound, hypnotised by words. They did not understand his philosophy; they could not follow his reasoning; they were altogether fogged as to whether he decided upon the one side or the other; and at the end, when he raised his two hands according to custom and said, "The palaver is finished," they went away pleasantly confounded.

"We have a chief," said the headman of the fishing village by the river, "who is wiser than all other men; so wise that we cannot understand him."

K'maka busied himself with mundane affairs. He even took a girl of the Isisi to wife. Also he allowed free passage to Isisi and Ochori alike. Both nations sent him presents, which he accepted. On the third day of his chieftainship his headman had come to tell him that the Ochori were fishing in Lombobo waters, and that the Isisi were hunting in the Lombobo forests.

"Let this be," said M'maka, "for the forests and the rivers are for all, and there are no boundaries to necessity. For this is not my land nor my river; nor is it yours; being rather for all men, who find therein certain requirements."

This was as Sanders required, and when the news came to the Commissioner, as it did, he was pleased.

Then an evil gossip brought to K'maka stories of his girl-wife, who was attractive.

"I am no man to set a fence about desire," said K'maka; "nor shall man or woman in this, my land, be enslaved by custom."

Two months passed smoothly. K'maka grew in influence daily, his crowning achievement being a judgment which took nine days to deliver.

Then a headman came with a plaint against the Ochori.

"Lord, they cut wood in the Lombobo country and carry it to their city," he said.

"The wood is free to all," said K'maka.

He sat on the little carved stool in the centre of the half-moon of huts which constituted his administrative headquarters.

"Yet," he went on, "since this is my land and the

people my people, and since I have been set to guard them, it is a shameful thing that robbers should spoil this land."

A fortnight after this a party of Ochori hunters came into the Lombobo country hot on the trail of an elephant. K'maka sent a regiment to seize them and impound the elephant.

"For this I say," said he to his captives, "and my words are of such wisdom that even Sandi bows before them: That which is on one side of a certain tree on the Ochori side is mine and what is on the other side is your master's."

"Lord," said the chief huntsman, "it was a palaver that there should be free hunting in your land."

"And free fishing," said K'maka with savage sarcasm, "and free wood-cutting by Death! And that thief, your master, would spoil my beautiful land, sucking it dry, and make mock of me—a chief of a thousand spears! Go back to Bosambo and summon him to meet me by the gum-tree on the road."

The empty-handed huntsmen returned home to meet with the wrath of their lord.

Bosambo swore in Karo, in Arabic, in Bomongo, in Swahili, and in English, calling K'maka a "dam black nigger," and casting reflections upon his parentage.

At an appointed time the two chiefs met, K'maka being late in arriving.

"Lord Bosambo," said he, speaking from a place which was on the Lombobo side of the gum-tree, "I have shame in my heart that I did not come at the hour. But I have a wife who had a lover, putting shame on me, and this day I killed her and him according to the law."

"These things happen," said Bosambo. "Now have I come to you, K'maka the Thinker, because of certain strange occurrences which have come to my ears. It is said that you have forbidden the Ochori to hunt or chop wood in your territory."

"That is true," said K'maka, "for the land this side of the gum-tree is mine, and I am chief of the country as far as your eye sees."

"The land is for all," said Bosambo with some unction.

"The world is for all," corrected the Thinker; "yet rabbits do not nest in trees or eagles burrow in the earth. Each kind lives in the place appointed, and it is appointed the Ochori should live on the one side and the Lombobo on the other."

Bosambo was aroused.

"It seems that you are an avaricious dog," he said, "and if I chop wood to the edge of my country, behold I begin!"

He called for an axe, and they brought him one, thin of blade and very sharp.

He struck twice at the tree.

"Bosambo," said K'maka, quivering with rage, "what do you do?"

"Dispenser of Justice," mocked Bosambo, "former of fat words, talking fish and breeder of wisdom as a dirty hut breds vermin, I go to cut my tree."

"It is my tree!" roared K'maka and reached behind him for a throwing spear.

"One half is yours," said Bosambo, chopping steadily, yet with an eye to danger, "and behold! I cut down that half which is mine. And if by your wisdom you keep your half standing, then you are a prince amongst thinkers."

He continued cutting whilst K'maka watched, boiling with rage.

"If you continue in your evil practice," he said, "what shall prevent the tree falling."

"Nothing," said Bosambo significantly, "for the nights of wind are coming, and the wind blows towards the Ochori—and behold! when the tree falls it shall belong to——"

K'maka drew back his hand swiftly and threw his spear.

    *   *   *   *   *

"They are in that clump of bush," said Sanders.

His face was reeking wet, and there was a thin trickle of blood on his face.

"I'll put a couple of shells into 'em," said the Houssa captain. "These Lombobo people fight fairly well."

Sanders said nothing. He bared his white teeth in a smile, but he was not really amused.

"Ahmet," said the Houssa captain, kneeling on the deck and keeping his field glasses fixed on the little patch of wood that hid the enemy, "as you love the faith and hate all Kaffirs, do not drop your shell short again, or I will beat you on the feet."

"Lord, the light is bad," said the gunner. He brought the muzzle of the gun a little higher and fired.

This time the shell fell true. Over the trees a white ball of smoke came into existence, and they heard the "krock" of its shell as it burst.

The Houssa captain rose and walked to where Sanders stood.

"Exactly what is all the bother about?" he asked.

Sanders said nothing for a while.

"Bosambo had something to do with it," he said, "yet the rascal was only acting according to his rights. K'maka is raising Cain. He has fought the Isisi and raided their territory; he has pushed back the Ochori to the edge of their city—they had to fight like the devil to save it. K'maka has proclaimed himself king of the Ochori, the Isisi, and the Lombobo, and has sent to the Akasava and the N'Gombi to bring him presents and do homage."

His voice choked; then the humour of it appealed to him, and he laughed.

He went ashore with the Houssas, and led the section which stormed the last stockade.

Revolver in hand, he raced across the little clearing, the Houssas, with fixed bayonets, flanking him.

K'maka, surrounded by the remnant of his captains, made a fierce resistance, but it was futile.

Suddenly his men flung down their spears and bolted.

"Take that man!"

A group of Houssas flung themselves upon the struggling philosopher and bore him down.

They brought him, bleeding but defiant, before Sanders, and for the space of two minutes they looked at one another.

"K'maka," said Sanders at length, "you have done a terrible thing, for you have brought war to this land by your arrogance and pride."

"White man," said K'maka haughtily, "I am a king and the master of these countries—I do not speak with servants—therefore, O little man, bring me before your king that we may speak, equal to equal."

Sanders said nothing, then:

"Catch him!" he said quickly.

For K'maka went suddenly limp, his knees gave way and he slid down to the earth.

He was wounded to death, as Sanders saw when he examined him.

They carried the man to the shade of a tree, and Sanders sat by him.

The man looked up at the Commissioner.

"Lord," he said faintly, "I think I go beyond your punishment."

"That is true, K'maka," said Sanders softly, "and I could have wished you had gone before you brought all this sorrow to the Lombobo people."

K'maka shook his head.

"This is the way," he said drowsily, "for the living things prey upon the living things, birds upon insects, leopards upon birds, men upon leopards, and, since there is nought greater than man, then man preys upon himself. This is ordained——"

They gave him water and he opened his eyes again.

"Lord," he said, and now he spoke with difficulty, "I have discovered in my thinking the greatest truth in the world."

A strange light came into his eyes; they danced eagerly with the greatness of his discovery.

"All your wise men do not know this," he whispered; "death is——"

Sanders waited, but K'maka the Thinker carried his secret with him to the land of sleep.

VIII

NINE TERRIBLE MEN

THERE were nine terrible men in the Forest of O'tomb', so native report had it.

Nine terrible men who lived on an island set in a swamp. And the swamp was hard to come by, being in the midst of a vast forest. Only a monkey or a leopard could find a way to the inhabitants of this island— they themselves being privy to the secret ways.

No man of the Isisi, of the N'Gombi, of the Akasava, or of the river tribes, attempted to track down the nine, for, as it was generally known, most powerful ju-jus guarded all paths that led to the secret place.

Nine outlawed men, with murder and worse upon their souls, they came together, God knows how, and preyed upon their world.

They raided with impunity, being impartial as to whether Isisi or N'Gombi paid toll.

By night they would steal forth in single file, silent

as death, no twig cracking in their path, no word spoken. As relentless as the soldier ant in his march of destruction, they made their way without hindrance to the village they had chosen for the scene of their operations, took what they wanted and returned.

Sometimes they wanted food, sometimes spears—for these lords of the woods were superior to craftsmanship—sometimes a woman or two went and never came back.

Such lawless communities were not uncommon. Occasionally very ordinary circumstances put an end to them; some there were that flourished, like the People-Who-Were-Not-All-Alike.

The Nine Terrible Men of the O'tomb' existed because nothing short of an army corps could have surrounded them, and because, as Sanders thought, they were not a permanent body, but dispersed at times to their several homes.

Sanders once sent two companies of Houssas to dislodge the nine, but they did nothing, for the simple reason that never once did they get within shooting distance. Then Sanders came himself, and caught little else than a vicious attack of malarial fever.

He sent messages to all the chiefs of the people within a radius of a hundred miles to kill at sight any of the nine, offering certain rewards. After three palpably inoffensive men of the Ochori tribe had been killed, and the reward duly claimed, Sanders countermanded the order.

For two years the nine ravaged at will, then a man of the Isisi, one Fembeni, found grace.

Fembeni became a Christian, though there is no harm in that. This is not satire, but a statement with a reservation. There are certain native men who embrace the faith and lose quality thereby, but Fembeni was a Christian and a better man—except——

Here is another reservation.

Up at Mosunkusu a certain Ruth Glandynne

laboured for the cause, she, as I have previously described, being a medical missionary, and pretty to boot.

White folk would call her pretty because she had regular features, a faultless complexion, and a tall, well-modelled figure.

Black folk thought she was plain, because her lips were not as they should be by convention; nor was she developed according to their standards.

Also, from N'Gombi point of view, her fair, long hair was ridiculous, and her features "like a bird."

Mr. Commissioner Sanders thought she was very pretty indeed—when he allowed himself to think about her.

He did not think about her more often than he could help, for two reasons—the only one that is any business of yours and mine being that she was an enormous responsibility. He had little patches of white hair on either side of his temple—when he allowed his hair to grow long enough for these to become visible—which he called grimly his "missionary hairs." The safety of the solitary stations set in the wilds was a source of great worry.

You must understand that missionaries are very good people. Those ignoramuses who sneer at them place themselves in the same absurd position as those who sneer at Nelson or speak slightingly of other heroes.

Missionaries take terrible risks—they cut themselves adrift from the material life which is worth the living; they endure hardships incomprehensible to the uninitiated; they suffer from tempestuous illnesses which find them hale and hearty in the morning and leave their feeble bodies at the edge of death at sunset.

"And all this they do," said Bosambo of Monrovia, philosophically and thoughtfully, "because of certain mysteries which happened when the world was young and a famous Man called Hesu.* Now I think that is the greatest mystery of all."

Sanders appreciated the disinterestedness of the work, was immensely impressed by the courage of the people who came to labour in the unhealthy field, but all the time he fretfully wished they wouldn't.

His feelings were those of a professional lion-tamer who sees a light-hearted amateur stepping into the cage of the most savage of his beasts; they were feelings of the skilled matador who watches the novice's awkward handling of an Andalusian bull—a troubled matador with a purple cloak held ready and one neatly-shod foot on the barrier, ready to spring into the ring at the novello's need.

The "missionary patches" grew larger and whiter in the first few months of Ruth Glandynne's presence at Musunkusu, for this village was too near to the wild N'Gombi, too near the erratic Isisi, for Sanders' liking.

Sanders might easily have made a mistake in his anxiety. He might have sent messengers to the two peoples, or gone in person—threatening them with death and worse than death if they harmed the girl.

But that would have aroused a sense of importance in their childlike bosoms, and when the time came, as it assuredly would come, when their stomachs were angry against him, some chief would say:

"Behold, here is a woman who is the core of Sandi's eye. If we do her harm we shall be revenged on Sandi."

And, since children do not know any other tomorrow than the to-morrow of good promise, it would have gone badly with the lady missionary.

Instead, Sanders laid upon Bosambo, chief of the Ochori, charge of this woman, and Bosambo he trusted in all big things, though in the matter of goods movable and goods convertible he had so such confidence.

* The Third Person of the Trinity is so called in some dialects.

When Fembeni of the Isisi was converted from paganism to Christianity, Sanders was fussing about the little creeks which abound on the big river, looking for a man named Oko, who after a long and mysterious absence had returned to his village, killed his wife, and fled to the bush.

The particular bush happened to be in the neighbourhood of the mission station, otherwise Sanders might have been content to allow his policemen to carry out the good work, but no sooner did news come that Oko had broken for that section of the N'Gombi country which impinges on Musunkusu, than Sanders went flying up river in his steamer because something told him he had identified one of the nine men.

Wrote Sergt. Ahmed, the Houssa, who prided himself on his English, to his wife at headquarters:

"At daylight, when search for murderer was officially resumed, came our Lord Sundah very actively angry. By orders I took left bank of Kulula River with three men, being ordered to shoot aforesaid Oko if resistance offered. Abiboo (sergeant) took right or other bank, and our lord searched bush. Truly Oko must be a very important man that Sundah comes officially searching for same, saying bitter reproach words to his humble servants."

Ahmed's picture of his chief's agitation may be a little exaggerated, but I do not doubt that there was a substratum of fact therein.

On the second day of the hunt, Sanders' steamer was tied up at the mission station, and he found himself walking in the cool of the evening with Ruth Glandynne. So he learnt about Fembeni, the Isisi man who had found the light and was hot and eager for salvation.

"H'm!" said Sanders, displaying no great enthusiasm.

But she was too elated over her first convert to notice the lack of warmth in his tone.

"It is just splendid," she said, her grey eyes alight and her pretty face kindling with the thought, "especially when you remember, Mr. Sanders, that I have only an imperfect knowledge of the language."

"Are you sure," asked the incredulous Sanders, "that Fembeni understands what it is all about?"

"Oh, yes!" She smiled at the Commissioner's simplicity. "Why, he met me half-way, as it were; he came out to meet the truth; he——"

"Fembeni?" said Sanders thoughtfully. "I think I know the man; if I remember him aright he is not the sort of person who would get religion if he did not see a strong business end to it."

She frowned a little. Her eyebrows made a level line over resentful eyes.

"I think that is unworthy of you," she said coldly.

He looked at her, the knuckle of his front finger at his lips.

She was very pretty, he thought, or else he had been so long removed from the society of white women that she seemed beautiful only because she stood before a background of brutal ugliness.

Slim, straight, grave-eyed, complexion faultless, though tanned by the African sun, features regular and delicate, hair (a quantity) russet-brown.

Sanders shook his head.

"I wish to heaven you weren't monkeying about in this infernal country," he said.

"That is beside the question," she replied with a little smile. "We are talking of Fembeni, and I think you are being rather horrid."

They reached the big square hut that Sanders had built for her, and climbed the wooden steps that led to the stoep.

Sanders made no reply, but when she had disappeared into the interior of the hut to make him some tea, he beckoned to Abiboo, who had followed him at a respectful distance.

"Go you," he said, "and bring me Fembeni of the Isisi."

He was stirring his tea whilst the girl was giving him a rosy account of her work, when Fembeni came, a tall man of middle age, wearing the trousers and waistcoat which were the outward and visible signs of his inward and spiritual grace.

"Come near, Fembeni," said Sanders gently.

The man walked with confidence up the steps of the stoep, and without invitation drew a chair towards him and seated himself.

Sanders said nothing. He looked at the man for a very long time, then:

"Who asked you to sit in my presence?" he said softly.

"Lord," said Fembeni pompously, "since I have found the blessed truth——"

Something in Sanders' eyes caused him to rise hurriedly.

"You may sit—on the ground," said Sanders quietly, "after the manner of your people, and I will sit on this chair after the manner of mine. For behold, Fembeni, even the blessed truth shall not make black white or white black; nor shall it make you equal with Sandi, who is your master."

"Lord, that is so," said the sullen Fembeni, "yet we are all equal in the eyes of the great One."

"Then there are a million people in the Isisi, in the N'Gombi, the Akasava, and the Ochori, who are your equals," said Sanders, "and it is no shame for you to do as they do."

Which was unanswerable, according to Fembeni's sense of logic.

The girl had listened to the talk between her novitiate and the commissioner with rising wrath, for she had not Sanders' knowledge of native people.

"I think that is rather small of you, Mr. Sanders,"

she said hotly. "It is a much more important matter that a heathen should be brought to the truth than that your dignity should be preserved."

Sanders frowned horribly—he had no society manners and was not used to disputation.

"I do not agree with you, Miss Glandynne," he said a little gruffly, "for, whilst the Isisi cannot see the ecstatic condition of his soul which leads him to be disrespectful to me, they can and do see the gross materialism of his sotting body."

A thought struck him and he turned to the man. That thought made all the difference between life and death to Fembeni.

"Fembeni," he said, relapsing into the language of the Isisi, "you are a rich man by all accounts."

"Lord, it is so."

"And wives—how many have you?"

"Four, lord."

Sanders nodded and turned to the girl.

"He has four wives," he said.

"Well?"

There was a hint of defiance in the questioning "Well?"

"He has four wives," repeated Sanders. "What is your view on this matter?"

"He shall marry one in the Christian style," she said, flushing. "Oh, you know, Mr. Sanders, it is impossible for a man to be a Christian and have more wives than one!"

Sanders turned to the man again.

"In this matter of wives, Fembeni," he said gently; "how shall you deal with the women of your house?"

Fembeni wriggled his bare shoulders uncomfortably.

"Lord, I shall put them all away, save one," he said sulkily, "for that is the blessed way."

"H'm!" said Sanders for the second time that morning.

He was silent for a long time, then:

"It is rather a problem," he said.

"It presents no difficulty to my mind," said the girl stiffly.

She was growing very angry, though Sanders did not realise the fact, being unused to the ways of white women.

"I think it is rather horrid of you, Mr. Sanders, to discourage this man, to put obstacles in his faith——"

"I put no obstacle," interrupted the Commissioner. He was short of speech, being rather so intent upon his subject that he took no account of the fine feelings of a zealous lady missionary. "But I cannot allow this to happen in my district; this man has four wives, each of them has borne him children. What justice or what Christianity is there in turning loose three women who have served this man?"

Here was a problem for the girl, and in her desperation she used an argument which was unanswerable.

"The law allows this," she said. "These things happen all over the world where missionary work is in progress. Perhaps I could bring the women to understand; perhaps I could explain——"

"You couldn't explain the babies out of existence," said Sanders brutally.

That ended the discussion, for with a look of scorn and disgust she passed into the hut, leaving Sanders a prey to some emotion.

He turned a cold eye to the offending Fembeni.

"It seems," he said, "that a man by becoming a Christian has less mouths to fill. Now I must investigate this matter."

Fembeni regarded him apprehensively, for if a woman is questioned, who knows what she will say? And it was fairly unimportant to the man if he had one wife or forty.

There was no possibility of searching any farther that night for the erring Oko, and Sanders was rowed

8

across the river in his canoe to interview the wives of the new convert.

He found one woman who viewed the coming change with considerable philosophy, and three who were very shrill and very voluble.

"Lord," said one of these three in that insolent tone which only native women assume, "this white witch has taken our man——"

"I do not hear well," said Sanders quickly, "yet I thought I heard a word I do not like."

He whiffled a pliant stick till it hummed a tune.

"Lord," said the woman, dropping her voice and speaking more mildly, "this God-lady has taken our man."

"God-ladies do not take men," said Sanders; "rather they influence their spirits that they may be better men."

"Fembeni will be no better and no worse," said the woman bitterly, "for he goes to the forest by night; often he has risen from my side, and when he has gone, behold the Nine Terrible Men have come from near by and taken that which they wanted."

She stopped abruptly. There was horror in the eyes which met the Commissioner's; in her anger she had said too much.

"That is foolish talk," said Sanders easily.

He knew there would be no more information here and he played to quieten her fears.

He strolled through the village, talked awhile with the headman, and returned to his canoe.

Once on the *Zaire* he summoned Abiboo.

"Take three men and bring Fembeni to me," he said, "and be very ready to shoot him, for I have heard certain things."

He waited for ten minutes, then Abiboo returned—alone.

"Fembeni has gone into the forest," he said; "also the God-lady."

Sanders looked at him.

"How?"

"Lord, this Fembeni is a Christian, and desired to speak with the God-woman of the new magic. So they walked together, the God-woman reading from a book. Also he had a gift for her, which he bought from a Frenchi trader."

"I see," said Sanders.

He poured himself out a stiff glass of whiskey, and his hand shook a little.

Then he lifted down a sporting rifle that hung on the wall of his cabin, broke open two packets of cartridges, and dropped them into his coat pocket.

"Let the men come on quickly," he said, "you commanding."

"Lord, there are other Sergeants," said Abiboo. "I will go with you, for I am at your right hand, though death waits me."

"As you will," said Sanders roughly.

He went through the missionary compound, stopping only that a boy should point out the direction the two had taken, then he moved swiftly towards the forest, Abiboo at his heels.

He followed the beaten track for a hundred yards. Then he stopped and sniffed like a dog.

He went on a little farther and came back on his tracks.

He stooped and picked up some pieces of broken glass and turned aside from the path, following his nose.

*　　*　　*　　*　　*

Ruth Glandynne had supreme faith in the power of the Word which makes martyrs.

"You must have no doubt, Fembeni," she said in her halting Isisi, "for with Light, such things as the Word brings, all things will be made plain to you."

They were beyond the confines of the little mission station, walking slowly towards the forest.

She read little extracts from the book she carried, and so full of her subject was she that she did not observe that they had passed the straggling trees, the outposts of the big forest.

When she did notice this she turned.

"More I will tell you, Fembeni," she said.

"Lady, tell me now," he begged, "for Sandi has made me doubt."

She frowned. What mischief can a materialist work! She had liked Sanders. Now for one resentful moment she almost hated him.

"There are white men who doubt," she said, "and who place pitfalls in the way——"

"Also this have I bought for you," said Fembeni, "paying one bag of salt."

From the leather pouch at his side he produced a long flat flask.

She smiled as she recognised the floral label of the abominable scent beloved of the natives.

"This I bought for you, teacher," he said, and removed the stopper so that the unoffending evening reeked of a sudden with the odour of musk, "that you might protect me against Sandi, who is no God-man but a devil."

She took the bottle and hastily replaced the stopper.

"Sandi is no devil," she said gently, "and will do you no harm."

"He has crossed the river," said Fembeni sulkily, and there was a curious glitter in his eyes, "and he will speak with my wives, and they will tell him evil things of me."

She looked at him gravely.

"What evil things can they say?" she asked.

"They can lie," he said shortly, "and Sandi will bring his rope and I shall die."

She smiled. "I do not think you need fear," she said,

and began to walk back; but he stood in front of her, and at that instant she realised her danger, and the colour faded from her face.

"If Sandi comes after me to kill me," he said slowly, "I shall say to him: 'Behold, I have a woman of your kind, and if you do not pardon me you will be sorry.'"

She thought quickly, then of a sudden leapt past him and fled in the direction of the station.

He was after her in a flash. She heard the fast patter of his feet, and suddenly felt his arm about her waist.

She screamed, but there was none to hear her, and his big hand covered her mouth.

He shook her violently.

"You live or you die," he said; "but if you cry out I will beat you till you die."

He half carried, half dragged her in the direction of the forest.

She was nearly dead with fear; she was dimly conscious of the fact that he did not take the beaten path, that he turned at right angles and moved unerringly through the wood, following a path of his own knowing.

As he turned she made another attempt to secure her liberty. She still held the scent flask in her hand, and struck at him with all her might. He caught her arm and nearly broke it.

The stopper fell out and her dress was drenched with the vile perfume.

He wrenched the flask from her hand and threw it away.

Grasping her by the arm he led her on. She was nearly exhausted when he stopped, and she sank an inert heap to the ground.

She dare not faint, though she was on the verge of such a breakdown. How long they had been travelling she had no idea. The sun was setting; this she guessed rather than knew, for no sunlight penetrated the aisles.

Fembeni watched her; he sat with his back to a tree and regarded her thoughtfully.

After a while he rose.

"Come," he said.

They moved on in silence. She made no appeal to him. She knew now the futility of speech. Her mind was still bewildered. "Why, why, why?" it asked incoherently.

Why had this man professed Christianity?

"Fembeni," she faltered, "I have been kind to you."

"Woman," he said grimly, "you may be kinder."

She said no more.

The horror of the thing began to take shape. She half stopped, and he grasped her arm roughly.

"By my head you shall live," he said, "if Sandi gives his word that none of us shall hang—for we are the Terrible Men, and Sandi has smelt me out."

There was a gleam of hope in this speech. If it was only as a hostage that they held her——

Night had fallen when they came to water.

Here Fembeni halted. He searched about an undergrowth and dragged to view a section of hollow tree-trunk.

Inside were two sticks of iron wood, and squatting down before the lokali he rattled a metallic tattoo.

For ten minutes he played his tuneless rhythm. When he stopped there came a faint reply from somewhere across the lake.

They waited, the girl and her captor, for nearly half an hour. She strained her ears for the sound of oars, not knowing that the water did not extend for more than a hundred yards, and that beyond and around lay the great swamp wherein stood the island headquarters of the Nine.

The first intimation of the presence of others was a stealthy rustle, then through the gloom she saw the men coming toward her.

Fembeni grasped her arm and led her forward.

He exchanged a few words with the new-comers in a dialect she could not understand. There was a brief exchange of questions, and then the party moved on.

The ground beneath her feet grew soft and sodden. Sometimes the water was up to her ankles. The leader of the men picked his way unerringly, now following a semi-circular route, now turning off at right angles, now winding in and out, till she lost all sense of direction.

Her legs were like lead, her head was swimming and she felt she was on the point of collapse when suddenly the party reached dry land.

A few minutes later they reached the tumbledown village which the outlaws had built themselves.

A fire was burning, screened from view by the arrangement of the huts which had been built in a crescent.

The girl was shown a hut and thrust inside.

Soon afterwards a woman brought her a bowl of boiled fish and a gourd of water.

In her broken Isisi she begged the woman to stay with her, but she was evidently of the N'Gombi people and did not understand.

A few minutes later she was alone.

*　　*　　*　　*　　*

Outside the hut about the fire sat eight of the Nine Terrible Men. One of these was Oko of the Isisi, a man of some power.

"This woman I do not like," he said, "and by my way of thinking Fembeni is a fool and a son of a fool to bring her unless she comes as other women have come—to serve us."

"Lord Oko," said Fembeni, "I am more skilled in the ways of white folk than you, and I tell you that if we keep this woman here it shall be well with us. For if Sandi shall catch you or me, or any of us, we shall say to him: 'There is a woman with us whom you greatly prize, and if you hang me, behold you kill her also.' "

Still Oko was not satisfied.

"I also know white people and their ways," he said. "Sandi would have left us, now he will not rest till we are scattered and dead, for Sandi has a memory like the river, which never ceases to flow."

A man of the Akasava suggested an evil thing.

"That we shall consider," said Oko.

He had already decided. He had none of the subtlety of mind which distinguished Fembeni. He saw an end, and was for crowding in the space of life left to him as much of life as his hand could grasp.

They sat in palaver till early in the morning, the firelight reflected on the polished skin of their bodies.

Then Oko left the circle and crept to the girl's hut. They saw him stoop and enter, and heard a little scream.

"Oko has killed her," said Fembeni.

"It is best," said the other men.

Fembeni rose and went to the hut.

"Oko," he called softly, then stooped and went in.

Facing him was a ragged square of dim light, where a great hole had been cut in the farther side of the hut.

"Oko," he called sharply, then two hands of steel caught him by the throat and two others pulled his legs from under him.

He went to the ground, too terrified to resist.

"Fembeni," said a soft voice in his ear, "I have been waiting for you."

He was rolled on to his face and he made no resistance. His hands were pulled behind, and he felt the cold steel bands encircle his wrist and heard a "snick" as they fastened.

He was as expeditiously gagged.

"As for Oko," said Sanders' voice, "he is dead, and if you had heard him cry you also would have been dead."

That ended the one-sided conversation, Sanders and his sergeant sitting patiently in their little lair waiting for the rest of the men to come.

* * * * *

With the morning arrived a detachment of Houssas under Sergeant Ahmed, following the trail Sanders had followed.

There were four dead men to be buried—including him who had stood on guard at the edge of the swamp.

There was a white-faced girl to be guarded back across the swamp to the seclusion of the forest, and with her went the women of the outlaws' village.

Fembeni and his four companions stood up for judgment.

"One only thing I would ask you, Fembeni," said Sanders, "and that is this: you are by some account a Christian. Do you practise this magic, or are you for the ju-jus and gods of your fathers?"

"Lord," said Fembeni eagerly, "I am a Christian in all ways. Remember this, master, I am of your faith."

Sanders, with his lips parted, and his eyes narrowed, looked at the man.

"Then it is proper that I should give you time to say your prayers," he said. "Abiboo, we hang this man last."

"I see that you are a devil," said Fembeni, "otherwise you would not follow us in the night with none to show you the way. Now I tell you, Sandi, that I am no Christian, for all God-folk are foolish save you, and I know that you are no God-man. Therefore, if I am to hang, let me hang with the rest."

Sanders nodded.

IX

THE QUEEN OF THE N'GOMBI

THERE are certain native traits, certain inherent characteristics, which it is inexpedient to describe in print.

The N'Gombi people had a weakness for forbidden fruit; they raided and burnt and pillaged, but in the main the treasure which they carried away with them took the shape of eligible women.

Sanders was at some pains to teach them that this was one of the forms of hunting which his soul loathed. He pointed his lesson with whippings, banishments, and once, after a particularly unpleasant episode, by a hanging from a gallows which he caused to be erected in the N'Gombi city of Shusha.

Here, before the duly impressed people, in the presence of a puisne judge brought especially from the coast—there had been a little trouble over a summary execution—and in a space kept clear by a half-battalion of Houssas (imported for the occasion), Lombasi, a king of the N'Gombi, died the death amidst the plaudits of his fickle subjects. And this happened in the sight of every chief, every headman, and the new king of the N'Gombi.

Yet three weeks later the offence for which the king suffered was repeated by his successor.

"Make your own arrangements," telegraphed the Administration when a despairing Sanders had reported the fresh crime. "Hang Bogali at your discretion; if necessary, burn crops and village."

Sanders did neither. He deposed the king as he had deposed half a dozen other kings, thrashed him publicly, distributed his property, and appointed—whom should be appoint?

He had half a mind to send for Bosambo of the

neighbouring Ochori, but that would be a dangerous experiment.

The deposed Bogali had two sons and a daughter. One of the sons was far gone in sleeping sickness, and the other was a fairly easy-going, foolish youth, who would be in the hands of his councillors.

"It shall be the woman," decided Sanders; and so, against all precedent, he set up E'logina as Queen of the N'Gombi.

A tall, resolute girl of sixteen, she was at that time with a husband of no great character and several lovers, if there was any truth in popular rumour.

With fitting solemnity Sanders placed her in the chair of state, and she was very grave and very stately —accepting her new position as by right.

"E'logina," said Sanders, "you shall rule this country, and there shall be no women palavers. And I am behind you to enforce your order. If any man say to you: 'I will not obey you because you are a woman,' behold! he shall obey because I am a man; and whosoever sets your authority at defiance shall suffer very painfully."

"Lord!" said the girl, "I will rule wisely."

"As for your lovers," said Sanders, "of whom I have heard, you shall give them no preference over other councillors, or they will lead you to destruction."

"Master!" said the girl, "it is said in the N'Gombi country, 'A lover has strong arms, but no brains.'"

"That is true in other countries," said Sanders.

There were no more women palavers in the N'Gombi from that day. A minor chief who raided an outlying village and carried away girls was summoned to her presence, and certain things happened to him which changed his habits of life, for this lady of the N'Gombi was elementary but effective.

Sanders heard of the happening, and wisely pretended ignorance. The art of government lies in knowing nothing at the proper moment.

She ruled as she had promised—with wisdom. There came the inevitable moment when her chief lover sought to influence affairs of state.

She sent him a long green leaf, which meant that she was in mourning for him. He accepted this as an augury of what might happen and left the city with commendable expedition.

The chiefs and kings of other countries paid her visits of ceremony, bringing her rich presents. Not least of these was Bosambo of the Ochori.

His state rivalled in magnificence a combination of the sunset and the morning star, but the girl on her daïs was not noticeably affected.

"Lady Queen," said Bosambo, "I have come a long journey because I have heard of your greatness and your beauty, and, behold, you are wonderful to see, and your wisdom blinds me like the sun on still water."

"I have heard of you," said E'logina. "You are a little chief of a little people."

"The moon is little also, when seen from a muck-heap," said Bosambo calmly. "I return to my moon."

He was ruffled, though he did not betray the fact.

"To-morrow," he said, as he prepared to depart, "I send word to Sandi, who, as all the world knows, is my nephew—being the son of my sister's husband's brother, and therefore of my blood—and I will say to him that here in the N'Gombi is a queen who puts shame upon our house."

"Lord Bosambo," said the girl hurriedly, "we know that you are nearly related to Sandi, and it would be wrong if my foolish tongue made you ashamed."

"We are proud men, Sandi and I," said Bosambo, "and he will be very terrible in his anger when he knows in what way you have spoken."

The girl rose and came toward him.

"Lord Bosambo," she said, "if you leave me now it will be dark and there will be no sun. For often I have spoken of you till my councillors weary of your name

and deeds. Therefore, stay with me a little that I may
drink of your understanding."

But Bosambo was dignified and obdurate.

"Also, Lord Bosambo," she said, "there are many
presents which my people are gathering for you, for it
would be shameful if I sent you back to your great
nation empty-handed."

"I will stay," said Bosambo, "though presents I do
not value—save meal and a little water—and my hut
is filled with presents from Sandi." He observed the
look of relief on the girl's face, and added without a
tremor, "So that I have room only for precious gifts
as your ladyship will give me."

He stayed that day, and the queen found him agreeable; he stayed the next day, and the queen was
fascinated by his talk. On the third day he was indis-
pensable.

Then came Bosambo's culminating effort.

He had a passion for discussing his kinship with
Sanders, and she was an attentive listener. Also she
had that day given him many tusks of ivory to carry
with him to his home.

"My brother Sandi," said Bosambo, "will be pleased
already; he loves you and has spoken to me about you.
Now I will not doubt that his love will be greater than
it is for me—for you are a woman, and Sandi has
sighed many days for you."

She listened with a kindling eye. A new and splendid thought came into her head. Bosambo departed
that evening, having compressed more mischief into
three days than the average native man crowds into a
lifetime.

It was six months before the result of Bosambo's
extravagance was seen. Sanders came north on a tour
of inspection, and in due course he arrived at Shusha.

All things were in order on the river, and he was
satisfied. His experiment had worked better than he
had dared to hope.

"Queen," he said, as he sat with her in the thatched palaver-house, "you have done well."

She smiled nervously.

"Lord, it is for love of you that I did this," she said; and Sanders, hardened to flattery, accepted the warmth of her pronouncement without blushing.

"For I have put away my lovers," she went on, "and my husband, who is a fool, I have banished to another village; and, my lord, I am your slave."

She slipped from the seat which was by her side, and knelt before him in the face of the city and before all the people.

She grasped his foot with her strong young hands and placed it on her head.

"Phew!" said Sanders, breaking into a sweat—for by all custom this was not an act of fealty, but the very act of marriage.

"Stand up, queen!" said the Commissioner when he had got his breath, "lest your people think foolish thoughts."

"Lord," she murmured, "I love you! and Bosambo, your nephew, looks favourably upon our marriage."

Sanders said nothing. He reached down, and catching her by the arm, drew her to her feet.

"Oh, people!" he said loudly to the amazed throng at the foot of the little hill on which the palaver house stood, "your queen is, by her act, wedded to my government, and has sworn to serve me in all matters of queenship—be faithful as she is. The palaver is finished."

It was an ingenious escape—though the girl's eyes narrowed as she faced him, and her bare bosom rose and fell in her anger.

"Lord," she breathed, "this was not as I meant."

"It is as I mean," said Sanders gently.

She faced him for a moment; then, turning swiftly, walked to her hut, and Sanders saw her no more that day.

"We stay till to-morrow," said Sanders to his sergeant as he went on board the *Zaire* that evening. "Afterwards we go to Ochori—I will have a palaver with Bosambo."

"Master," said Abiboo, "Bosambo will be pleased."

"I doubt it," said Sanders.

He went to bed that night to sleep the sleep of one who had earned the daily two pounds with which a grateful government rewarded him.

He was dead tired, but not too tired to slip the fine-meshed wire fly-door into its place, or to examine the windows to see if they were properly screened.

This must be done in the dark, because, if by chance a window or a door is open when a light appears, certain it is that the cabin will be filled with tiny little brothers of the forest, a hundred varieties of flies, winged beetles, and most assuredly musca—which, in everyday language, is the fever-carrying mosquito. With the habit formed of long practice, Sanders' hand touched the three windows, found the screens in their place and latched.

Then he switched on the electric light—a luxurious innovation which had come to him with the refitment of the *Zaire*. Leading from his cabin was a tiny bathroom. He pulled his pyjamas from under his pillow and disappeared into the cupboard—it was nothing more—to reappear at the end of five minutes arrayed in his grey sleeping kit.

He turned on a light over his pillow, switched out the other, and pulled back the clothes.

He did not immediately jump into bed, because, carefully arranged at regular intervals in the centre of the bed, were three round thorns.

Sanders turned on the other light, opened his desk, and found a pair of tweezers. With these he removed the uncomfortable burrs, placing them under a glass on his table.

After this he made a very thorough search of the

room—especially of the floor. But whosoever had placed the thorns had evidently forgotten the possibilities of a man walking bare-footed—nor was there any sign of the unknown's thoughtful attention in the bathroom.

He pulled the bed to pieces, shaking every article carefully; then he remade his couch, turned out the lights, climbed into bed, and went to sleep.

Two hours before dawn he woke. This was the time he intended waking. He sat up in bed and groaned—deliberately and inartistically. He groaned at intervals for five minutes, then he was quiet.

He listened and thought he heard a slight movement on the bank to which the *Zaire* was moored.

He bent his head and waited.

Yes, a twig snapped.

Sanders was out of the door in a second; he flew across the gangway which connected the steamer with the bank, and plunged into the forest path that led to the village of E'tomolini. Ahead of him he heard a patter of bare feet.

"Stop! O walker of the night," called Sanders in the Bomongo dialect, "or you die!"

The figure ahead halted and Sanders came up with it.

"Walk back the way you came," he said, and followed the shadowy form to the boat.

Sanders observed that the night-wanderer was a little taller than a boy, and had a method of walking which was not inconsistent with the theory that it was a girl.

"Go straight to my cabin," said the Commissioner, "if you know it."

"Lord, I know it," quavered the other, and Sanders learnt that it was indeed a girl.

A girl of fifteen, he judged, as she stood in the glare of the electric light—shapely of build, not bad-looking, and very frightened.

"I am plagued by women," said Sanders wrathfully. "You shall tell me how it comes about that you spy upon me in the night, also how you come to be abroad so early."

The girl hesitated, casting a bewildered glance round the cabin.

"Lord," she said, "I did that which seemed best."

"Who sent you here?"

Again she hesitated.

"I came for no reason, lord, but that I wish to see the strange devil-light."

This was a reasonable excuse, for the new electric installation had proved irresistibly fascinating to the raw folk of the upper river.

Sanders uncovered the three thorn burrs, and she looked at them curiously.

"What do they call you?" asked Sanders.

"Medini, the woman with nine lovers," she said simply.

"Well, Medini," said Sanders with a grim little smile, "you shall pick up those thorns and hold them in your hand—they will wound you a little because they are very sharp."

The girl smiled.

"A little thorn does not hurt," she quoted, and stretched out her hand fearlessly.

Before she could touch the thorns Sanders' hand shot out and caught her wrist.

The girl was puzzled and for a moment a look of apprehension filled her eyes and she shrank back, dragging her wrist from the Commissioner's hand.

"Sit down," said Sanders. "You shall tell me before you go who sent you to the bank to watch my boat."

"None, lord," she faltered.

Sanders shook his head.

"I have a ju-ju," he said slowly, "and this ju-ju has told me that somebody said, 'Go you, Medini, to the bank near where Sandi lies and listen. And when you

9

hear him groan aloud like a man in great pain, you shall come and tell me."

Consternation and horror were on the girl's face.

"Lord," she gasped, "that is true—yet if I speak I die!"

"Also, if you do not speak, I shall take you away from here to a place far from your own people," said Sanders.

The girl's eyes dropped.

"I came to see the devil-lights," she said sullenly.

Sanders nodded.

He went out from the cabin and called up the guard —an alert guard which had watched a flying Commissioner in pyjamas cross the plank gangway and reappear with a prisoner.

"Keep this woman under your eyes," he said. "Let none speak with her."

When daylight came he removed a spike from the thorn and placed it under his microscope. What he saw interested him, and again he had recourse to the microscope—scraping another spike and placing the shavings between two slides.

Native people have a keen sense of humour, but that humour does not take the form of practical joking.

Moreover, he had detected blood on the spike, and an organism which old blood generates.

Thus the bushmen poison their arrows by leaving them in the bodies of their dead enemies.

He sent a guard for the queen and brought her on board.

"I shall take you away," he said, "because you have tried to kill me by placing poisoned thorns in my bed."

"Medini, my woman, did this, because she loved me," said the queen, "and if she says I told her to do the thing she lies."

"You have said enough," said Sanders. "Abiboo, let there be steam quickly, for I carry the queen with me to the Ochori country."

Bosambo was not prepared for the Commissioner's arrival. He was a man singularly free from illusions, and when they brought him word that Sanders was accompanied by the Queen of the N'Gombi he had no doubt in his mind that the times ahead were troublesome.

So they proved.

Sanders cut short the flower of his welcome. He nipped it as the frost nips young buds, and as coldly.

"You have put foolish ideas into this woman's head," he said, "and I have brought her here that you might do that which is honourable."

"Lord, I am your man," said Bosambo, with proper humility.

"And my uncle also," said Sanders, "if all that you said to her was true."

The girl stood by listening.

"Now you have told her that she should marry into my house," said Sanders, "and, being a woman, her mind is set upon this matter."

Bosambo saw what was coming, and hastened to avert the evil.

"Lord," he said, in his agitation dropping into the English he had spoken on the coast, "she be number one women; dem wife she not be fit for nudder woman."

"I do not speak that monkey talk," said Sanders calmly. "You marry this woman to-day and she goes back to rule the N'Gombi—to-night."

"Lord," pleaded Bosambo, "I am of the Faith—the one Prophet of the one God."

"But not the one wife, I think," said Sanders. "You marry her or I whip you."

"Lord, I will be whipped," said Bosambo promptly.

"Also, I will place another chief over the Ochori."

"That is too great a shame," said Bosambo aghast. "For as you know, lord, my father and his father were chiefs of this tribe, and I have the blood of kings in my veins."

"You have the blood of Monravian thieves, and your fathers you never knew," said Sanders patiently. "You marry to-day!"

"It is as you will, oh, my uncle!" said Bosambo.

Sanders said nothing, though his hands clutched his stick the tighter.

After all, he had brought that insult upon himself.

X

THE MAN ON THE SPOT

ONCE upon a time a man went up to the Calali River to buy rubber from the natives. He had a permit signed by the new Administrator and a licence to trade, and he had come into Sanders' territory by a back way and did not trouble to have this permit viséd.

Now the permit bore the signature of His Excellency the Administrator, him and none other, and the name of His Excellency "goes," and people have been known to bow their heads most respectfully at the mention of his name.

Sanders did not respect him, but called him "your Excellency," because it was lawful.

Anyway, this trader to whom I have referred went up the Calali River and bought rubber. He bought it and sometimes paid for it. He did not give its exact value, and after three weeks of bartering his business came to an end, because native folk would not bring any further rubber to his big canoe. Whereupon Tinkerton—such was his name—had recourse to other methods. He sat down in a likely village and instructed the headman to produce for him so many kilos of rubber in so many days, promising remuneration which by every standard was absurd. The headman refused, whereupon Tinkerton tied him up to a tree and whipped him with a chicotte.

"Now you'll change your point of view," said Tinkerton, "and fetch me rubber—quick!"

The chief sent twenty young men into the forest to find rubber, and four men who were his best paddlers to find Mr. Commissioner Sanders, collecting hut tax with some labour in the Akasava country.

Rubber and Sanders arrived at the Calali River at the same time.

Tinkerton explained his position and the chief exhibited his back.

"My permit is quite in order, I think," said Tinkerton.

"Up to a point," admitted Sanders carefully, "it is. But, as you know, a licence to trade becomes invalid when the holder is convicted of any breach of the common law."

Tinkerton smiled uneasily.

"That doesn't affect me, I think," he said.

He always added "I think" to everything he said, lest the hearer should labour under the impression that he spoke without thinking.

"It affects you considerably," said Sanders; "for I am sentencing you to six months' hard labour for your assault on this native, and I am sending you to the coast to serve that sentence."

Tinkerton went crimson with rage.

"Do you know what I think of you?" he asked loudly.

"No," said Sanders, "but I can guess it, and if you open your mouth uncivilly I shall take you by the scruff of the neck and kick you into the river."

Tinkerton went down to the coast under escort, and he never forgave the Commissioner.

The major portion of his sentence was remitted by the Administrator, because it happened that the Administrator was a sort of cousin to Tinkerton's father.

So that to the patent fury of Tinkerton was added the coldly polite disapproval of an Administrator who is remembered best on the coast by his mistakes.

Now, although it is amusing to recall the blunders of a high official after his departure, it is not so entertaining to furnish material for subsequent anecdote, and one must be possessed of a peculiarly poignant sense of humour to thoroughly appreciate the travail in which these jests were born.

The Administrator may or may not have deliberately set himself the task of annoying Sanders.

From a strictly service aspect, a service which has for its ideal the perfection of British administration, to the exclusion of all personal ambition, the idea is preposterous. From the standpoint of one who has some knowledge of human nature, it seems very likely that there was something in the suggestion that His Excellency had his administrative knife in the executive ribs of Mr. Commissioner Sanders.

One spring morning Sanders received a big blue letter. It came in his mail bag with other communications but bore, in addition to the notification that it was "On His Majesty's Service," the legend "Department of His Excellency the Administrator," and was moreover subscribed "Strictly confidential."

Now, when a high official of state writes in strictest confidence to his subordinate, he is not telling him his troubles or confessing his guilt, or even trying to borrow money.

He is, as a rule, delivering a kick with all the force of his strong right leg.

Sanders looked at the letter, picked it up gingerly, held it up to the light, and weighed it in his hand. It was heavy. The bulk of it was eloquent of reproof, because administrators do not expend overmuch energy in praising the works of their underlings.

Sir Harry Coleby, K.C.M.G., had a reputation which he had acquired in Bermuda, Jamaica, and the

Straits Settlements. It was not a reputation for loving kindness exactly. His nickname—he came by this when he was a secretary of Legation at Madrid—was "Calliente," which he pronounced "Cally-enty," and means "hot." And hot he was of head and temper, and the men who worked for him and with him lived in a mild perspiration.

He was extravagant of speech and quick of temper, and he wrote letters which were vitriolic without being offensive within the meaning of the act.

Sanders opened the blue envelope reluctantly and smoothed out the typewritten sheets and read:

"Sir,—I have the honour to inform you that His Excellency the Administrator has received your half-yearly report on the conditions of the tribes and peoples under your honour's administration.

"His Excellency regrets that the reports you send concerning the spread of sleeping sickness in the Calali district are not as satisfactory as His Majesty's Government could wish. The measure framed for the restriction of this disease does not seem to have been effectively applied, and he requests that a further report on this matter should be furnished at the end of the present quarter."

Sanders read so far without being seriously troubled. The Administration was covering itself against any kicks which might come from Downing Street, and by Sanders' code was justified.

He read on:

"The state of lawlessness which prevails in the Akasava and Ochori countries is, in His Excellency's opinion, a matter for regret, and he expects your honour to take immediate steps to deal drastically with this condition of affairs. A suggestion which His Excellency makes is that the chief Bosambo should be deposed, and that the Akasava and Ochori should be combined under one chief."

Sanders, who knew the Ochori and Akasava for hereditary enemies, mopped his forehead with a gaudy bandana handkerchief and swore softly.

"His Excellency desires me to state that considering the natural resources of the lands under your honour's dominion, the amount of taxes collected would appear to be inadequate and he sends you herewith a revised scale of taxation which shall come into operation as from July 1st of the current year."

That was all.

The reference to the Akasava and Ochori crime left him unmoved. The crime was of no great importance, and was, in point of fact, less serious than in previous years. He could afford to ignore the suggestion concerning Bosambo, though he knew it was made to annoy Bosambo's patron. But the taxation was another matter—a very serious matter indeed, and he sat down to write on the subject. He pointed out the consequences of increasing the demand upon uncivilised people. He reported means by which an increased revenue might be secured without adding to the burden of the individual, and he ended his letter by expressing his absolute disagreement with the Administration.

"Whilst noting your Excellency's instructions," he said, "I decline to accept any responsibility whatsoever for the effect the new imposition may produce."

In reply, he received a most unpleasant letter which told him, in the stilted and official language of special correspondence, to do as he was bid.

"You will make whatsoever arrangements you deem necessary, without any further reference to His Excellency, to deal with the disorder which in your view will arise as a result of the new taxation. I am to say that in His Excellency's opinion no such danger is to be apprehended."

Now Sanders' position was a difficult one. He was bound hand and foot by service regulations. He knew that the new Administrator was acting off his own bat, and that were the Home Government aware of the innovation of the new taxes, it would make short work of them.

But Sanders could not communicate with Downing Street direct. It would be an unpardonable thing to go behind his superior. In another land where white men were, a newspaper correspondent might reveal the trouble brewing without Sanders being in any way responsible; such things are done—as I know. But the only white men in Sanders' territory were three missionaries, separated from him by hundreds of miles, a captain of Houssas and himself.

Sanders thought the matter over day and night for a week. Once he almost decided to break through all rules, notify the Government, and resign. He was in the act of penning the cablegram when an inspiration came to him.

"You will make whatsoever arrangements . . ."

The concluding paragraph of the Administrator's letter occurred to him.

Very slowly and thoughtfully he tore up the draft of his cable into little pieces and called his orderly, who was half-asleep on the verandah outside.

"Tell Yoka," he said, "that I will have fire in the *Zaire* by sunset—take food on board for three weeks. I go to make palaver with the God-men."

When the sun was throwing mile-long shadows upon the beach, he began his cruise.

His first call necessitated a twenty-mile march through the Isisi country to a place called Konshinda.

Here was the mission station of the Jesuits, and he found Father Wells, a tall, spare man in white, superintending the erection of a new hut.

He was a middle-aged man, grey-haired and clean-shaven, and he greeted Sanders with a smile. Together they went to the mission-house with its big cool stoep.

"Sit down, Commissioner," said the missionary. He took off his white topee and produced a well-burnt pipe, and Sanders, declining the jar of tobacco the other pushed toward him, lit a cheroot.

"Well," said the first, "what is the trouble? Have some of my converts been raiding or is this a visit of ceremony? If it is, I am sorry Father Vettechi is not here—he's rather keen on ceremonies."

He laughed with the happy boyish laugh of one who has no cares.

"I'm going to turn you out of the country," said Sanders calmly.

The other looked up quickly, with a smile which was half quizzical and half earnest.

"What is this?" he asked, "a new Expulsion of the Jesuits?"

"Something like that," said Sanders, "it is a long time since I persecuted anybody."

"But seriously——"

Sanders told the story of the new taxation. He was immensely serious, painting the consequence of the new tariff with vividness of detail.

"I am inclined to agree with you," said the Jesuit; "but I shall have to protest against being sent down, even though I know that you are acting in my best interest."

"Protest away," said Sanders cheerfully.

Father Wells was troubled.

"But I shall have to wire my protest to England," he said.

"I will give you every facility," said Sanders.

He left, carrying with him the Jesuit's cablegram, and when he reached the river sent a special courier to headquarters with orders to dispatch it.

A day later, he entered the narrow river which leads to the Modern Baptist Mission Station.

Along this stream for forty miles Sanders proceeded with caution. It was not easy to navigate. Beneath the smiling surface of smooth waters lay the gentle, sloping crests of sandbanks. These in themselves were fairly innocuous. But the Tembolini River flowed in its earlier stages through miles of primeval forest, and trees would sometimes float down to be caught and embedded in the sand, a blunt branch peeping from its sandy covering. Woe betide the steamer that struck these "snags"; for a mahogany brand backed and supported by a buried tree offered more resistance than anything smaller than an Atlantic steamer could resist, and striking at full speed, the bottom would be ripped from the best of steamers.

Tiny fishing villages were met at rare intervals, for this is part of the Isisi, isolated from the main country for many reasons, not the least of which was M'shimba-M'shamba, the green devil who walks by night and is very terrible to the dwellers of cities.

Sanders, who never wasted a journey if he could help it, stopped at each village for an hour, adjusted such differences as needed his help (there was a very bad murder palaver at one to which he had to return later) and on the morning of the second day he arrived at the Baptist Mission.

He had different material to deal with here. A little man, immensely important as little men sometimes are, slightly aggressive in the name of the Lord and "not quite."

You meet people who are "not quite" in all branches of life, but curiously enough they are to be met with most frequently in a certain type of foreign mission. God forbid that I should speak disparagingly of the devoted men and women who sacrifice health and life in the execution of their duty and in the fulfilment of their faith.

Mr. Haggins, of the Modern Baptist Mission, was "not quite," however.

He had been a London street preacher, hot for glory, and a radical constitutionally opposed to government, whatsoever and whichever party was for the moment in power. Sanders represented government, was popularly supposed to be antagonistic to the Word and its carriers. He whipped people, hanged a few with scanty trial, and had been accused by Mr. Haggins' predecessor of having committed atrocities. It cost the proprietors of the Modern Baptist Mission, which printed the wild and whirling accusation, exactly a thousand pounds, and if Mr. Haggins ever wrote tremendous things about Sanders you may be sure that the editor of the magazine never published them.

"I am glad to see you, Mr. Sanders," said the missionary with ominous politeness, as Sanders stepped ashore; "there are one or two matters on which I wished to see you. Particularly in regard to your atrocious treatment of one of my native evangelists, Balibi——"

"He can keep," said Sanders shortly; "your evangelist amused himself in his spare time with certain women of the Akasava——"

"That's not true," said Mr. Haggins rudely.

Sanders looked at him queerly.

"If you call me a liar," he said, "I shall——"

He checked himself.

"It isn't true," said Mr. Haggins with vehemence. "I believe in our brother——"

"That is neither here nor there!" interrupted Sanders. "What I have come to tell you is that you are to close up your station and bring all your belongings to headquarters."

Mr. Haggins was dumbfounded.

"Close—my—station?" he repeated.

"That is it," said Sanders blandly; "I expect trouble with my people over the new taxation."

"But I will not go," said Mr. Haggins, very wrathful and suspecting the worst; "it is an outrage; it is an attempt to ruin my station—I shall make representations to England, Mr. Sanders—we are not without friends in Parliament——"

He said much more in the same strain, speaking with great heat.

"If you like to send a telegram," said Sanders, calling into play all his patience, "I shall be most happy to send it."

Sanders made other calls, including one upon that medical missionary lady, Miss Glandynne, and at each station he met with an unpleasant reception.

* * * * *

Sir Harry Coleby, K.C.M.G., occupied a magnificent white palace at a coast town, with the name of which you are tolerably sure to be familiar. It was set on the side of a great mountain and looked down upon a town of broad streets, in the main populated and inhabited by coal-black negroes who spoke English and affixed "Mr." to their name.

Sir Harry was stout, white of hair, bristling of moustache, and pink of face. He referred to himself as the "man on the spot"; this was an idiosyncrasy of his.

He worked as a motor engine worked, by a series of explosions. He exploded at his overworked secretary, he exploded at his officers; he exploded at anything and anybody that thwarted or annoyed him.

He damned people's eyes with a persistency and a fury which suggested that he had a near and dear relative in the optical line of business, and was trying to do him a turn.

I add the indisputable fact that though he had only been six months on the coast he was cordially hated.

Mr. Commissioner Sanders of the Isisi, Mr. Commissioner de la Court of the Kroo River, numerous deputy commissioners, inspectors and officers of state, living meanly along a hot slip of coast, daily thought of him and cherished next to their hearts the news—it was cut from an impudent Lagos journal—that His Excellency found the climate very trying.

Sir Harry came into his office one day—it was the morning after the official dinner at Government House and he was lively—to find Sanders' final letter on the subject of taxation.

"By God, if I have any more of that fellow's insolence I will pack him off to England!" he roared, and proceeded to invoke Divine interference with Sanders' eyesight.

"Tell him——" he shouted, banging his desk with his clenched knuckles.

"I'm sorry to interrupt your Excellency," said the secretary, "but ought we not to notify the Colonial Office about this change——"

He was a permanent official who had spent his life on the coast, and he knew more about West Central Africa than most secretaries.

"Notify nothing," snapped his chief, "I administrate here, I am the man on the spot; I am going to increase revenue, sir."

"There will be trouble, your Excellency," said the secretary quietly.

Sir Harry drew a long breath, and in one long and comprehensive sentence consigned the secretary, Sanders, and the native peoples of his kingdom to the devil.

A negro clerk brought in a cablegram and handed it to the Administrator.

"Here's a 'confidential,' Browne," he snarled; "decode the damn thing and don't bother about matters which do not concern you."

The secretary took the four closely written forms.

It began:

"Airlight, Transport, Divine, Sunlight, Meridan."

"Airlight" meant "confidential"; "transport" meant "act at once"; this he knew, and settled down to decode the wire.

The further he got, consulting the two books with the double code, the higher rose the spirits of His Excellency's secretary. When he had finished he laid the decoded message before his chief, and Sir Harry read:

"Very urgent. Act at once. Representation made by missionary societies that their stations being closed in Isisi, Akasava, Ochori, N'Gombi countries by order Sanders. Understand he fears disturbances as a result of new taxation. Before enforcing new taxation communicate particulars to Colonial Office."

It is said that Sir Harry Coleby went stark, staring mad when this communication was read. He was not used to being dictated to from Downing Street. He was of a régime which held the Colonial Office in good-natured contempt. Whether he went mad or whether this is an exaggerated description of the secretary, I do not know. Certainly he sent a wire to His Majesty's Secretary of State for Colonial Affairs which reminded that gentleman of communications which came to him in the stormy days of the first Home Rule Bill. It was not a mad wire, or a bad wire, it was penned in Sir Harry's best style, and it hinted to the Colonial Office in London that Sir Harry was the man on the spot and would use his own discretion, and he would not submit to outside interference, and that if anybody interfered with him—my word!

Sir Harry had once sent such a wire before and the Colonial Secretary of the day had surrendered. Unhappily for the Administrator, there was a man at the Colonial Office.

At ten o'clock that night a cable was received by

His Excellency. It was in plain English and the Administrator read it and sat looking at it for quite a long time before he understood it. It ran:

"Your successor sails on ninth. Hand over your work to your attorney-general and return by first available steamer."

It was signed "Chamberlain."

XI

THE RISING OF THE AKASAVA

A NATIVE alone may plumb the depths of the native mind with any accuracy. Sanders was remarkable because he was possessed of a peculiar quality—the quality of comprehension.

He made few mistakes because he applied no rules. He knew, for instance, that native memory is short, yet he was prepared to hear a greybeard of forty contest his finding in some particular suit with a precedent created twenty years before and entirely obliterated from Sanders' memory.

A scientific expedition once again went through the Ochori country—and I think it had to do with astronomical observation—and in the language of Kipling:

> " What they thought they might require,
>   They went an' took."

Bosambo, the chief, complained, for he knew the value of money to such an extent that he never accepted a Spanish douro without biting it, or confused a mark with a shilling.

Sanders was secretly annoyed with the behaviour of the expedition, but felt it necessary to keep up the end of his fellow-countrymen.

"They were of the Government," he said at the time; "and, moreover, white men. And it is the white man's way."

Bosambo said nothing, but remembered.

Years later something happened in the Akasava, and by a distressing string of circumstances Sanders found himself confronted with a two-million-pound war, the undoing of all his work, and a most ignominious death.

This happened in the autumn of the year. At the time of harvest the lands under Mr. Commissioner Sanders were quiet and peaceable. The crop had been a good one, the fish plentiful in the river, serious sickness of no account.

"And no crime," said Sanders to himself, and pulled a little face. "I would welcome a little earthquake just now."

The European reader might stand aghast at this callousness, but Sanders knew.

The reports that came down-river were satisfactory —if one gained satisfaction from the recital of virtuous behaviour. Isisi, N'Gombi, Akasava, Bolegi, Bomongo —all these peoples were tranquil and prosperous.

The only adverse report was from the Ochori. There a mysterious fire had destroyed one-half of the crops—a fire that had appeared simultaneously in twenty gardens. Also it was reported that Bosambo, the chief, was treating his people with unusual severity.

Sanders grew very thoughtful when this news came, for Bosambo was a wise and cunning man, who knew native folk as well as Sanders himself. Sanders drew his own conclusions, and made preparations for a long cruise.

He stepped on board his little stern-wheeler at dawn one day.

For days previous men had been piling wood on the

10

lower deck till the *Zaire* looked for all the world like a timber ship. On the steel deck below, in double banks, in the well before the tiny bridge deck, in the space at the stern which is usually occupied by drowsy Houssas, wood was piled to the height of a man's head.

In addition there were many stacks of a bright, black stone, which Yoka, the engineer, regarded with unusual pride; as well he might, for coal is not a customary sight on the big river.

The *Zaire* had recently come newly furnished from the slips. White workmen, brought at great expense from Lagos or Sierra Leone, or one of those far-distant and marvellous cities, had replaced certain portions of the machinery and had introduced higher power, and, most wonderful of all, a new engine which worked from the main boiler and which by magic turned a strange, clumsy wheel at an incredible speed. From this coiled two fat ropes of wire, covered so that no wire could be seen.

They disappeared through a hole in the deck and came to light again in the bridge, being attached to a big lamp working on a swivel.

Nor was this the only innovation. The two Maxims which had stood on either corner of the bridge deck had been moved to amidships, and in their places were long steel-barrelled Hotchkiss guns with rubber-covered shoulder pieces. Beneath, by the bulwarks, were polished wooden chests, where fat brass cartridges lay stored like wine in bins.

Sanders went aboard with a picked crew and half a company of Houssa rifles, and set forth with little idea as to where his journey would end.

He had not left headquarters far behind when the steersman who stood by his side uttered an exclamation, and Sanders looked up.

Overhead in the blue, two birds were wheeling and circling frantically.

The smaller bird darted this way and that.

Sanders sprang into his cabin and snatched up a shot-gun.

The bigger bird was a hawk, going about his proper business; but his quarry, as the Commissioner recognised at a glance, was a faithful servant of the Government—a carrier-pigeon.

The birds had closed in one furious bunch of whirling feathers and talons when Sanders raised his gun and fired. The first barrel missed, but the second brought them down to the water.

A dozen men sprang overboard and swam to the spot where the birds struggled convulsively in their death-grip.

One of the men reached them, deftly wrung the neck of the hawk, and came back to the boat.

The pigeon was dead—had probably died before the shots hit him. Round one red leg was a rubber band and a torn piece of paper.

Sanders smoothed it out and read. It was in Arabic, and all that was left consisted of three words:

" . . . Akasava . . . war . . . King."

"H'm!" said Sanders.

He had a man watching the Akasava, a reliable spy whose judgment was beyond doubt. There was urgency in the fact that the message had been sent by carrier-pigeon, and Sanders put the nose of his steamer to the north and prepared for the worst.

At two o'clock in the afternoon, two days' steaming from headquarters, he came to the junction of three rivers where, according to all plans, his spy should have waited him with further intelligence.

But there was no sign of the man, and, though the steamer cruised about, crossing from one bank to the other, the spy did not put in an appearance. Sanders had no other course than to continue his voyage. He arrived at the Akasava city at midnight, picking his way through the shoals and sand-banks without difficulty, thanks to his new searchlight.

He "tied up" to one of the many middle islands in the centre of the river and waited for light. At dawn the *Zaire* came sidling to the Akasava bank, her soldiers sitting on the iron lower deck, their legs dangling over the side, their loaded rifles at their knees.

Yet there was no sign of perturbation amongst the people. They flocked down to the beach to watch the steamer come to her moorings, and in half an hour Toloni, the King, came in state with his drummers, his spearmen and his councillors—to pay their respects.

Sanders went ashore with an orderly, walked through the city's street by the King's side, and listened to such news as he had to tell him.

Sanders made no inquiry as to his spy, because that would be futile, but he kept a sharp look-out.

The scene was a peaceful one. The women ground corn before their huts, naked babies strutted daringly in the streets, their shrill laughter rising as hut called to hut, and, best of all, the men were in good humour.

"Lord," said the King as Sanders took his departure, "all things are well, as you see, and my people are full of food and lazy. There is no sickness, and no man injures another."

"Thus it is," said Sanders, who never failed to take advantage of any opportunity for drawing a moral, "because my lord the king has given you his protection so that every man may live fearless of his enemies."

"That is so," said the other humbly. "We are dogs before your presence, and blinded by the bright face of the Great King our master."

Sanders took a short cut to the *Zaire*.

There was a little path which led through the tall, rank, elephant grass.

"Lord," said Toloni, hesitating at the entrance of the path, "this is not a proper way for your greatness, for there is water in the path, and many snakes who live in the marsh."

"This is the way," said Sanders briefly.

The Akasava monarch hesitated, then led the way.

It was, as he had said, an unpleasant road, for the rains had been very heavy and in places the path was ankle-deep in ooze.

Sanders was regretting his obstinacy when, half-way to the beach, he came upon a place where the earth had been recently dug, and there was a raised mound.

"What man is buried here?" asked the Commissioner.

The King looked at him steadfastly.

"One Karama," he said.

"This is not the place of burying," said Sanders; "for if my memory serves me your dead people sleep in one of the middle islands."

"That is so, lord," replied the chief, "yet this man was dead a long time, and only his bones were left. And because my people feared his spirit they buried him where he was found."

The explanation was satisfactory and Sanders passed on, though the grave was the grave of Ali Hazrah, a reliable spy of his, who had been caught by the King's men and speared to death whilst the pigeon he had just released was still circling above in the blue sky.

"My lord goes far?" asked the King as he stood by the gangway of the ship.

"I go north," said Sanders. "Why do you ask?"

"There have been heavy rains," said the King, "and many rivers are swollen. And in such times strangers from the Frenchi and Portagasi lands come into these territories; also, I have heard of an Arabi who is buying people, ten days' journey from here, on the Calali River."

Was this the message Ali had sent?

The possibility struck Sanders as being a reasonable one.

The man might have heard something of the sort,

sent his message, and gone north in search of further news.

Sanders cast off, and, leaving the Isisi River on his right, took the Calali—a little-known stream.

Toloni, the King, might be sending him on a fool's errand, but he had to take that chance. As it happened, the Akasava overlord had spoken the truth for a certain purpose.

*　　*　　*　　*　　*

El Mahmud, a notorious trader, found his way into Sanders' territory one spring-time when the rivers were flooded and when certain streams were navigable which had never before known canoe, much less El Mahmud's gay felucca.

He brought with him rich bales of merchandise, secret bottles of gin, tobacco, hemp, and his own elegant person.

He was a sallow-faced man who sat under an awning on a silken cushion and smoked, and he was possessed of an insatiable curiosity.

He had large ideas, and was a man of many schemes.

He was engaged in arming a Calali village with rifles which had rendered good service to France in '75, when Sanders came suddenly upon him.

El Mahmud was warned, and put his craft, with all sails set, in the direction of safety, which was represented by a creek four miles up river, into which no steamer of the *Zaire* size could penetrate.

His little plan, admirable in intention, was somewhat upset by the disconcerting fact that the *Zaire* had recently been re-equipped. The first shot from Sanders' new Hotchkiss gun smashed the side of the felucca as a rifle bullet would smash a match-box. The second carried away the roof of El Mahmud's private cabin.

The *Zaire* swung up to the sinking felucca, and a rope being passed she was towed to shallow water.

Taking all things into consideration, El Mahmud, who knew something of the English-speaking people and their peculiar ways, would much rather have seen his boat sunk.

"Sheik," said his headman as the *Zaire* took the boat in tow, "there is time to get rid of much that will do us harm when the Englishman inspects this boat."

El Mahmud was silent, and his headman drew a long knife from his belt and tested its edge.

He looked inquiringly at his master, but El Mahmud shook his head.

"You are a fool! This Americano will hang you like a pig if he smells a spot of blood. Let us wait—what is written must be."

He had not long to wait. As soon as the *Joy of Night* —such was the felicitous name of the craft—was beached, he was escorted before Sanders.

"How came you here?" demanded the Commissioner, and El Mahmud explained calmly and logically that owing to the heavy rains he had adventured along a new river which had never before existed, and thus had come to the Isisi. That was a good excuse, as Mahmud knew. It was more difficult to explain the selling of rifles, for it is a practice which all civilised nations very properly hold as unpardonable. Much more difficult was it to account for twenty-one slaves discovered in the bottom of the felucca. Yet the man had a permit to "recruit labour," signed by one Dom Reynaldo de Costa y Ferdinez, Portuguese governor of a coast colony.

Sanders had a horror of "complications," especially with Portuguese authorities, for complications meant long, long letters, reports, minutes, memoranda, and eventually blue books. This meant years of correspondence, official investigations, and a kick at the end, whether he was right or wrong.

"By all laws, El Mahmud," he said, "you have for-

feited your life, yet I accept part of your story, though,
God knows, I believe you lie! My steamer shall take
you to a place which is twenty miles from the Portuguese, and there you shall be set free with food and
arms."

"What of my ship and cargo?" asked El Mahmud.

"I shall burn the one and confiscate the other," said
Sanders.

El Mahmud shrugged his shoulders.

"All things are ordained," he said.

Sanders took him on board and steamed to a place
indicated by the trader—it was nearer his camp—and
released him with rifles and ammunition for his followers and ten days' supply of food.

"Go with God," said Sanders in the vernacular.

El Mahmud stood on the bank and watched the
steamer sweeping out to mid-stream.

He waited till its nose was turned down-stream and
Sanders was plainly to be seen on the bridge, then sat
down carefully, raised his rifle, taking deliberate aim,
and fired.

Sanders was giving instructions to Abiboo concerning the repacking of Hotchkiss cartridges which had
been laid on the deck in preparation for eventuali-
ties.

"These——" he said, then stumbled forward.

Abiboo caught him in his arms, and lowered him to
the deck.

"The man—do not let him escape," said Sanders
faintly.

Abiboo picked up a cartridge, opened the breech of
the long-barrelled Hotchkiss, and slipped it in.

El Mahmud was running swiftly toward the cover of
the forest. He had two hundred yards of bare ground
to cover, and Abiboo was firing a gun which was as
accurately sighted as a rifle. Moreover, he had plenty
of time, and was not flurried.

The terrified followers of El Mahmud, returning

that night to search for their master, were constantly finding him.

* * * * *

The moon came up over the forest and fretted the river with silver, and Toloni, King of the Akasava, watched from the shore for the omen which Tilagi, the witch-doctor, had promised.

He had long to wait before he saw the ripple which a swimming crocodile makes, but when it came into view, crossing the river in a straight line from shore to shore, he had no eyes for aught else.

Straight as an arrow it sped, undeviating by a single curve from the true line.

"That is a good omen," said Toloni, and rose from the shadow of the bush which hid him from view.

He waited a little while, then struck noiselessly into the forest, swinging his spears.

He came upon his six councillors sitting patiently by the side of the forest path.

"All is as should be," he said. "Tilagi has spoken the truth, for the crocodile crossed from bank to bank, and the day of the Akasava has come."

He led the way back to the sleeping city and gained his big hut. It was empty, by his orders. A fire smouldered in the centre of the hut, and his bed of skins was ready for him on the raised frame bedstead.

He went out again into the open.

"Send Tilagi to me," he said to the waiting headman.

When the old man came—a skinny old man, walking laboriously by the aid of a stick, Toloni called him into the hut.

"Father," he said, "at the full of the moon, as the tide was high, I saw the black crocodile leave his pool on the Isisi bank, and he swam from shore to shore even as you said."

The old man said nothing, nodding his head.

"All this is favourable to my plans," said the King, "and it shall fall out as you say."

"You are a great king," croaked the old man. "There never was in this land so great a king, for you have the mind of a white man, and are greater than Sandi. Other kings and chiefs of the Akasava were fools, and died like fools on a certain high tree, Sandi putting a rope about their necks; but they had black men's brains."

The King walked up and down the length of his hut. He was a tall man, splendidly built, and he carried his head high.

"All men are with me," he said. "Isisi, N'Gombi, Bomongo——"

He paused.

"And the Ochori, lord king," said the witch-doctor. "Yes, they are with you, though the foreigner who rules them is one with Sandi."

"That is a matter which needs settlement," said the King; "yet we must move quickly, for Sandi will soon be back. It is now three days since he left, and the boat-with-the-wheel travels swiftly."

Messengers came and went all that day. Five times was the King aroused from his slumbers to receive messages and to answer questions. The Isisi people were nervous; they feared Sandi.

Would the King swear by death that if the plan did not prosper he would tell Sandi that he forced the Isisi to act by threats and cruelties? The N'Gombi had a queen of Sandi's house; should they slay her? She had a lover who would kill her very quickly, having access to her hut.

"Do not kill her," was the message Toloni sent, "for I know she is very beautiful. She shall have a hut in the shadow of my great house."

The Lesser Isisi people were impatient. There were two mission stations in their country; should they stay and burn?

"These are small matters," said Toloni the King. "First we must take Sanders, and him we will sacrifice according to ancient practice. Then all other matters will be simple and easy."

That night when darkness came and his unconscious people gossiped about the fires—none were in the secret of the coming great events save Toloni's councillors and certain headmen of other tribes—a lokali rattled musically on the outskirts of the town.

The King, in his hut, heard the signal-drum, and knew from its note that it answered some far-off fellow.

Very faintly the distant drum was sounding news from village to village, every roll, every staccato tap, every crescendo having its special meaning.

Before his hut, with both hands to his ears, the King listened.

Three rolls, rising and falling, a slow rattle, a roll, a tattoo, another roll.

That stood for Sandi—Sandi the swift, Sandi the sharp in anger, Sandi the alarmer, Sandi the giver of justice.

All these qualities and characteristics were expressed by the distant drummer.

Twice the far-away lokali spoke Sandi's name, then a long roll, a short roll, and silence.

Again—a long roll, a short roll—silence.

"Sandi dies!"

Toloni's voice was harsh and exultant.

"Listen!" he whispered.

A metallic tattoo, punctuated by an irregular procession of low, deep notes—that stood for the Arabi.

"Tap—tap—tap—tap."

There had been more shooting.

Then Sanders' name occurred again—the long roll, the short roll, and silence.

It was clear to those who could read the message— the message that ten miles away had been received by the lokali man and hammered forth from his hollow tree trunk to yet another village.

Even now Toloni's signaller was sending the message on. All night long, through the length and breadth of the land, the message would be repeated till it came to the edges of wild lands, where Sandi was unknown and the message itself incomprehensible.

"All gods and devils are with me," said the King of the Akasava. "Now is the time."

Stretched on his bunk, Sanders, with the aid of Abiboo and a small hand-mirror, located his injury.

He had suffered the slightest of wounds—the bullet had struck a steel chain purse he carried in his pocket and had deflected and taken a piece of flesh out of his left forearm, and had fetched up in the roof of the cabin before which he had been standing.

Beyond a pained bruised side and the wound in his arm, he had suffered no hurt. Abiboo dressed both places from the medicine chest, and there the matter should have ended, for Sanders was a healthy man.

But the next morning found him in a highly feverish condition. The arm had swollen to twice its normal dimensions, and was terribly painful. Sanders suspected a poisoned bullet, and was probably justified. He did not consider the matter very fully, for he was too busily engaged in an impossible argument with the Administration to give much heed to such trivialities. It was a tedious argument about a tall hat. Should Sanders wear a tall hat for the Coronation Naval Review, or should he not? The Administration was firm, but Sanders was equally determined.

"I've a shocking headache, and you ask me to wear a tall hat, your Excellency," he said in anger, and burst into tears.

It was so unlike Sanders, and he knew it was so unlike him, that by a tremendous effort of will, he came back to actualities.

He was lying in his cabin. His head and his arm

ached diabolically. His face was wet with perspiration and his tongue was like a strip of leather.

Abiboo, squatting by the side of the bed, rose as Sanders opened his eyes.

"Where do you go?" asked Sanders.

"To the God-woman who gives medicine," said Abiboo, without any display of emotion. "For I fear that you will die, and I wish for a book that I did everything properly."

"Cautious devil," muttered Sanders, and relapsed again into unconsciousness.

When he awoke again he did not hear the beat of the steamer's paddles. It was to a surprising calm and ease he awoke. He was lying in a big room in a small bed, and the sheets were of the finest linen—which on the steamer they had not been.

There was a big bowl of blue flowers on a table near the bed, and a strange fragrance.

It cannot be said that he recognised the place, because he had never before seen the interior of Miss Glandynne's bedroom; but he had a dim recollection that somebody had said he was to be taken to her. His first conscious emotion was one of extreme annoyance that he had been a nuisance to somebody, his second was one of doubt as to his own condition.

He turned his head slowly to view the erring arm. He would not have been surprised if he had found it missing. It was here safe enough, and he sighed his relief. Also it was near enough to normal size to be comforting.

He ventured to move the hand of the injured limb, and to his great pleasure found no difficulty to and experienced no pain.

Then Ruth Glandynne came in—a beautiful vision in that dark land.

She smiled, lifted a warning finger, shifted his pillow a little, and sat down by his side.

"What is wrong with the Akasava?" he asked suddenly. It was àpropos of nothing; he had not even been thinking of the Akasava, but something impelled the question.

He saw her face go suddenly grave.

"I—I think you had better not bother about the Akasava," she faltered. "You must keep very quiet."

"I must know!" he said.

His voice was cracked and weak, but she knew that, whatever might be the result, she must tell him.

He lay quietly with closed eyes while she spoke, and when she had finished he lay silent—so silent that she thought he had relapsed into unconsciousness.

Then he opened his eyes.

"Send a messenger to the Ochori," he said, "and bid Bosambo the chief come to me."

Bosambo was immensely unpopular amongst all other chiefs and peoples.

Bosambo was an alien—being a Krooman who had fled from Liberia owing to the persecutions of the government of that model republic. If you should ask how it came about that the majestic machinery of state came to be put into motion against so insignificant a man as Bosambo—a common man, if you might judge him by his place in the state—I enlighten you by offering the explanation that Bosambo had killed a warder at the convict settlement whither he had been sent for theft. The adventurer wandered across Africa till he came to the milk-hearted Ochori, in which he became paramount chief of the tribe on the sudden and inexplicable death of its rightful chief.

It is sufficient to say that this ex-convict made men of a timid people, giving them pride and a sort of spurious courage which was made up as to three-parts of fear—for Bosambo had pliant whips of rhinoceros hide, and was very quick to take offence.

One morning, in the spring of the year, Bosambo came out of his hut to find the world exquisitely beautiful—being covered with the freshest green of growing things, the sky flecked with white clouds, and a gentle breeze wrinkling the surface of the big river.

The city of the Ochori was built on the slope of a hill, and you looked across the N'Gombi Forest to the faint blur of the mountain of trees, which is in the Akasava territory.

Bosambo, who was no poet and admired only those beauties of nature which were edible, glanced disconsolately along the broad street of his city, where women were preparing the morning meals, and where the smoke of a score of little fires drifted lazily. Bosambo's three common wives were engaged before the next hut in a similar operation; his chief wife was not visible, being of the faith which requires that woman shall have no existence save to her lord.

He turned his face to the western end of the city and walked slowly.

Bosambo was no fool. He had lived amongst civilised people, he spoke English, he was a thief who had made his living in a nation of thieves.

He was aware of the happenings in the Akasava. There had been a rising—a section of the people which had declared against rebellion and had been wiped from the face of the earth. Also the Isisi had joined in the general movement, had destroyed the timid of their number, and forced the folk of the Bolenzi to servitude.

Bosambo had received an invitation to do homage to Toloni, the King, and had sent back a message which was at once comprehensive and coarse. He was safe from reprisals for a week or so. Between him and the Akasava lay the mission station where Sandi was—dying, by all accounts, but certainly there. And tied up to the mission bank was the *Zaire* and half a company of Houssas, to say nothing of two immense guns.

But if Bosambo was contemptuous of the self-appointed King of the World—as Toloni called himself—there were men of the Ochori who, remembering Bosambo's pliant whip, and his readiness to exercise it, corresponded with Toloni, and Bosambo knew that half the Ochori people were far gone in sedition.

Yet he was not over-distressed—that worried him less than another matter.

"Light of my life and joy of my soul," he said to the woman who shared the gaudy magnificence of his thatched harem. "If Sandi dies there is no virtue in religion, for I have prayed to all gods, to the Prophets, and to the lords Marki, Luko, and Johanni—also to the Virgin of whom the Marist Brothers told me; and I have prayed to crosses and to ju-jus, and have sacrificed a goat and a chicken before the Ochori fetish."

"Mahomet," she said reprovingly, "all this is evil, for there is but one God."

"He will praise my diligence in seeking Him," said Bosambo philosophically. "Yet, if Sandi recover, I will thank all gods lest I miss the Him who benefited my master."

His position was a delicate one, as he knew. Only the previous night he had caught a secret messenger from Toloni, who came to call upon the Ochori to attack Sandi's men from the north, driving them towards the waiting legions of the rebel king. Bosambo extracted the full message from the courier before he disposed of him.

Two more days of anxious waiting followed. A headman of the Ochori, who had been promised the chiefship of the tribe, decided to rush matters, and crept into Bosambo's hut one evening to create the necessary vacancy.

Bosambo, who was waiting for him, clubbed him into insensibility with promptitude and dispatch, dragged him in the darkness of the night to the river bank, and slid him into the water with a rope about his neck and a stone attached to the rope.

It brought matters to a head in one sense, for, missing their leader, his faction called upon Bosambo and demanded that the missing man be handed over to them. Their chief's reply was an emphatic one. The spokesman carried the marks of Bosambo's eloquence to the grave. How matters might have developed it is difficult to guess, but Sandi's summons came to Bosambo, and he called his people together.

"I go to Sandi," he told them, "Sandi who is my master and yours, in addition to being my relative, as you know. And behold I leave behind me a people who are ungrateful and vicious. Now I say to you that in my absence you shall go about your work and do nothing evil—that you shall neither attend to the council of fools nor follow your own wicked fancies—for when I return I shall be swift to punish; and if any man disobey me, I will put out his eyes and leave him in the forest for the beasts to hunt. I will do this by Ewa, who is death."

After which Bosambo departed for the mission station, taking with him his favourite wife and fifty fighting men.

He came to Sandi's within forty-eight hours of the Commissioner's summons, and squatted by his master's bedside.

"Bosambo," said Sandi, "I have been very ill, and I am still too weak to stand. And whilst I am lying here, Toloni, King of the Akasava, has risen, and with him the countryside."

"Lord, it is as you say," said Bosambo.

"In time there will come many white men," said Sandi, "and they will eat up this foolish king; but in the meantime there will be much suffering, and many innocent people will be slain. I have sent for you because I trust you."

"Lord," said Bosambo, "I am a thief and a low man, and my heart is full of pride that you should stoop toward me."

Sandi detected the tremor in Bosambo's voice, and he knew he was sincere.

"Therefore, O chief, I have placed you in my place, for you are skilled in war. And I give over to you the command of my ship and of my fighting men, and you shall do that which is best."

Bosambo sprang noiselessly to his feet, and stood tense and erect by the bedside. There was a strange light in his eyes.

"Lord Sandi," he said in a low voice, "do you speak true—that I"—he struck his broad chest with both his clenched fists—"I stand in your place?"

"That is so," said Sandi.

Bosambo was silent for a minute, then he opened his mouth to speak, checked himself, and, turning without a word, left the room.

Which was unlike Bosambo.

They were prepared for his coming. Abiboo stood at the end of the gangway and raised his hand in salute.

"I am your man, chief," he said.

"Abiboo," he said, "I do not lie when I say that I am of your faith; and by Allah and his Prophet I am for doing that which is best for Sandi, our master."

"So we both desire," said Abiboo.

Bosambo's preparations were quietly made.

He sent half of his fighting men to the mission house to guard Sandi, and with them twenty Houssas under a sergeant.

"Now we will call upon Toloni the king," he said.

The King of the Akasava sat in palaver. His force was camped on the edge of the N'Gombi country, and a smoking village spoke of resistance offered and overcome—for the N'Gombi had at last declined to join the coalition, and the lover, who had undertaken to persuade the queen, and, failing persuasion, to take more effective action, had failed.

The queen notified his failure by sending his head to Toloni.

Not even the news that Sandi was sick to death served to shake them in their opposition. It may have been that the vital young queen cherished ambitions of her own.

The king's palaver was a serious one.

"It seems that the N'Gombi people must be eaten up village by village," he said, "for all this country is with me save them only. As to this queen, she shall be sorry."

He was within striking distance of the N'Gombi queen. His legions were closing steadily in upon the doomed city. By nightfall he was within reach, and at dawn the following morning Toloni carried the city by assault and it was a beastly business.

They carried the queen back to the king's headquarters, and there was a great dance.

By the light of a dozen fires the king sat in judgment.

The girl—she was little more—stood up before him, stripped of her robes, and met the king's eyes without fear.

"Woman," he said, "this night you die!"

She made no answer.

"By fire and by torment I will kill you," said Toloni, and told her the means of her death.

He sat on his carved stool of state beneath a tree. He was naked, save for the leopard robe that covered one shoulder, and his cruel eyes glittered in anticipation of the spectacle she would afford.

She spoke calmly enough.

"If I die to-night and you die to-morrow, O king, what is a day? For Sandi will come with his soldiers."

"Sandi is dead," said the king thickly. He had drunk heavily of the maize beer that natives prepare. "And if he lived——"

There came to his hearing a faint wail that grew in shrillness until it became a shriek. Shrieking it passed over his head and died away.

He struggled to his feet unsteadily.

"It was a spirit," he muttered, then——

The wailing sound came again—a shriek this time of men. Something struck the tree, splintering the bark.

The faint and ghastly light of dawn was in the sky; in a second the world went pearl-grey and, plain to be seen, hugging the shore on the opposite bank, was the *Zaire*.

As the king looked he saw a pencil of fire leap from the little ship, heard the whine of the coming shell, and realised the danger.

He gave a hurried order, and a regiment ran to the river-bank where the canoes were beached. They were not there. The guards left to watch them lay stretched like men asleep on the beach, but the canoes were in mid-stream five miles away, carried down by the river.

In the night Bosambo's men had crossed the river.

The story of the fall of Toloni is a brief one. Trapped on the middle island, at the mercy of the long-range guns of the *Zaire*, Toloni surrendered.

He was conducted to the *Zaire*.

Bosambo met him on the bridge.

"Ho, Bosambo!" said Toloni, "I have come to see Sandi."

"You see me who am as our lord," said Bosambo.

Toloni spat on the deck.

"When a slave sits in the king's place only slaves obey him," he quoted a river saying.

"Kings have only one head, and the slave's blood is also red," said Bosambo readily. "And it seems to me, Toloni, that you are too full of life for our lord's happiness. But first you shall tell me what has come to the Queen of the N'Gombi."

"She died," said Toloni carelessly; "very quickly she died."

Bosambo peered at him. It was a trick of Sandi's

this peering, and the Chief of the Ochori was nothing if not imitative.

"You shall tell me how she died," said Bosambo.

The king's face twitched.

"I took her by the throat," he said sullenly.

"Thus?" said Bosambo, and his big hand closed on the king's strong neck.

"Thus!" gasped the king, "and I struck her with my knife—ah!"

"Thus?" said Bosambo.

Twice his long, broad-bladed knife rose and fell, and the king went quivering to the deck.

*   *   *   *   *

Sandi was strong enough to walk to the beach to meet the *Zaire* on its return—strong enough, though somewhat dazzled by his splendour, to greet Bosambo, wearing a sky-blue robe laced with tinsel, and a tall and napless hat.

Bosambo came mincing down the gangway plank swinging a brass-headed stick and singing a low song such as Kroomen sing on the coast when they receive their pay and are dismissed their ships.

He was beautiful to behold—feathers were in his hair, rope after rope of gay beads about his neck.

"I have slain Toloni," he said, "even as your lord would have done—he turned his face from me and said, 'It is honourable to die at your hands, Bosambo,' and he made little moaning noises thus——"

And Bosambo, with his heart in the task, made an admirable effort of mimicry.

"Go on," said Sandi hastily.

"Also I have sent the Isisi and the Akasava to their homes to await your honour's judgment, even as you would have done, master."

Sandi nodded.

"And these?" he asked, indicating the chief's finery.

"These I stole from the camp of Toloni," said Bosambo. "These and other things, for I was working for government and lord," he said with becoming simplicity. "It is according to the white man's custom, as your lordship knows."

XII

THE MISSIONARY

THIS is a moral story. You may go to the black countries for your morals and take from cannibal peoples a most reliable code of ethics. For cannibal folk are fastidious to a degree, eminently modest—though a photograph of the average Bogra native would leave you in some doubt—clean of speech and thought and habit. If they chop men it is because they like food of that particular type. They are no better and no worse than vegetarians, who are also faddy in the matter of foodstuffs.

Native peoples have a code of their own, and take some account of family obligations.

There were two brothers who lived in the Isisi country in a small village, and when their father died they set forth to seek their fortune. The name of the one was M'Kamdina, and of the other M'Kairi. M'Kamdina being the more adventurous, crossed the border of the lawful land into the territory of the Great King, and there he sold himself into captivity.

In those days the Great King was very great and very ancient; so great that no British Administrator did more than reprove him mildly for his wanton cruelty.

This M'Kamdina was a clever youth, very cunning in council, very patient of abuse. He had all the qualities that go to the making of a courtier. It is not surprising, therefore, that he gained a place in the King's household, sat at his right hand at meat, and married such of the King's light fancies as His Majesty was pleased to discard.

He grew wealthy and powerful; was the King's Prime Minister, with power of life and death in his master's absence. He went afield for his lord's dancing girls and, having nice taste in such matters, was considerably rewarded.

So he lived, happy and prosperous and content.

The other brother, M'Kairi, had no such enterprise. He settled in a small village near the Pool of Spirits, and with great labour, being a poor man and only affording one wife, he cleared a garden. Here he sowed industriously, and reaped with a full measure of success, selling his stock at a profit.

News came to him of his brother's prosperity, and once, in contempt of all Sanders' orders, the painted canoe of the Great King's Premier came flashing down the river bearing gifts to the poor brother.

Sanders heard of this when he was on a tour of inspection and went out to see M'Kairi.

"Lord, it was so," said the man sadly. "These rich gifts come from my brother, who is a slave. Salt and corn and cloth and spearheads he sent me."

Sanders looked round at the poor field the man worked.

"And yet, M'Kairi," he said, "this is not the garden of a rich man, nor do I see your fine cloth nor the wives that salt would bring you."

"Lord," said the man, "I sent them back, for my heart is very sore that my brother should be a slave and I a free man, toiling in the fields, but free; and I would give my life if I could pay the price of him."

He told Sanders he had sent a message asking what that price was, and it happened that Sanders was close at hand when the Great King, for his own amusement, sent back word saying that the price of M'Kamdina was ten thousand matakos—a matako being a brass rod.

Now it is a fact that for seven years—long, patient, suffering, lean years—M'Kairi laboured in his garden, and sold and bought and reared and bargained until he had acquired ten thousand matakos. These he put into his canoe and paddled to the edge of the land where the Great King ruled, and so came to the presence of his brother and the master of his brother.

The Great King was amused; M'Kamdina was not so amused, being wrathful at his brother's simplicity.

"Go back with your rods," he said. He sat in his grand hut, and his smiling wives and his slaves sat about him. "Take your rods, M'Kairi my brother, and know that it is better to be a slave in the house of a king than a free man toiling in the fields."

And M'Kairi went back to his tiny plantation sick at heart.

Three weeks later the Great King died. That is the station where the moral of this little story steps off. For according to custom, when the Great King lay stretched upon his bier, they took the principal slave of the great one—and that slave was M'Kamdina—and they cut off his head that his body might be buried with his master to serve his soul's need in another land.

And the son of the Great King reigned in his stead, and in course of time died violently.

"There's the basis of a good Sunday school yarn in that story," said the Houssa captain.

"H'm!" growled Sanders, who was innocent of any desire to furnish material for tracts.

"Rum beggar, that old king!" said the Houssa thoughtfully, "and the new fellow was a rummer. You hanged him or something, didn't you?"

"I forget," said Sanders shortly. "If your infernal troops were worth their salt there would be no hangings. What is it?"

His orderly was standing in the doorway of the Houssa skipper's hut.

"Lord, there is a book,"* said the man.

Sanders took the soiled envelope from the man's hand. It was addressed in flowing Arabic:

"The Lord Commissioner, Who is at the town where the river is broadest near the sea. Two flagstaffs standing up and many soldiers will be seen. Go swiftly, and may God be with you."

It was an address and an instruction.

"Who brought this?"

"An Arabi," said the man, "such as trade in the high land."

Sanders tore open the letter. He sought first the signature at the top of the letter and found it to be that of Ahmed, a reliable chief of his secret service.

Sanders read the letter, skipping the flowery introduction wherein Ahmed asked Providence and its authorised agents to bring happiness to the house of the Commissioner.

"It is well that I should tell you this, though I hide my face when I speak of a woman of your house."

(Sanders accepted the innuendo which coupled the name of an innocent missionary lady with himself.)

"Of this God-woman, who is at present on the river, many stories come, some being that she cries at night because no men of the Akasava take God-magic.

"And I have heard from an Isisi woman who is her servant that this God-woman would go back to her own land, only she is ashamed because so few have learnt the new God. Also, she has fever. I send this by an Arabi, my friend Ahmed, who is my messenger, being five days in search of an Akasava man who has stolen goats."

Sanders laughed helplessly.

"That girl will be the death of me," he said.

* A letter.

He left for the mission station that very hour.

The girl was well enough, but very white and tired; she was obviously glad to see Sanders.

"It was so good of you to come," she said. "I was getting a little dispirited; I had half made up my mind to go back to England."

"I wish I hadn't come if that's the case," said Sanders bluntly.

The girl smiled.

"That isn't very nice of you, Mr. Sanders," she said.

"Nice! Look here."

He took off his helmet and pointed to his closely cropped head.

"Do you see those?" he asked.

She looked curiously.

She saw nothing except a face burnt brick-red by the sun, two steady grey eyes in such odd contrasts to the tan that they seemed the lightest blue.

She saw the lean face, the straight thin nose, the firm jaw and the almost hairless head.

"What am I looking for?" she asked.

"Grey hairs," said Sanders grimly.

She frowned in pretty perplexity.

"It is difficult to see any hair at all," she confessed. "But will you turn your head a little? Yes, I see something which might be grey."

"They're grey enough," said Sanders with a little smile. He was more at home with her than he had ever been with a white woman.

"And exactly what do they signify?" she asked.

"Worry—about you," said Sanders. "Good Lord! Haven't you had enough of these infernal people? I seem to spend half my life running up and down this river keeping people in order who are anxious to chop you. You cannot build on sand, and you are trying to lay a foundation on water."

"You mean religious teaching must have a basis of civilisation?" she asked quietly.

"Something like that. Look here, Miss Glandynne; that man who is working in your garden, he's one of your converts, isn't he?"

She nodded.

"He is the most helpful man I have; he goes into the outlying villages and holds services."

"What is his name?"

"Kombolo," she said.

Sanders called the man to him. He was a stout, good-humoured native, the "outward and visible sign of whose inward and spiritual grace" was a pair of trousers and a waistcoat.

"Kombolo," said Sanders in the Isisi dialect, "they tell me you are a fine God-man."

"Lord, that is so," said the man, beaming, "for I have the blessed Spirit in me which makes me talk wonderfully."

"And you go to many villages?"

"Preaching the Word, master," said the man, nodding.

"And do you go ever to the people of the Forest-of Happy-Thought?" asked Sanders quietly.

The man shuddered.

"Lord, I do not go there," he said.

"Why?"

Kombolo shuffled his bare feet and stood on one leg in his embarrassment.

"Lord, there are devils and ghosts in the wood, as you know," he said.

"Do you ever go to the people of the N'Gombi Forest?" asked Sanders innocently.

Again the man shivered.

"Never do I go there, Sandi," he said, "because, as your lordship knows, M'shimba-M'shamba walks therein."

The girl was following the conversation with knitted brows.

"Who is M'shimba-M'shamba?" she asked.

"He is the green devil who walks by night," said Sanders blandly, "and he is very terrible."

Kombolo nodded his head vigorously.

"That is true, mamma," he said earnestly. "I myself have seen him."

The girl's face wore a look of shocked surprise.

"But, Kombolo," she said in distress, "you know there are no such things as devils."

Kombolo was frankly puzzled.

"Lady," he said slowly, "it is certain that there are devils, for do we not read of him—the Devil, the old One—who fills us with bad thoughts?"

"But that is different," she began helplessly.

"A devil is a devil," said Kombolo philosophically, "and, though there be only one devil in your land, there are many here; for, lady, here, as you have told me, there are many flies and many beasts such as you do not see in your own country. So also there must be devils, though perhaps not so mighty as the lord Devil of the white people."

Sanders dismissed him with a nod, and sat whistling cheerfully to himself whilst the girl laid reason under tribute to fact.

"Well?" he said at last.

"You don't make things easy," she said, and Sanders, to his horror, discovered that she was on the verge of tears. "I think it was unkind of you to sow doubt in Kombolo's mind. It is hard enough to fight against their superstition——"

"But——" protested the agitated Commissioner.

"——without having to combat superstition and ignorance fortified by authority."

She checked a sob.

"But, Miss Glandynne——"

"I know what you are going to say—you want me to go home. I'm too much bother to you. I give you grey hairs and take up all your time. But I'm going to stay."

She rose and stamped her foot vehemently.

"Don't get angry——"

"I'm not angry——"

"Don't be annoyed——"

"I'm not annoyed. I know I'm unfitted for the work; I never intended doing evangelical work. I came out for the medical side, and if I'd known I had to work alone I shouldn't have come at all."

"Then go back," said Sanders eagerly; "go back to the life you ought to be living. I'll get Father Wells to come up and take over your station."

"A Catholic!" she said scornfully.

"Is he?" asked Sanders, who never worried about creeds. "Anyway——"

"And besides," she said, and her voice shook, "I've nothing to hand over. I've been here nearly a year, and my only convert is a man who believes in green devils. Oh, Mr. Sanders!"

She broke down and tugged furiously for a handkerchief in her belt.

"Oh, Lord!" said Sanders, and beat a hasty retreat.

He saw her again in the evening. She was calmer and inclined to listen to reason.

"Give the station another three months," he said. "The country has been a bit upset since you've been here. I can understand you not wishing to admit your failure."

She caught her breath ominously.

"Not that you've been a failure," Sanders went on with frantic haste; "far from it. But it would be different, wouldn't it, if you could point to some work——"

"Of course it would," she said shortly; then, realising that she was being a little ungracious, she smiled through the gathering tears. "I'm afraid I'm too worldly for this work. I'm not satisfied with the knowledge that I am doing my best. I want to see results."

Sanders, in his intense astonishment, patted her hand.

More to his astonishment, he told her the story of the two brothers, and she was greatly impressed.

"That is the best missionary moral I have ever heard," she said.

"I am leaving to-morrow," he said, after he had stopped to curse himself under his breath. "I go to Lukalela for a wife-beating palaver, and afterwards to the black country."

He did not mention the fact that he was going to the Ochori—for reasons of his own. Yet it was to the Ochori country that he headed. It was peculiar to his office that no man knew to whither the Commissioner was bound. He stood by the steersman, and by a wave of his hand, this way or that, set the steamer's course.

If he so willed, the *Zaire* would deviate to the left or right bank—if he wished the steamer kept a straight course till night fell, when the nearest wooding was his apparent objective.

Before night came, late in the afternoon, he fetched up at a wooding where a year before he had felled ten trees, leaving them to season and to dry. For two hours the men of the *Zaire* sawed and chopped at the fallen trunks, stacking the wood on the well-deck below.

At night the *Zaire* resumed her journey. The big lamp on the right of the steersman hissed and spluttered as Sanders switched on the current, and a white fan of light shot ahead of the ship.

It searched the water carefully—a great unwinking eye which looked closely for shoal and sandbank.

At midnight Sanders tied up to give himself a little rest.

He reached the Ochori city in the afternoon, and his interview with Bosambo was a brief one.

By evening he was gone, the steamer sweeping back to Lukalela.

*   *   *   *   *

Bosambo held a court every morning of his life, save on those mornings when work and pleasure were forbidden by the Koran, which he imperfectly knew, but which he obeyed at second hand—his wife was of the faith, and had made an obedient, if a careless, convert in her husband.

In the time of the Ramadhan, Bosambo did no work, but fasted in the privacy of the forest—whither on the previous day he had removed a store of food and water sufficient to last him over a very trying twenty-four hours. For, though it was his pleasure to humour his wife, it was not his wish to humour her to his own discomfort.

On the morning after Sanders' visit, Bosambo sat upon a wooden chair—a gift of Sanders—painted alternately red, green, and yellow—the paint also being a gift of Sanders, though he was unaware of the fact—and dealt with the minor offences and the little difficulties of his people.

"Lord Bosambo," said a thin young man from an outlying village, "I bring salt to your justice."*

"Speak, my brother," said Bosambo; "you shall have your meal."

"I have two wives, lord; one I bought from her father for three skins, and one came to me after the great [Akasava] war. Now the woman I bought has put shame upon me, for she has a lover. In the days before you came, lord, it would be proper to put her to death; but now she and other women laugh at our beatings, and continue in sin."

"Bring the woman," said Bosambo.

The young man dragged her forward, a comely girl of sixteen, with defiant laughter in her eyes, and she was unabashed.

"Woman," said Bosambo severely, "though no death awaits you by Sandi's orders, and my pleasure, yet

* A River saying, meaning: "I am so certain of the meal, I have brought the flavouring."

there are ways, such as you know, of teaching you wisdom. I have built a prison in the Forest of Dreams, where devils come nightly, and it seems a proper place for you."

"Lord," she gasped, "I am afraid."

"Yet I will not send you there, for I love my people," said Bosambo. "Now you shall go to the God-woman who dwells by Kosumkusu, and you shall do as she tells you. And you shall say that you have come to learn of the new God-magic, and you shall do all the strange things she desires, such as shutting your eyes at proper moments and saying 'Ah-min.'"

"Lord, I will do this," said the girl.

"It will be well for you if you do," said Bosambo.

The next case was that of a man who claimed goats from his neighbour in lieu of other benefits promised.

"For he said, speaking with an evil and a lying tongue, 'If you help me with my fishing for a year I will give you the first young of my goat after the rains,'" said the man.

The dispute centred in the words "after the rains," for it would appear that the goats were born before the rains came.

"This is a difficult palaver," said Bosambo, "and I need time to take the counsel of Sandi. You, Kalo, shall go to the God-woman by Kosumkusu; and you too," he said, addressing the other party to the dispute, "and there you shall learn the God-magic and do all the things she desires, telling her that you come to learn of her wisdom, and in course of time it shall be revealed to me who is right and who is wrong."

And for every man and woman who came before him he had one solution, one alternative to punishment—a visit to the God-woman and the cultivation of a spirit of humility. Some there were who demurred.

"Lord, I will not go," said a man violently, "for this

God-woman speaks slightingly of my god and my ju-ju, and I do not want to know the new God-magic."

"Tie him to a tree," said Bosambo calmly, "and whip him till he says 'Ah-min.' "

Willing hands bound the unfortunate to a tree, and a rhinoceros whip whistled in the air and fell once, twice, thrice——

"Ah-min!" yelled the malcontent, and was released to make his pilgrimage to Kosumkusu.

At the close of the palaver, Bosambo, with his chief councillor, Olomo, a wise old man, walked through the street of the city together.

"Lord," said Olomo, shaking his head, "I do not like this new way of government, for it is not proper that the young people of the Ochori should——"

Bosambo stopped and looked at him thoughtfully.

"You are right, Olomo," he said softly; "it is not wise that only the young people should go. Now I think it would please me if you went with them that they might feel no shame."

"Lord, I do not desire," said the alarmed old man.

"For I should like you to bring me news of my people," Bosambo went on, "and you could teach them, being so full of wisdom, how to shut their eyes and say 'Ah-min' when certain words are spoken; also, you could prevent them running away."

"By Ewa, I will not go!" said the old man, trembling with passion.

"By Ewa, you will go," said Bosambo, "or I will take you by the beard, old he-goat, and pull you through the village."

"I am your slave," muttered Olomo, and tottered off to make preparations for the journey.

* * * * *

Sanders made a longer stay in Kukalala than he had expected. And there had been an outbreak of beri-

beri in an interior village which made his presence necessary.

He came to the mission station, wondering, hoping, and a little fearful.

He went ashore and walked up the little path and through the garden she had made for herself; the girl came to meet him half-way.

A radiant, happy girl, showing no sign of her illness. Sanders' heart smote him.

"Oh, Mr. Sanders," she said, stretching out both hands in welcome, "I cannot tell you how glad I am to see you! I have wonderful news!"

Sanders blushed guiltily, and felt monstrously uncomfortable.

"Indeed!" was all he could say.

And then she told him the splendid happening. How her little flock had grown with a rapidity which was little short of marvellous; how the news had gone out, and pilgrims had arrived—not singly, but in fours and fives—for days on end—men and women, old and young.

"Extraordinary!" said Sanders. "Now I suppose you will not object to handing over the station to Father——"

"Hand it over!" she exclaimed in amazement. "Leave all those poor people! Abandon them! Of course, I shall do nothing so criminal."

Sanders did not swoon.

"But—but," he said, "do they want to stay?"

"They did not at first, but after I had told them your story they understood something of their position."

"Oh!" said Sanders. He gathered himself together and walked back to the boat.

*　　*　　*　　*　　*

Bosambo paddled down-stream to meet the Commissioner and lay his troubles before him.

"Lord," he said ruefully, "I did not know that this new palaver would be pleasing to my people. I have sent the flower of my nation to the God-woman, and they will not come back."

"It is written," said Sanders.

They had met in the middle of the river. Just as the *Zaire* was turning Bosambo had come alongside, and now they stood on the deck together, silent in the consciousness of their mutual failure.

From the shore came a sound of singing. It was the evening hymn of the new converts.

The music came to an end, there was a pause, and then a sharp roll of melody.

"Ah-min!" echoed Bosambo bitterly. "And, lord, I taught them that word."

XIII

A MAKER OF SPEARS

NORTH of the Akasava country and on the left bank of the Isisi is a veritable forest of elephant grass. Here in the cool of the evening, and later, the hippo come to wallow and for social intercourse. Here, too, buck and the small but terrible buffalo come to bathe and drink.

For ten miles without a break the jungle runs and there is no tree or hill behind the green curtain to reveal what manner of country lies beyond.

It is a marsh for fifty miles and in the centre is an island unapproachable save by secret ways such as a few Akasava men know and jealously preserve.

No corporation working under a charter or great seal of state is so close, so exclusive as is that of "The Keepers of the Water Path."

The secret is kept in one family and is known only

to the male members. There is a story that a woman once discovered the mystery of the open water—for open water there is in the maze of grass—and that she unwittingly betrayed her knowledge. They took her, so the story runs, her own brothers and blood kindred, and they drowned her in the water. This must have been calacala—long ago—before keen-eyed and swift-handed justice made its appearance in the shape of Mr. Commissioner Sanders.

To the uninitiated it might seem that the secret way was not of any great importance. True, the best fish came into the creek and the family had that advantage. But as Sanders discovered, the marsh land was of some strategical importance, for it effectively separated the Akasava from the Isisi. It made sudden raidings such as are common between tribes with contiguous frontiers impossible, also it offered no hiding place to malefactors, and for this reason alone it was wiser to preserve the Keepers of the Marsh in their mystery.

Sanders was in the Akasava territory, in the village nearest the marsh, when an unfortunate thing occurred.

There was a woman of the frontier who had been married to an old chief whose name was Likilivi. He was chief not only of the village, but of the family which kept the marsh, and he was an important man —but old.

Now all men know that the makers of spears, and of iron work generally, are the N'Gombi people.

They are born craftsmen, skilful and very cunning. Also, in parenthesis, they are great thieves and once stole a little anvil from the *Zaire*, which was converted into spear heads and steel cups before the anvil was missed.

Yet Likilivi, a man of the Akasava, was the most famous worker of spears on the river. So famous that hunters and warriors came from all parts to buy his weapons. His father before him, and his father, had also made spears, but none equal in keenness or in temper to those which Likilivi made in his big work hut. And he made them with extraordinary rapidity, he and the two sons of his house, so that he grew rich and powerful.

He was old, too old for the girl his wife, who hated him from the first, hated him fiercely till her young heart nearly burst with the fury of her emotions.

She ran from him, was brought back and beaten. She sat down to brood and find a way out, whilst from the adjoining hut came the "tink—tink—tink" of hammered steel, as Likilivi and his grown sons pounded spear heads into shape.

*   *   *   *   *

If you take a piece of glass no bigger than the top of your thumb, place it in a mortar and industriously pound and grind at it, you will, in course of time, produce a fine white powder smooth to the touch and, though insoluble, yet easily administered to man.

You must be patient, and have plenty of time to make your powder "fit," as they say on the coast, but M'ciba (this was the girl's name) had all the time there was to prepare her release.

Old Likilivi came from his workshop one afternoon; he was a little soured because some innocent villager with a taste for crude arithmetic had asked him how it came about that so few men made so many spears.

He was at best an old and sour man, he was no more amiable because of this embarrassing question.

"The sun has come to me," his wife should have said politely, as he came to the hut where she sat crushing corn. (The white powder and the mortar and iron-wood pestle were discreetly hidden.)

She said nothing.

"If you do not speak to me," said the old man sourly, "I will break your head."

The girl did not speak.

She went about her work, which was the preparation of his food. She made him a mess of manioc, and fish, and she added a judicious quantity of fine white powder.

The old chief ate his meal, muttering to himself and casting evil eyes at her.

When he had finished he beat her for no particular reason save that he felt like beating her, then he went to bed.

He woke up in the night. She was not lying at his side as was her duty. By the dull red light of the fire he saw her sitting with her back against the hut wall, her hands clasping her knees, watching him with grave eyes.

"M'ciba," he gasped, and the sweat was standing on his forehead, "I have the sickness-mongo."

She said nothing and he did not speak again.

An hour later she covered her body with dust and sitting down before the hut wailed her grief, and the awakened village hurried forth to find Likilivi near to death, with his face twisted painfully.

By the aid of an extraordinary constitution and the employment of a drastic but effective native remedy the chief did not die. M'ciba had wailed too soon.

It was many weeks before Likilivi recovered. He suspected nothing. As soon as he was well he took the pliant half of his hunting spear and thrashed her.

"For you are a fool," he said, "or you would have called for help sooner, and I should have recovered more quickly."

She took her beating meekly, knowing that she deserved more, but her hatred grew.

Her treatment by her husband was scandal in the village, for native folk are kind, and it is not customary or good form to beat one's womenkind.

Then M'ciba committed her crowning indiscretion.

Likilivi, his cousin and his sons, prepared to make one of their periodical visits to the marsh—a matter of some importance and considerable secrecy. There was to be a great netting of fish, and other high mysteries were to be enacted—foolish mysteries, you might think them, such as the sacrificing of chicken and the like, but which were very real and important to Likilivi and his kin. Also there were other matters to be seen to.

By some means M'ciba came to know of the intended visit, and spoke to a woman about the event. It was unforgivable. It was against all tradition. Likilivi, for the honour of his house, ordered a public whipping.

And at sunset one evening, before the assembled visitors, with the chief sitting on his stool, M'ciba was led forth, and whilst his sons held her the chief took the hide.

"Woman," he said, "I do this that all the world may know you as shameless and a destroyer of honour—behold . . ."

So far he got, when the crowd opened to allow of the passage of a dapper man in white, a broad and spotless helmet on his head, an ebony stick in his hand.

Likilivi was staggered.

"Lord Sandi," he said in confusion, "this woman is my wife, and I go to whip her because of certain abominations."

Sanders eyed him unpleasantly.

"Release this woman," he said, and the two sons obeyed instanter.

"It seems," he said to the embarrassed chief, "that you are old and evil. And when I place a man above others to be chief of those people, I desire that he shall so live that all common people shall say 'Lo! as our lord lives, so shall we.' And if he is evil, then all the village is evil. You are certainly no chief for me."

"Lord," said the old man tremulously, "if you take from me my chieftainship I shall die of shame."

"That I shall certainly do," said Sanders, "and whip you also if you injure this woman, your wife."

And Sanders meant it, for he respected only the law which has neither age nor sex.

He took the girl apart.

"As to you, M'ciba," he said, "be pleasant to this man who is your husband, for he is old and will soon die."

"Lord, I pray for his death," she said passionately.

Sanders looked at her from under his brows.

"Pray," he said drily, "yet give him no glass in his food, or I shall come quickly, and then you will be sorry."

She shivered and a look of terror came into her eyes.

"You know all things, master," she gasped.

Sanders did not attempt to disabuse her mind. The faith in his omnipotence was a healthy possession.

"You shall be beaten no more," he said, for she was in a state—being prepared for a further whipping—that revealed something of her husband's previous ferocity.

Sanders dismissed the people to their homes—some had departed quickly on his appearance, and he had a few words with Likilivi.

"O chief," he said softly, "I have a mind to take my stick to you."

"I am an old man," quavered the other.

"The greater evil," said Sanders, "that you should beat this child."

"Lord, she spoke with women of our Marsh Mystery," said the chief.

"More of this mystery," warned Sanders, "and I will bring my soldiers and we will clear the grass till your infernal mystery is a mystery no longer."

In all his long life Likilivi had never heard so terrible a threat, for the mystery of the Marsh was the most sacred of his possessions.

Sanders was smiling to himself as the *Zaire* went speeding down the river. These childish mysteries amused him. They were part of the life of his people.

Admitting the fact that the Marsh was an impenetrable buffer state between Isisi and Akasava, it was less a factor in the preservation of peace than it had been in the bad years of long ago.

Sanders' trip was in a sense a cruise of leisure. He was on his way to the N'Gombi to make an inquiry and to point a lesson.

N'Gombi signifies forest. When Stanley first penetrated the interior of the great land, he was constantly hearing of a N'Gombi city of fabulous wealth. Not until he had made several ineffective expeditions did he discover the true significance of the name.

Though of the forest, there are N'Gombi folk who live on the great river, and curiously enough whilst they preserve the characteristic which distinguishes them from the riverain people in that they cannot swim, are yet tolerable fishermen.

Sanders was bound for the one N'Gombi town which stands on the river, and his palaver would be, as he knew, an unsatisfactory one.

He saw the smoke of the N'Gombi fires—they are great iron workers hereabouts—long before he came in sight of the place.

As he turned to give directions to the steersman, Abiboo, who stood on the further side of the helmsman, said something in Bomongo, and the man at the wheel laughed.

"What was that?" asked Sanders.

"Lord, it was a jest," said Abiboo; "I spoke of the N'Gombi people, for there is a saying on the river that N'Gombi crocodiles are fat."

The subtlety of the jest may be lost to the reader, but to Sanders it was plain enough.

The town is called Oulu, but the natives have christened it by a six-syllable word which means "The Town of the Sinkers."

Sanders nodded.

An extraordinary fatality pursued this place. In the

last four or five years there had been over twenty drowning accidents.

Men had gone out in the evening to fish. In the morning their waterlogged canoes had been found, but the men had disappeared, their bodies being either carried away by the swift stream, or, as popular legend had it, going to some secret larder of the crocodile in the river bed.

It was on account of the latest disaster, which had involved the death of three men, that Sanders paid his visit.

He swung the *Zaire* to shallow water and reached the N'Gombi foreshore.

The headman who met him was grimed with smoke and very hot. He carried the flat hammer of his craft in his hand, and was full of grievances. And the least of these was the death of three good workmen by drowning.

"Men who go on the water are fools," he said, "for it is not natural that any should go there but fish and the dogs of Akasava."

"That is not good palaver," said Sanders sharply. "Dogs are dogs and men are men; therefore, my man, speak gently in my presence of other tribes or you will be sorry."

"Lord Sandi," said the man bitterly, "these Akasava would starve us and especially Likilivi the chief."

It was an old grievance between the two villages, the N'Gombi holding themselves as being chartered by Providence to supply all that was crafty and cunning in iron work.

"For as you know, master," the man went on, "iron is hard to come by in these parts."

Sanders remembered a certain anvil stolen at this very village, and nodded.

"Also it is many years before young men learn the magic which makes iron bend. How it must be heated so, cooled so, tapped and fashioned and hammered."

"This I know," said Sanders.

"And if we do not receive so much salt and so many rods for each spear head," the headman continued, "we starve, because . . ."

It was the old story, as old as the world, the story of fair return for labour. The N'Gombi sold their spears at the finest margin of profit.

"Once we grew fat with wealth," said the headman, "because for every handful of salt we ate, when we worked two handfuls came for the spears we made. Now, lord, few spears go out from the N'Gombi and many from Likilivi, because he sells cheaper."

Sanders sighed wearily.

"Such things happen in other lands," he said, "and folks make palaver—just as you, M'Kema. Yet I know of no way out."

He inspected the town, received two oral petitions, one for the restoration to liberty of a man who had stolen government property (to wit the aforesaid anvil) and one for a dissolution of marriage, which he granted. He stayed at the town, holding a palaver in the cool of the evening, in the course of which he addressed the people on the necessity for learning to swim.

"Twenty men have been drowned," he said, "and yet none learn the lesson. I say that you either do not go upon the water at all, or else learn to walk-in-water as the Isisi and the Ochori and the Akasava walk."

After dinner, that night, being in a frame of mind agreeable to the subject, he sent again for the headman.

"O chief," he said, looking up from the book he was reading, "I have been thinking about this matter of spears. For it seems to me that Likilivi, for all his skill, cannot make so many spears that you are inconvenienced."

"Master, I speak the truth," said the man emphatically.

"Yet the people hereabout are hunters," said Sanders, puzzled.

"Lord," said the headman with considerable emphasis, "if all the world wanted spears Likilivi would supply them."

That was an exaggeration, but Sanders passed it over. He dismissed the man and sat down in solitude to reason the matter out.

Likilivi was an old man, and if he were of our faith we should say that he would be well employed if he were engaging himself in the preparation for another and a better world. Certainly he should not be considering means of reprisal against his young wife. She had put him to shame before his people. She had called down upon him a public reproof from Sandi, moreover, had caused Sandi to threaten an end to the Marsh Mystery and that was the worst offence of all.

Likilivi calmly considered in what way he might bring about her death without Sandi knowing by whose instrumentality she perished. There were many ways suggested to his mind. He could easily bring about her disappearance . . . there would be no inquiries, but the matter might be readily explained.

He came back from his workplace and found her in the hut he had set aside for her, for she was no longer a Wife of the House—degradation for most women, but happiness for little M'ciba. She looked up apprehensively as he stooped to enter the hut.

"M'ciba, my wife," he said with a twisted smile; "you sit here all day as I know, and I fear that you will have the sickness mongo, for it is not good for the young that they should shun the sunlight and the air."

She did not speak but looked at him, waiting.

"It will be good," he said, "if you go abroad, for though my heart is sore within me because of your ingratitude, yet I wish you well. You shall take my little canoe and find fish for me."

"If I find no fish you will beat me," she said, having no illusions as to his generosity.

"By my heart and my life," he swore, "I will do none of these things; for I desire only your health, knowing that if you die of sickness Sandi will think evil things of me."

Thus it came about that M'ciba became a fisher girl. From her babyhood she had been accustomed to the river and its crafts. She made good catches and pleased her husband.

"You shall find me a great fish," he said to her one evening; "such as few fisherfolk find—that which is called Baba, the father of fish."

"Master and husband," said M'ciba sulkily, "I do not know where such fish are found."

He licked his thin lips and stroked his little grizzled beard.

"I, Likilivi, know," he said slowly. "These fish come in the dark of the night to the edge of the Mystery. And when the moon is newly risen you shall take your canoe to the place of elephant grass which hides my marsh and catch such a fish. And if you do not catch it, M'ciba, I shall not beat you, for such fish are very cunning."

When night came she took food and drink and placed it in the tiny canoe, Likilivi helping her.

"Tell none that you go to find the fish," he said, "lest the people of the village discover where the fish feeds and trap it for themselves."

It was then moonlight when she pushed off from the shore. She paddled close to the shore, keeping to the slack water until she was out of sight of the village, then brought her canoe out into the river as it sweeps around the little headland which marks the beginning of the Mystery Marsh.

Again she sought for slack water and having found it paddled leisurely to the place which her husband had indicated.

She saw a hippo standing belly high in mud; once she crossed the path of a cow hippo swimming to shore with a little calf on its back.

She steadied the canoe and waited for it to pass, for a cow hippo with young is easily annoyed.

At last she found the spot. The water was calm and almost currentless and she threw over her lines and sat down to wait.

Such drift of the water as there was set toward the shore, very slowly, imperceptibly. Hereabouts there was no sign of solid earth. The green reeds grew thickly from the water. Once the canoe drifted till its blunt bow went rustling amongst the grass and she was forced to take her paddle and stroke away for a few yards.

Once she thought she heard a sound in the bushes, but there was a gentle night wind and she paid no heed to the noise.

She pulled in her lines, baited them again with the little silver fish such as is used for the purpose and threw them out again.

This made a little noise and drowned the click of a tiny steel grapnel thrown by somebody hiding in the grass.

She felt the boat drifting in again and paddled. But there were two strong arms pulling the canoe. Before she realised her danger, the boat was pulled into the rushes, a hand at her throat strangled her screams.

"Woman, if you make a noise I will kill you!" said a voice in her ear, and she recognised the elder son of her husband.

He stepped from the darkness into the canoe ahead of her—he must have abandoned his own—and with strong strokes sent the boat into the darkness of the marsh. She could not see water. The jungle surrounded them. Putting out her hand she could touch the rank grass on either side.

This way and that the canoe went deeper and

deeper into the marsh, and as he paddled her stepson sketched with frankness the life which was ahead of her.

Strapped to her thigh, hidden by the dyed grass waist skirt, was a thin knife.

She had kept it there for reasons of her own. She slipped it out of its case of snake skin, leant forward and with the other hand felt his bare back.

"Do not touch me, woman!" he snarled over his shoulder.

"I am afraid," she said, and kept her hand where it was, a finger on each rib.

Between her fingers she pushed the thin knife home.

Without a word he slid over the side of the canoe, and she threw her weight on the other gunwale to prevent it filling.

His body fell into the water with a loud "plop" and she waited for him to come up again. He gave no sign, though she peered into the water, the knife in her hand.

Then she paddled back the way she came, driving the canoe stern first.

There was little mystery about the waterway save the mystery of the spot where creek and river met, and she had little difficulty in reaching open water. She had nearly come to safety when a sound reached her and she stopped paddling. Behind her she could hear the beat of another canoe, the very swishing of the grass as it forced its passage.

With quick silent strokes she sent her tiny craft the remainder of the journey, and came into the river just as the moon was sinking behind the N'Gombi Forest. Keeping to the shadow of the jungle she passed swiftly along to the north. They could not see her, whoever the mysterious "they" were, and had she reasoned clearly she was safe enough. But she could not reason clearly at the best of times, being but an Isisi girl whose mental equipment found no other stimulus than the thought of lovers and their possibilities. Her breath came quickly in little sobs as she plied her paddles. She skirted the grass until she reached the second headland—the horn of the bay in which the marsh stands.

Clear of this she paddled boldly into midstream. Looking behind her she saw nothing, yet there were vague, indefinite shadows which might have been anything.

Her nerve had gone; she was on the point of collapse, when suddenly ahead of her she saw something and dropped her paddles.

A steamer was coming toward her, its funnel belching sparks, and ahead, as though to feel its way through the darkness, a broad beam of light, a dazzling whiteness.

She sat spellbound, breathing quickly, until the current carried her into the range of the searchlight.

She heard the voice of Sanders in the black darkness behind the light, and the tinkle of the engine telegraph as he put the *Zaire* astern.

*   *   *   *   *

Likilivi believed in the impenetrability of the Marsh as whole-heartedly as he believed in M'shimba-M'shamba and other strange gods.

"The woman is dead," he said to his son, "and your brother Okora also, for M'ciba was a wicked woman and very strong."

He did not doubt that somewhere in the depths of the lagoon the two lay locked in the grip of death.

The villagers accepted the drowning of M'ciba philosophically and made no inquiries.

"I will report this matter to Sandi," said Likilivi.

"Father," said his son, "Sandi passed on the night of the killing, which was six nights ago, for men who were fishing saw his devil light."

"So much the better," said Likilivi.

There had been other deaths in the Marsh, for sickness readily attacks slaves who are chained by the leg and beaten, and who moreover do their work by night, lest the smoke of their fires invites suspicion.

Likilivi, his two remaining sons and two cousins, set themselves to recruit new labour.

Three nights they waited on the edge of the Marsh, and on the fourth they were rewarded, for two men came paddling carelessly with trailing fish lines.

They sang together a N'Gombi song about a hunter who had trusted an Akasava spear and had died from over-confidence.

Listening in the darkness Likilivi cursed them silently.

The canoe was close in shore when the elder of the chief's sons threw the grapnel, and the canoe was drawn into the rushes.

Two canoes closed in upon it.

"You come with us or you die," said Likilivi.

"Lord, we go with you," said the N'Gombi promptly.

They were transferred to the chief's canoe carrying their blankets, and their boat was taken by the other canoe, turned bottom upwards, and allowed to drift.

The chief waited until the canoe returned, then the two boats made for the heart of the Marsh.

For an hour they twisted and turned along the meandering fairway until at length the nose of the foremost canoe grounded gently on a sandy beach.

They were on the island. The pungent smell of smoke was in the air—Likilivi had wood to spare— and to the ears of the captives came a monotonous "clank, clank, clank." of steel against steel.

Likilivi hurried them along a narrow path which ended abruptly in a clearing.

By the light of many fires the prisoners saw.

There were two big huts—long and low roofed. They were solidly built on stout, heavy stakes, and to each stake a man was fastened. A long chain clamped about his legs gave him liberty to sleep on the inside of the hut and work at the fire outside.

There they sat, twelve men without hope, hammering spear heads for Likilivi, and each man was a skilled N'Gombi workman, artistically "drowned" for Likilivi's profit.

"Here shall you sit," said Likilivi to the two silent watchers, "and if you work you shall be fed, and if you do not work you shall be beaten."

"I see," said one of the captured.

There was something strange in his tone, something dry and menacing, and Likilivi stepped back showing his teeth like an angry dog.

"Put the chain upon them," he commanded, but his relatives did not move, for the prisoner had dropped his blanket from his arm, and his revolver was plain to be seen.

Likilivi saw it too and made a recovery.

"You are one of Sandi's spies," he said thickly. "Now I swear to you that if you say nothing of this I will make you rich with ivory and many precious things."

"That I cannot do," said the man, and Likilivi, peering at the brown face closely, saw that this N'Gombi man had grey eyes, and that he was smiling unpleasantly, just as Sanders smiled before he sent men to the Village of Irons to work in bondage for their crimes.

XIV

THE PRAYING MOOR

ABIBOO told Sanders that an Arabi had come to see him, and Arabs are rare on the coast, though certain dark men of Semitic origin have that honorary title.

Sanders came out to his stoep expecting to find a Kano, and was surprised to see, squatting by the edge of the raised verandah, a man of true Moorish type. He sat with his hands about his knees wrapped in a spotless white djellab.

"You are from Morocco," said Sanders in Arabic, "or from Dacca?"

The man nodded.

"The people of Dacca are dogs," he said, in the sing-song voice of a professional story-teller. "One man, who is a cousin of my mother's, stole twenty douros from my house and went back to Dacca by a coast boat before I could catch him and beat him. I hope he is killed and all his family also. Bismallah. God is good!"

Sanders listened, for he knew the Tangier people for great talkers.

The man went on. "Whether a man be of the Ali or Sufi sect, I do not care. There are thieves of both kinds."

"Why do you come here?" asked Sanders.

"Once I knew a man who sat in the great sok." (Sanders let him tell his story in his own way.) "And all the country people who brought vegetables and charcoal to the market would kiss the edge of his djellab and give him a penny.

"He was an old man with a long white beard, and he sat with his beads in his lap reciting the Suras of the Koran.

"There was not a man in Tangier who had not

kissed the edge of his djellab, and given him five centimos except me.

"When the people from far-away villages came, I used to go to a place near the door of his little white house and watch the money coming to him.

"One day when the sun was very hot, and I had lingered long after the last visitor had gone, the Haj beckoned me and I went nearer to him and sat on the ground before him.

"He looked at me, saying no word, only stroking his long white beard slowly. For a long time he sat like this, his eyes searching my soul.

" 'My son,' he said at last, 'how are you called?'

" 'Abdul az Izrael,' I replied.

" 'Abdul,' he said, 'many come to me bringing me presents, yet you never come.'

" 'Before God and His prophet,' I swore, 'I am a poor man who often starves; I have no friends.'

" 'All that you tell me are lies,' said the holy man, then he was silent again. By and by he spoke.

" 'Do you say your prayers, Abdul?' he asked.

" 'Four times every day,' I replied.

" 'You shall say your prayers four times a day, but each day you shall say your prayers in a new place,' and he waved his hand thus."

Abdul Azrael waved his hand slowly before his eyes.

Sanders was interested. He knew the Moors for born story-tellers, and was interested.

"Well?" he said.

The man paused impressively.

"Well, favoured and noble master," he said, "from that day I have wandered through the world, praying in new places, for I am cursed by the holy man because I lied to him, and there is that within me which impels me. And, lord, I have wandered from Damaraland to Mogador, and from Mogador to Egypt, and from Egypt to Zanzibar."

"Very pretty," said Sanders. "You have a tongue

like honey and a voice like silk, and it is written in the Sura of the Djinn, 'Truth is rough and a lie comes smoothly. Let him pass whose speech is pleasing.'"

Sanders was not above taking liberties with the Koran, as this quotation testifies.

"Give him food," said Sanders to his orderly, "later I will send him on his way."

A little later, the Commissioner crossed over to the police lines, and interrupted the Houssa Captain at his studies—Captain Hamilton had a copy of Squire's Companion to the British Pharmacopæia open before him, and he was reading up arsenic (1) as a cure for intermittent fever; (2) as an easy method of discharging himself from the monotony of a coast existence.

Sanders, who had extraordinary eyesight, comprehended the study at a glance and grinned.

"If you do not happen to be committing suicide for an hour or so," he said, "I should like to introduce you to the original Wandering Jew from Tangier."

The Houssa closed his book with a bang, lit a cigarette and carefully extinguished the match.

"This," he said, addressing the canvas ceiling of his hut, "is either the result of overwork, or the effect of fishing in the sun without proper head protection."

Sanders threw himself into a long seated chair and felt for his cheroots.

Then, ignoring the Houssa's insult, he told the story of Abdul Azrael, the Moor.

"He's a picturesque mendicant," he said, "and has expressed his intention of climbing the river and crossing Africa to Uganda."

"Let him climb," said the Houssa; "from what I know of your people he will teach them nothing in the art of lying. He may, however, give them style, and they stand badly in need of that."

Abdul Azrael accordingly left headquarters by the store canoe which carried government truck to the Isisi villages.

There was a period of calm on the river. Sanders found life running very smoothly. There were returns to prepare (these his soul loathed), reports from distant corners of his little empire to revise; acts of punishments administered by his chiefs to confirm—and fishing.

Once he ran up the river to settle a bigger palaver than the new king of the Akasava could decide upon, but that was the only break in the monotony. There was a new Administrator, a man who knew his job, and knew, too, the most important job of all was to leave his subordinates to work out their own salvation.

Sanders finished his palaver with the Akasava, gave judgment, which was satisfactory to all parties, and was returning to the enjoyment of that contentment which comes to a man who has no arrears of work or disease of conscience.

He left the Akasava city at sunset, travelling through the night for his own convenience. The river hereabout is a real river, there being neither sand-bank nor shoal to embarrass the steersman. At five o'clock he passed Chumbiri.

He had no reason to believe that all was not well at Chumbiri, or cause to give it anything but a passing glance. He came down-stream in the grey of dawn and passed the little village without suspicion. He saw, from the bridge of the *Zaire*, the dull glow of a fire on the distant foreshore—he was in midstream, and here the river runs two miles wide from bank to bank. Day came with a rush. It was little better than twilight when he left the village to starboard, and long before he came to the sharp bend which would hide Chumbiri from view, the world was flooded with strong white light.

One acquires the habit of looking all ways in wild Africa. It was, for example, a matter of habit that he cast one swift glance backward to the village, before he signalled to the helmsman with a slight bend of his

head, to bring the helm hard-a-port. One swift glance
he threw and frowned. The tiny town was clearly to
be seen. Three straight rows of huts, on a sloping
bank, with Isisi palms running the length of each
street.

"Turn about," he said, and the steersman spun the
wheel.

The little steamer listed over as the full power of
the swift current caught her amidships, then she
slowly righted and the waters piled themselves up at
her bows as she breasted the current again.

"Abiboo," said Sanders to his sergeant, "I see no
people in the streets of this village, neither do I see
the smoke of fires."

"Lord, they may go hunting," said Abiboo wisely.

"Fishermen do not hunt," said Sanders, "nor do
women and old people."

Abiboo did not advance the preposterous suggestion
that they might sleep, for if the men were sluggards
they would not be sufficiently lost to shame to allow
their womenfolk to escape their duties.

Sanders brought the steamer into slack water near
the beach and none came to meet him.

There was no dog or goat within sight—only the
remains of a big fire still smouldering upon the beach.

His men waded ashore with their hawsers and
secured the steamer, and Sanders followed.

He walked through the main street and there was
no sign of life. He called sharply—there was no response. Every hut was empty; the cooking pots, the
beds, every article of necessity was in its place. The
rough mills for the grinding of corn stood before the
huts, the matchets and crude N'Gombi axes for the
cutting of timber, the N'Gombi spades, all these
things were in evidence, but of the people, young or
old, man or woman or child, well or sick, there was no
trace. The only living being he saw was Abdul Azrael.
He came upon that pious man on a sheltered beach

near the village, his praying carpet was spread and he faced toward Mecca in rapt contemplation.

Sanders waited for the prayers to finish and questioned him.

"Lord, I have seen nothing," he said, "but I will tell you a story. Once——"

"I want no stories," snapped Sanders.

He put the nose of the steamer across the river. Exactly opposite was Fezembini, a larger town, and since constant communication was maintained between the two places, some explanation of the people's absence might be secured.

Fezembini was alive and bustling, and all that could walk came down to the beach to say "O ai!" to the Commissioner, but Mondomi, the chief, had no solution.

He was a tall, thin man, with a thin curl of beard on his chin.

"Lord, they were there last night," he said, "for I heard their drums beating and I saw their fires; also I heard laughter and the rattle of the dancers' little cages."*

"H'm!" said Sanders.

He pursued his inquiries at the neighbouring villages, but was no nearer a satisfactory explanation of the vanishing of three hundred people at the end of his investigation.

He sat down in the cool and quiet of his cabin to reason the matter out. The Chumbiri folk were as law-abiding as Akasava people can be; they had paid their taxes; there was no charge against any of them, yet of a sudden they had left their homes and gone into the forest. That they had not made for the river was evident from the discovery of their canoes, carefully docked in a convenient creek.

"I give it up," said Sanders. He had to be at head-

---

* A sort of wicker-work dumb-bell, containing stones—not unlike a double-headed baby's rattle.

quarters for a day or two. When he had finished his work there he returned to Chumbiri and its problem.

The people had not returned, nor had any of his spies news of them.

He sent Abiboo into the forest to find their trail, and the Houssa sergeant had no difficulty, for two miles into the forest he found an old man who had died by the way, and a little further he found an old woman, also dead.

Sanders went out to see the bodies. There was no sign of wound or injury. They had obviously died from fatigue.

"When daylight comes we will follow," said Sanders, "I will take ten men, and you will choose swift walkers."

He snatched a few hours' sleep, and before dawn Abiboo brought him the cup of tea without which Sanders never began a day.

Sanders, who had not an ounce of superfluous flesh, was an indefatigable walker, and the party covered twelve miles before noon—no easy task, for the forest path was little more than a grass track. The party rested through the three hot hours of the day, and resumed its journey at three o'clock.

They came upon a camping place with the ashes of the fires hardly cold and two newly-made graves to testify to the fate of age and infirmity suddenly called upon for effort.

At nine o'clock that night, just when Sanders was considering the advisability of camping, he saw the light of fires ahead and pushed on.

There were many young trees which hid the view of the camp, and the party had to take a circuitous route to reach the clearing where the people were.

It was an extraordinary view which met the eyes of our dumbfounded Commissioner.

Line upon line of kneeling forms were revealed by the light of the fire.

They faced in one direction, and as they swayed backwards and forward, one knelt in advance, whom Sanders had no difficulty in recognising as the chief headman.

"Lala is a great one," he sang.

"O Cala!" droned his people.

"Lala is high!"

"O Cala!" they repeated and bowed their heads.

The chief did not see Sanders, because Sanders came up behind him. He knew that Sanders was there, because Sanders kicked him very hard.

"Get up, O foolish man!" said Sanders.

He did not use those exact words, because he was very annoyed, but whatever he said had the desired effect.

"Now you shall tell me," said Sanders, "why you are so much bigger a fool than I ever thought you were."

"Lord," said the chief humbly, "we go to seek new lands, for an Arabi taught us that we should pray in a certain way, and that if we prayed in a different place every night, great blessings would come to us——"

A light dawned on Sanders.

"We will go back to-morrow," he said, after swallowing something in his throat, "and I will take my steamer and search for this Arabi."

Two days brought him to the village. He left the judgment of the chief to another day and hurried aboard.

As the *Zaire* was casting off that woe-begone individual came running to the beach.

"Master," he gasped, "we ask for justice!"

"You shall have it," said Sanders grimly.

"Lord, all our homes are stolen, nothing is left."

Sanders swore at him fluently, in a language which allows considerable opportunities for such exercise.

"Speak quickly, father of monkeys."

"Lord, they are gone," said the agitated headman,

"all our good pots and our mills, our spears, our hatchets and our fishing lines."

"Why did you leave them, O father of tom-cats?" said Sanders in exasperation.

"The Arabi told us," said the headman, "and we did that which we thought was best."

Sanders leant on the rail and spoke to the man.

They were not words of kindness and cheer, nor words of hope or comfort. Sanders drew upon forest and river for his illustrations. He told the headman all about his life and sketched his existence after death. He referred to his habits, his morals and his relations. He spoke feelingly of his head, his feet and his bodily infirmities, and the interested Houssas on the *Zaire* drew closer lest one word should escape them.

"And now," said Sanders in conclusion, "I call all men to witness that you and your people are bushmen."

"O Ko!" said the horrified villagers who had come to the beach at the heels of their headman, for "bushman" is the very summit of insults.

"Bushmen!" repeated Sanders bitterly as the boat drifted from the shore; "root-eaters, who talk with monkeys in their own language. . . ."

He left the people of the village considerably depressed.

First he crossed the river to Fezembini.

Yes, the chief had seen the Arabi, had indeed hired him two large canoes and six paddlers to each.

"He said he was of the Government, lord, on secret service," said the chief, "and desired to collect the things which the people of Chumbiri had left behind them."

These canoes had gone up river and they had some six days' start of the Commissioner.

Sanders lost no time. From a coop which was erected aft he took two pigeons. One had a red and the other had a tiny blue band about its leg. He wrote identical messages on sheets as thin in texture as a cigarette paper, bound them to the legs of the birds and released them. One pigeon he released, and that went north. He waited till it was out of sight, then he let the other go. That went north also, but a point or two west to its fellow.

Sanders sent the *Zaire* in the same general direction. Later in the afternoon he reached the Akasava city.

"What strangers have been here?" he asked the hastily-summoned chief.

"Master, no stranger," said the chief, "save only the new Arabi, whom your lordship has sent to sell us pots and knives."

Sanders gripped the rail of the boat, not trusting himself to speak.

"He sold you pots?" he asked chokingly.

"And spears," said the chief, "and many desirable things, and they were very cheap and all the people praised you, master, that you had done this kindness. For thus said the Arabi: 'Our lord Sandi desires that you should pay only a little for these precious articles —he himself has paid me that I should benefit you.'"

"Anything else?"

The chief hesitated.

"Lord, he told us a story about a certain evil devil who tormented the ungrateful, and my people were frightened lest they did not accept the benefits your lordship offered and——"

"Cast off!" roared Sanders.

Naked men jumped into the shallow water and waded ashore to where the wire hawsers were fastened.

"As for you," said Sanders to the chief, "go tell your master the king that he has set up a child as chief of this city. For when was I so mad that I gave gifts to lazy people? Have I sickness that I should pay a thieving Arabi money to benefit evil and foolish men?"

"Lord," said the chief simply, "knowing that you were a mean and cruel man we felt great joy, thinking that the gods had touched your hard heart."

Sanders looked round for something to throw at him, for time was precious.

He found only valuable things and allowed the matter to drop.

At a village ten miles away he found further evidence of the Moor's perfidy. Here the praying pilgrim had rested for a night and had borrowed three bags of salt, some dried fish and a store of manioc. He had done this in the name of the Government.

"And gave me," said the wizened headman, "a book with devil marks."

He handed a paper to Sanders.

It was in Arabic, and the Commissioner read it with some emotion.

"From Abdul Azrael, the servant of God, the one, true, beneficent and merciful.

"To the giaour Sanders whom may God preserve and lead to the true faith.

"Peace be on your house. This is written on the fourth day of the third week following Ramazin.

"I go to my brethren who live beyond the Cataracts of the Great River. I pray for you, therefore pay these people for all that I have taken."

Sanders read it again.

If Abdul took the river which passes Ochori and turned sharply to the right into the creek of Bamboo he would come in time to the Arab settlements which were beyond the Commissioner's jurisdiction. Moreover, he would be beyond his reach, for the *Zaire* drew a fathom and a half of water and the creek of Bamboo averaged half a fathom.

"Did this Arabi say which way he would go?" asked Sanders.

The old man nodded.

"By the Ochori country, lord," he said, and Sanders

groaned. "And he asked what manner of people the Ochori were."

"And what said you?" asked Sanders, interested.

"I said they were fools," said the headman, "and very fearful."

"And how long have you sat in this village?" asked Sanders.

"Lord, I was born here and here I have lived."

There was a twinkle in the eyes of Mr. Commissioner Sanders. This old man had never heard of Bosambo the chief. Suppose Abdul yielded to temptation and arrested his flight at the city of that great man?

Abdul Azrael came to the Ochori village singing a song. He was cheerful because a few miles up the river was a crocodile creek, broad enough and deep enough for a fast canoe, but having neither depth nor the width for a steamer such as the *Zaire*.

He had intended going straight to his hiding-place, but judged very shrewdly that so far he had a day the better of the chase.

It would have been wiser of him to continue his journey, but this he did not know. He was in high spirits, for a few hours before he had sold one of the canoes he had borrowed to a N'Gombi chief, who had, moreover, paid him in Frankies.*

In various portions of his attire Abdul Azrael secreted the result of many pilgrimages. He had dirty Turkish notes, golden coins of Tunis, English sovereigns, marks, twenty-peseta pieces, heavy golden eagles from a land he had never seen, not a few black and chocolate hundred-franc notes of the Bank Nationale de Belgique (these he had come by on the Congo), to say nothing of the silver coinage of dubious quality which the Shereefian Government issue at odd moments.

* The franc was the only coinage known in Sanders' territory, and on the Upper River. It came from the adjoining French territories.

He strutted through the main street of the Ochori city and came before Bosambo.

"Peace be upon your house," he said, and Bosambo, who had a working knowledge of Arabic, bade him welcome.

"I have come from Sandi, our lord," said Abdul gravely; "he has sent me with these words, 'Give unto Abdul Azrael the best of your hospitality and regard him as me.'"

"I am Sandi's dog," said Bosambo, "though he is, as you know, my half-brother of another mother."

"This he has often told me," said Abdul.

They exchanged compliments for twenty minutes, at the end of which time the Moor excused himself.

"For I must say my prayers," he said.

"I will also say my prayers," said Bosambo promptly, "according to my custom, and I thank Allah that you are here that I may pray in peace."

Abdul had been on the point of telling his story of the Holy Man of Tangier, but stopped.

"That is strange talk," he said, "for there is one custom as there is one God. And all men pray in peace."

Bosambo shook his head sadly.

"I live amongst thieves," he said, "and I am a rich man. It is the custom in this part of the country to remove all clothes, placing them before the door of the dwelling, then to enter the hut and pray."

"That is a good custom," said Abdul eagerly. "It is one I have often practised."

"Yet," Bosambo went on, "how may a believer go about his proper business? For if I leave my clothes, with all my precious jewels concealed, my people will rob me."

"Bismallah!" cried the pious Moor, "this is a happy day, for we will pray together, you and I. And whilst I am at prayers you shall guard my robes, and whilst you are at your prayers, behold, I will be Azrael, the

Angel of the Sword, and none shall touch your jewels
by my life."

It is said that they embraced. Abdul in the excess
of his emotion running his deft fingers lightly over the
other's waist, noting certain bulky protuberances
which were unknown to nature.

"I will pray first," said Abdul, "and I will pray for
a long time."

"I also will take a long time," said the simple
Bosambo.

Abdul stripped to his under robe, collected his
djellab and his long gabardine into a convenient
bundle and placed them on the ground before the hut
and entered.

*   *   *   *   *

Sanders arrived six hours later and Bosambo
awaited him.

"Lord," said the chief, "the Arabi I have arrested
as your lordship directed, for your pigeon was a cunning one and came swiftly though there are many
hawks."

"Where is he?" asked Sanders.

"He is in my hut," said Bosambo, "and, master,
deal gently with him, because he is of my faith; also
he is a little mad."

"Mad?"

Bosambo nodded his close-cropped head.

"Mad, master," he said sadly, "for he says I have
robbed him, taken from him such as gold and book
money—a large fortune."

Sanders eyed him keenly.

"Did you?" he asked.

"Lord," said Bosambo with simple dignity, "he was
my guest and of my faith, how could I rob him?"

Sanders' interview with the wrathful Moor was not
a protracted one.

"I send you to labour in the Village of Irons for a

year," he said, "for you are a liar, a thief, and a maker of mischief."

"I will go to your prison, lord," said Abdul; "but tell this black man to restore the money he has stolen from me; lord, it was hidden in my clothes, and by a trick——"

"That is not my palaver," said Sanders shortly.

The Houssas were marching the Moor away when he turned to Bosambo.

"After I come back from the Village of Irons," he said, "I will come to you, Bosambo, thou infidel, and eater of pig. And——"

Bosambo waved his hand with an airy gesture.

"You will never come from the Village of Irons," he said, "for Sandi, who is my cousin, has told me secretly that you will be poisoned. As to the money, I think you are an evil liar."

"Six hundred Spanish dollars!" hissed Abdul.

"Four hundred and half a hundred," corrected Bosambo blandly, "and much of the silver breaks when you bite it. Go in peace, O my angel!"

XV

THE SICKNESS MONGO

SANDERS taught his people by example, by word of mouth, and by such punishment as occasion required. Of all methods, punishment was the least productive of result, for memory lasts only so long as pain, and men who had watched with quaking hearts a strapped body as it swayed from a tree branch, straightway forgot the crime for which the criminal died just as soon as the malefactor was decently interred.

Sanders taught the men of the *Zaire* to stack wood.

14

He showed them that if it was stacked in the bow, the vessel would sink forward, or if it was stacked all on one side, the vessel would list. He stood over them, day after day, directing and encouraging them, and the same men were invariably his pupils because Sanders did not like new faces.

He was going up river in some haste when he tied to a wooding to replenish his stock.

At the end of six years' tuition he left them to pile wood whilst he slept, and they did all the things which they should not have done.

This he discovered when he returned to the boat.

"Master," said the headman of the wooders, and he spoke with justifiable pride, "we have cut and stored the wood for the puc-a-puc in one morning, whereas other and slower folk would have worked till sundown, but because we love your lordship we have worked till the sweat fell from our bodies."

Sanders looked at the wood piled all wrong, and looked at the headman.

"It is not wise," he said, "to store the wood in the bow, for thus the ship will sink, as I have often told you."

"Lord, we did it because it was easiest," said the man simply.

"That I can well believe," said Sanders, and ordered the restacking, without temper.

You must remember that he was in a desperate hurry: that every hour counted. He had been steaming all night—a dangerous business, for the river was low and there were new sandbanks which did not appear on his home-made chart. Men fret their hearts out, dealing with such little problems as ill-stacked wood, but Sanders neither fretted nor worried. If he had, he would have died, for things like this were part of his working day. Yet the headman's remissness worried him a little, for he knew the man was no fool.

In an hour the wood was more evenly distributed

and Sanders rang the engines ahead. He put the nose of the boat to the centre of the stream and held on his course till at sunset he came to a place where the river widened abruptly, and where little islands were each a great green tangle of vegetation.

Here he slowed the steamer, carefully circumnavigating each island, till darkness fell, then he picked a cautious way to shore, through much shoal water. The *Zaire* bumped and shivered as she struck or grazed the hidden sandbanks.

Once she stopped dead, and her crew of forty slipped over the side of the boat, and wading, breast high, pushed her along with a deep-chested song.

At last he came to a shelving beach, and here, fastened by her steel hawsers to two trees, the boat waited for dawn.

Sanders had a bath, dressed, and came into his little deck-house to find his dinner waiting.

He ate the tiny chicken, took a stiff peg of whiskey, and lit his cigar. Then he sent for Abiboo.

"Abiboo," he said, "once you were a man in these parts."

"Lord, it is so," said Abiboo. "I was a spy here for six months."

"What do you know of these islands?"

"Lord, I only know that in one of them the Isisi bury their dead, and of another it is said that magic herbs grow; also that witch-doctors come thither to practise certain rites."

Sanders nodded.

"To-morrow we seek for the Island of Herbs," he said, "for I have information that evil things will be done at the full of the moon."

"I am your man," said Abiboo.

It happened two nights following this that a chief of the N'Gombi, a simple old man who had elementary ideas about justice and a considerable faith in devils, stole down the river with twelve men and with labour they fastened two pieces of wood shaped like a St. Andrew's Cross between two trees.

They bent a young sapling, trimming the branches from the top, till it reached the head of the cross, and this they made fast with a fishing line. Whatever other preparations they may have contemplated making were indefinitely postponed because Sanders, who had been watching them from behind a convenient copal-tree, stepped from his place of concealment, and the further proceedings failed to yield any satisfaction to the chief.

He eyed Sanders with a mild reproach.

"Lord, we set a trap for a leopard," he explained, "who is very terrible."

"In other days," mused Sanders aloud, "a man see-ing this cross would think of torture, O chief—and, moreover, leopards do not come to the middle island —tell me the truth."

"Master," said the old chief in agitation, "this leopard swims, therefore he fills our hearts with fear."

Sanders sighed wearily.

"Now you will tell me the truth, or I shall be more than any leopard."

The chief folded his arms so that the flat of his hands touched his back, he being a lean man, and his hands fidgeted nervously.

"I cannot tell you a lie," he said, "because you are as a very bat, seeing into dark places readily and mov-ing at night. Also you are like a sudden storm that comes up from trees without warning, and you are most terrible in your anger."

"Get along," said Sanders, passively irritable.

"Now this is the truth," said the chief huskily.

"There is a man who comes to my village at sunset, and he is an evil one, for he has the protection of the Christ-man and yet he does abominable things—so we are for chopping him."

Sanders peered at the chief keenly.

"If you chop him, chief, you will surely die," he said softly, "even if he be as evil as the devil—whichever type of devil you mostly fear. This is evidently a bad palaver indeed, and I will sit down with you for some days."

He carried the chief and his party back to the village and held a palaver.

Now Sanders of the River in moments such as these was a man of inexhaustible patience; and of that patience he had considerable need when two hours after his arrival there came stalking grandly into the village a man whose name was Ofalikari, a man of the N'Gombi by a Congolaise father.

His other name was Joseph, and he was an evangelist.

This much Sanders discovered quickly enough.

"Fetch this man to me," he said to Sergeant Abiboo, for the preacher made his palaver at the other end of the village.

Soon Abiboo returned.

"Master," he said, "this man will not come, being only agreeable to the demands of certain gods with which your honour is acquainted."

Sanders showed his teeth.

"Go to him," he said softly, "and bring him; if he will come for no other cause, hit him with the flat of your bayonet."

Abiboo saluted stiffly—after the style of native non-commissioned officers—and departed, to return with Ofalikari, whom he drew with him somewhat unceremoniously by the ear.

"Now," said Sanders to the man, "we will have a little talk, you and I."

The sun went down, the moon came up, flooding the black river with mellow light, but still the talk went on—for this was a very serious palaver indeed.

A big fire was built in the very middle of the village

street and here all the people gathered, whilst Sanders
and the man sat face to face.

Occasionally a man or a woman would be sent for
from the throng; once Sanders dispatched a messenger
to a village five miles away to bring evidence. They
came and went, those who testified against Ofalikari.

"Lord, one night we gathered by his command and
he sacrificed a white goat," said one witness.

"We swore by the dried heart of a white goat that
we would do certain abominable things," said another.

"By his order we danced a death dance at one end
of the village, and the maidens danced the wedding
dance at the other, then a certain slave was killed by
him, and . . ."

Sanders nodded gravely.

"And he said that the sons of the White Goat should
not die," said another.

In the end Sanders rose and stretched himself.

"I have heard enough," he said, and nodded to the
sergeant of Houssas, who came forward with a pair of
bright steel handcuffs.

One of these he snapped on the man's wrist, the
other he held and led him to the boat.

The *Zaire* swung out to midstream, making a difficult way through the night to the mission station.

Ill news travels faster than an eight-knot steamboat
can move up stream.

Sanders found the missionary waiting for him at
day-break on the strip of white beach, and the missionary, whose name was Haggin, was in one of those cold
passions that saintly men permit themselves, for right-
eousness' sake.

"All England shall ring with this outrage," he said,
and his voice trembled. "Woe the day when a British
official joins the hosts of Satan . . ."

He said many other disagreeable things.

"Forget it," said Sanders tersely; "this man of yours
has been playing the fool."

And in his brief way he described the folly.

"It's a lie!" said the missionary. He was tall and thin, yellow with fever, and his hands shook as he threw them out protestingly. "He has made converts for the faith, he has striven for souls . . ."

"Now listen to me," said Sanders and he wagged a solemn forefinger at the other. "I know this country. I know these people—you don't. I take your man to headquarters, not because he preaches the gospel, but because he holds meetings by night and practises strange rites which are not the rites of any known Church. Because he is a son of the White Goat, and I will have no secret societies in my land."

If the truth be told, Sanders was in no frame of mind to consider the feelings of missionaries.

There was unrest in his territories—unrest of an elusive kind. There had been a man murdered on the Little River and none knew whose hand it was that struck him down.

His body, curiously carved, came floating down stream one sunny morning, and agents brought the news to Sanders. Then another had been killed and another. A life more or less is nothing in a land where people die by whole villages, but these men with their fantastic slashings worried Sanders terribly.

He had sent for his chief spies.

"Go north to the territory of the killing, which is on the edge of the N'Gombi country and bring me news," he said.

One such had sent him a tale of a killing palaver— he had rushed north to find by the veriest accident that the threatened life was that of a man he desired most of all to place behind bars.

He carried his prisoner to headquarters. He was anxious to put an end to the growth of a movement which might well get beyond control, for secret societies spread like fire.

At noon he reached a wooding and tied up.

He summoned his headman.

"Lobolo," he said, "you shall stack the wood whilst I sleep, remembering all the wise counsel I gave you."

"Lord, I am wise in your wisdom," said the headman, and Abiboo having strung a hammock between two trees, Sanders tumbled in and fell asleep instantly.

Whilst he slept, one of the wooders detached himself from the working party, and came stealthily towards him.

Sanders' sleeping place was removed some distance from the shore, that the noise of chopping and sawing and the rattle of heavy billets on the steel deck should not disturb him.

Noiselessly the man moved until he came to within striking distance of the unconscious Commissioner.

He took a firmer grip of the keen steel machette he carried and stepped forward.

Then a long sinewy hand caught him by the throat and pulled him down. He twisted his head and met the passionless gaze of Abiboo.

"We will go from here," whispered the Houssa, "lest our talk awake my lord."

He wrenched the machette from the other's hand and followed him into the woods.

"You came to kill Sandi," said Abiboo.

"That is true," said the man, "for I have a secret ju-ju which told me to do this, Sandi having offended. And if you harm me, the White Goat shall surely slay you, brown man."

"I have eaten Sandi's salt," said Abiboo, "and whether I live or die is ordained. As for you, your fate is about your neck . . ."

Sanders woke from his sleep to find Abiboo squatting on the ground by the side of the hammock.

"What is it?" he asked.

"Nothing, lord," said the man. "I watched your sleep, for it is written, 'He is a good servant who sees when his master's eyes are shut.'"

Sanders heard the serious undertone to the proverb; was on the point of asking a question, then wisely checked himself.

He walked to the shore. The men had finished their work, and the wood was piled in one big, irregular heap in the well of the fore deck. It was piled so that it was impossible (1) for the steersman on the bridge above to see the river; (2) for the stoker to get anywhere near his furnace; (3) for the *Zaire* to float in anything less than three fathoms of water.

Already the little ship was down by the head, and the floats of her stern wheel merely skimming the surface of the river.

Sanders stood on the bank with folded arms looking at the work of the headman's hands. Then his eyes wandered along the length of the vessel. Amidships was a solid iron cage, protected from the heat of the sun by a double roof and broad canvas eaves. His eyes rested here for a long time, for the cage was empty and the emissary of the White Goat gone.

Sanders stood for a few moments in contemplation; then he stepped slowly down the bank and crossed the gangway.

"Be ears and eyes to me, Abiboo," he said in Arabic, "find what has become of Ofalikari, also the men who guarded him. Place these under arrest and bring them before me."

He walked to his cabin, his head sunk in thought. This was serious, though he reserved his judgment till Abiboo returned with his prisoners.

They arrived under escort, a little alarmed, a little indignant.

"Lord, these men have reason," said Abiboo.

"Why did you allow the prisoner to go?" asked Sanders.

"Thus it was, master," said the senior of the two; "whilst you slept the God-man came—him we saw at daybreak this morning. And he told us to let the prisoner come with him, and because he was a white man we obeyed him."

"Only white men who are of the Government may give such orders," said Sanders; "therefore I adjudge you guilty of folly, and I hold you for trial."

There was nothing to be gained by lecturing them.

He sent for his headman.

"Lobolo," he said, "ten years you have been my headman, and I have been kind to you."

"Lord, you have been as a father," said the old man, and his hand was shaking.

"Yonder," said Sanders, pointing with his finger, "lies your land and the village you came from is near enough. Let the storeman pay you your wages and never see me again."

"Lord," stammered the headman, "if the stacking of wood was a fault——"

"Well, you know it is a fault," said Sanders; "you have eaten my bread and now you have sold me to the White Goats."

The old man fell sobbing at his feet.

"Lord master," he moaned, "I did this because I was afraid, for a certain man told me that if I did not delay your lordship I should die, and, lord, death is very terrible to the old, because they live with it in their hearts."

"Which man was this?" asked Sanders.

"One called Kema, lord."

Sanders turned to his orderly.

"Find me Kema," he said, and Abiboo shifted his feet.

"Lord, he has died the death," he said simply, "for whilst you slept he came to slay you. And I had some palaver with him."

"And?"

"Lord, I saw him for an evil man and I smote his head from his body with a machette."

Sanders was silent. He stood looking at the deck, then he turned to his cabin.

"Master," said the waiting headman, "what of me?"

The Commissioner stretched his finger towards the shore, and with bowed shoulders Lobolo left the ship that had been his home for many years.

It took the greater part of an hour to trim the vessel.

"We will make for the mission station," said Sanders, though he had no doubt in his mind as to what he would find. . . .

The mission house was still burning when the *Zaire* rounded the river's head.

He found the missionary's charred body among the smouldering wreckage.

Of Ofalikari he found no trace.

There had been a secret society suppressed in Nigerland, and it had been broken by three regiments of native infantry, a battery of mountain guns and some loss of life. The "British victory" and the "splendid success of our arms" had given the people of the islands a great deal of satisfaction, but the Commissioner who let the matter get to the stage of war was a ruined man, for governments do not like spending the millions they have put aside for the creation of a national pension scheme which will bring them votes and kudos at the next election, on dirty little wars which bring nothing but vacancies in the junior ranks of the native army.

Sanders had a pigeon post from headquarters containing a straight-away telegram from the Administrator.

"Your message received and forwarded. Ministers wire settle your palaver by any means. For God's sake keep clear necessity employing army. Sending you one battalion Houssas and field gun. Do the best you can."

There was not much margin for wastage. The whole country was now rotten with rebellion. It had all happened in the twinkling of an eye. From being law-abiding and inoffensive, every village had become of a sudden the headquarters of the White Goats. Terrible rites were being performed on the Isisi; the N'Gombi had danced by whole communities the dance of the Goat; the Akasava killed two of Sanders' spies and had sent their heads to Sanders as proof of their "earnest spirits"—to quote the message literally.

There was a missionary lady at Kosumkusu. Sanders' first thought was for her. He steamed direct from the smouldering ruins of Haggin's hut to find her.

She was amused at the growth of the secret societies, and thought it all very interesting.

Sanders did not tell her the aspect of the situation which was not amusing.

"Really, Mr. Sanders," she smiled, "I'm quite safe here—this is the second time in three months you have tried to bring me into your fold."

"This time you are coming," said Sanders quietly. "Abiboo has turned my cabin into a most luxurious boudoir."

But she fenced with him to the limits of his patience.

"But what of Mr. Haggin and Father Wells?" she asked. "You aren't bothering about them."

"I'm not bothering about Haggin," said Sanders, "because he's dead—I've just come from burying him."

"Dead!"

"Murdered," said Sanders briefly, "and his mission burnt. I've sent an escort for the Jesuits. They may or they may not get down. We pick them up to-morrow, with luck."

The girl's face had gone white.

"I'll come," she said, "I'm not afraid—yes, I am. And I'm giving you a lot of worry—forgive me."

Sanders said something more or less incoherent, for he was not used to penitent womankind.

He took her straight away, and the *Zaire* was hardly out of sight before her chief convert set fire to the mission buildings.

Sanders picked up the Jesuits. His rescue party had arrived just in time.

He landed his guests at headquarters and went back to the Upper River to await developments.

The *Zaire* had a complement of fifty men. They were technically deck hands and their duty lay in collecting wood, in taking aboard and discharging such stores as he brought with him and in assisting in the navigation of the boat.

He went to a wooding on the Calali River to replenish his stock of fuel and very wisely he "wooded" by daylight.

The same night the whole of his men deserted, and he was left with twenty Houssas, Yoka, the engineer, and a Congo boy, who acted as his cook.

This was his position when he dropped down stream to an Isisi river where he hoped news would await him.

For all the volcano which trembled beneath his feet, he gave no outward sign of perturbation. The movement could be checked, might indeed be destroyed, if Ofalikari were laid by the heels, but the "missioner" had vanished and there was no reliable word as to his whereabouts.

Somewhere in the country he directed the operations of the society.

There was a lull; a sudden interval of inactivity That was bad, as bad as it could be.

Sanders reviewed the position and saw no good in it; he remembered the Commissioner who brought war to the Niger and shivered, for he loved the country and he loved his work.

There were two days of heavy rains, and these were followed by two days of sweltering heat—and then Bosambo, a native chief, with all a native's malignity and indifference to suffering grafted to knowledge of white men, sent a message to Sanders.

Two fast paddlers brought the messenger, and he stood up in his canoe to deliver his word.

"Thus said our lord Bosambo," he shouted, keeping a respectful distance from the little boat. "'Go you to Sandi, but go not on board his ship on your life. Say to Sandi: The White Goat dies, and the people of these lands come back to wisdom before the moon is full.'"

"Come to the ship and tell me more," called Sanders. The man shook his head.

"Lord, it is forbidden," he said, "for our lord was very sure on that matter; and there is nothing to tell you, for we are ignorant men, only Bosambo being wiser than all men save your lordship."

Sanders was puzzled. He knew the chief well enough to believe that he did not prophesy lightly, and yet——

"Go back to your chief," he said, "tell him that I have faith in him."

Then he sat down at the junction of the Isisi and Calali Rivers for Bosambo to work miracles.

Bosambo, chief of the Ochori, had had in his time many gods. Some of these he retained for emergencies or because their possession added to his prestige. He neither loved nor feared them. Bosambo loved or feared no man, save Sanders.

The White Goats might have the chief of the Ochori in a cleft stick; they might seduce from their allegiance half and more than half of his people, as they had done, but Bosambo, who knew that weak men who acquire strength of a sudden, invariably signalise their independence by acquiring new masters, accepted the little troubles which accompany the chieftainship of such a tribe as his with pleasing philosophy.

It was a trying time for him, and it was a period

not without some excitement for those who tried him.

A dish of fish came to him from his chief cook one morning. Bosambo ate a little, and sent for the same cook, who was one of his titular wives.

"Woman," said Bosambo, "if you try to poison me, I will burn you alive, by Ewa!"

She was speechless with terror and fell on her knees before him.

"As matters are," said Bosambo, "I shall not speak of your sin to Sandi, who is my sister's own child by a white father, for if Sandi knew of this, he would place you in boiling water till your eyes bulged like a fish. Go now, woman, and cook me clean food."

Other attempts were made on his life. Once a spear whizzed past his head as he walked alone in the forest. Bosambo uttered a shriek and fell to the ground and the thrower, somewhat incautiously, came to see what mischief he had wrought, and if need be to finish the good work. . . . Bosambo returned from his walk alone. He stopped by the river to wash his hands and scour his spears with wet sand, and that was the end of the adventure so far as his assailant was concerned.

But the power of the society was growing. His chief councillor was slain at meat, another was drowned, and his people began to display a marked insolence.

The air became electric. The Akasava had thrown off all disguise, the influence of the White Goat predominated. Chiefs and headmen obeyed the least of their hunters, or themselves joined in the lewd ritual celebrated nightly in the forest. The chief who had brought about the arrest of Ofalikari was pulled down and murdered in the open street by the very men who had lodged complaints, and the first to strike was his own son.

All these things were happening whilst Sanders waited at the junction of the Isisi and Calali Rivers, his Houssas sleeping by the guns.

Bosambo saw the end clearly. He had no illusions as to his ultimate fate.

"To-morrow, light of my eyes," he said to his first wife, "I send you in a canoe to find Sandi, for men of the White Goat come openly—one man from every tribe, calling upon me to dance and make sacrifice."

His wife was a Kano woman; tall and straight and comely.

"Lord," she said simply, "at the end you will take your spear and kill me, for here I sit till the end. When you die, life is death to me."

Bosambo put his strong arm about her and patted her head.

The following day he sat at palaver, but few were the applicants for justice. There was a stronger force abroad in the land; a higher dispenser of favour.

At the moment he had raised his hand to signify the palaver was finished a man came running from the forest. He ran unsteadily, like one who was drunken, throwing out his arms before him as though he was feeling his way.

He gained the village street, and came stumbling along, his sobbing breath being audible above the hum of the Ochoris' wondering talk.

Then suddenly a shrill voice cried a word in fear, and the people went bolting to their huts—and there was excuse, for this wanderer with the glazed eyes was sick to death, and his disease was that dreaded bush plague which decimates territories. It is an epidemic disease which makes its appearance once in twenty years; it has no known origin and no remedy.

Other diseases: sleeping sickness, beri-beri, malaria, are called by courtesy the sickness mongo—"The Sickness Itself"—but this mysterious malady alone is entitled to the description.

The man fell flat on the ground at the foot of the little hill where Bosambo sat in solitude—his head-

men and councillors fleeing in panic at the sick man's
approach.

Bosambo looked at him thoughtfully.

"What may I do for you, my brother?" he asked.

"Save me," moaned the man.

Bosambo was silent. He was a native, and a native
mind is difficult to follow. I cannot explain its
psychology. The coils were tightening on him, death
faced him as assuredly as it stared hollow-eyed on the
Thing that writhed at his feet.

"I can cure you," he said softly, "by certain magic.
Go you to the far end of the village, there you will
find four new huts and in each hut three beds. Now
you shall lie down on each bed and after you shall go
into the forest as fast as you can walk and wait for my
magic to work."

Thus spake Bosambo, and the man at his feet, with
death's hand already upon his shoulder, listened
eagerly.

"Lord, is there any other thing I must do?" he
asked in the thin whistling tone which is characteristic
of the disease.

"This you must also do," said Bosambo, "you must
go to these huts secretly so that none see you; and on
each bed you shall lie so long as it will take a fish
to die."

Watched from a hundred doorways, the sick man
made his way back to the forest; and the men of the
village spat on the ground as he passed.

Bosambo sent his messengers to Sanders then and
there, and patiently awaited the coming of the emis-
saries of the Goat.

At ten o'clock that night, before the moon was up,
they arrived dramatically. Simultaneously twelve
lights appeared, at twelve points about the village,
then each light advanced at slow pace and revealed a
man bearing a torch.

They advanced at solemn pace until they arrived

together at a meeting place, and that place the open roadway before Bosambo's hut. In a blazing semicircle they stood before the chief—and the chief was not impressed.

For these delegates were a curious mixture. They included a petty chief of the Ochori—Bosambo marked him down for an ignominious end—a fisherman of the Isisi, a witch doctor of the N'Gombi, a hunter of the Calali, and, chiefest of all, a tall, broad-shouldered negro in the garb of white men.

This was Ofalikari, sometime preacher of the Word, and supreme head of the terrible order which was devastating the territories.

As they stood the voice of a man broke the silence with a song. He led it in a nasal falsetto, and the others acted as chorus.

"The White Goat is very strong and his horns are of gold."

"O ai!" chorused the others.

"His blood is red and he teaches mysteries."

"O ai!"

"When his life goes out his spirit becomes a god."

"O ai!"

"Woe to those who stand between the White Goat and his freedom."

"O ai!"

"For his sharp feet will cut them to the bone and his horns will bleed them."

"O ai!"

They sang, one drum tapping rhythmically, the bangled feet of the chorus jingling as they pranced with deliberation at each "O ai!"

When they had finished, Ofalikari spoke.

"Bosambo, we know you to be a wise man, and acquainted with white people and their gods, even as I am, for I was a teacher of the blessed Word. Now the White Goat loves you, Bosambo, and will do you no injury. Therefore have we come to summon you to a big palaver to-morrow, and to that palaver we will summon Sandi to answer for his wickedness. Him we will burn slowly, for he is an evil man."

"Lord Goat," said Bosambo, "this is a big matter, and I will ask you to stay with me this night, that I may be guided and strengthened by your lordships' wisdom. I have built you four new huts," he went on, "knowing that your honours were coming; here you shall be lodged, and by my heart and my life no living man shall injure you."

"No dead man can, Bosambo," said Ofalikari, and there was a rocking shout of laughter. Bosambo laughed too; he laughed louder and longer than all the rest, he laughed so that Ofalikari was pleased with him.

"Go in peace," said Bosambo, and the delegates went to their huts.

In the early hours of the morning Bosambo sent for Tomba, an enemy and a secret agent of the society.

"Go to the great lords," he said, "tell them I come to them to-night by the place where the Isisi River and the big river meet. And say to them that they must go quickly, for I do not wish to see them again, lest our adventure does not carry well, and Sandi punish me."

At daybreak with his cloak of monkey tails about him—for the dawn was chilly—he watched the delegation leave the village and each go its separate way.

He noted that Tomba accompanied them out of sight. He wasted half an hour, then went to his hut and emerged naked save for his loin cloth, his great shield on his left arm, and in the hand behind the shield a bundle of throwing spears.

To him moved fifty fighting men, the trusted and the faithful, and each carried his wicker war shield obliquely before him.

And the Ochori people, cowards at heart, watched the little company in awe.

They stood waiting, these fierce, silent warriors, till at a word they marched till they came to the four huts where Bosambo's guests had lain. Here they waited again. Tomba came in time and stared uneasily at the armed rank.

"Tomba," said Bosambo gently, "did you say farewell to the Goat lords?"

"This I did, chief," said Tomba.

"Embracing them as is the Goat custom?" asked Bosambo more softly still.

"Lord, I did this."

Bosambo nodded.

"Go to that hut, O Tomba, great Goat and embracer of Goats."

Tomba hesitated, then walked slowly to the nearest hut. He reached the door, and half turned.

"Slay!" whispered Bosambo, and threw the first spear.

With a yell of terror the man turned to flee, but four spears struck him within a space of which the palm of a hand might cover and he rolled into the hut, dead.

Bosambo selected another spear, one peculiarly prepared, for beneath the spear head a great wad of dried grass had been bound and this had been soaked in copal gum.

A man brought him fire in a little iron cup and he set it to the spear, and with a jerk of his palm sent the blazing javelin to the hut's thatched roof.

In an instant it burst into flame—in ten minutes the four new houses were burning fiercely.

And on the flaming fire, the villagers, summoned to service, added fresh fuel and more and more, till the sweat rolled down their unprotected bodies. In the afternoon Bosambo allowed the fire to die down. He sent two armed men to each of the four roads that led into the village, and his orders were explicit.

"You shall kill any man or woman who leaves this

place," he said; "also you shall kill any man or woman who, coming in, will not turn aside. And if you do not kill them, I myself will kill you. For I will not have the sickness mongo in my city, lest our lord Sandi is angry."

*   *   *   *   *

Sanders, waiting for he knew not what, heard the news, and went steaming to headquarters, sending pigeons in front asking for doctors. A week later he came back with sufficient medical stores to put the decks of the *Zaire* awash, but he came too late. The bush plague had run its course. It had swept through cities and lands and villages like a tempest, and strange it was that those cities which sent delegates to Bosambo suffered most, and in the N'Gombi city to which Ofalikari stumbled to die, one eighth of the population were wiped out.

"And how has it fared with you, Bosambo?" asked Sanders when the medical expedition came to Ochori.

"Lord," said Bosambo, "it has passed me by."

There was a doctor in the party of an inquiring mind.

"Ask him how he accounts for his immunity," he said to Sanders, for he had no knowledge of the vernacular, and Sanders repeated the question.

"Lord," said Bosambo with simple earnestness, "I prayed very earnestly, being, as your lordship knows, a bueno Catolico."

And the doctor, who was also a "good Catholic," was so pleased that he gave Bosambo a sovereign and a little writing pad—at least he did not give Bosambo the latter, but it is an indisputable fact that it was in the chief's hut when the party had gone.

XVI

THE CRIME OF SANDERS

IT is a fine thing to be confidential clerk to a million-aire, to have placed to your credit every month of your life the sum of forty-one pounds thirteen shillings and fourpence.

This was the experience of a man named Jordon, a young man of considerable character, as you shall learn.

He had a pretty wife and a beautiful baby, and they were a contented and happy little family.

Unfortunately the millionaire died, and though he left "£100 to my secretary, Derik Arthur Jordon," the sum inadequately compensated young Jordon for the forty-one pounds thirteen shillings and fourpence which came to his banker with monotonous regularity every month.

A millionaire's confidential clerk is a drug on the market which knows few millionaires, and those ad-mirably suited in the matter of secretaries. The young man spent six months and most of his money before he came to understand that his opportunities were limited.

Had he been just an ordinary clerk, with the re-quisite knowledge of shorthand and typewriting, he would have found no difficulty in securing employ-ment. Had he had an acquaintance with a thousand and one businesses he might have been "placed," but he had specialised in millionaires—an erratic million-aire whose memory and purse and *Times* he was—and the world of business had no opening for his undis-puted qualities. He had exactly £150 left of his savings and his legacy, when the fact was brought home to him.

Then it happened, that returning to his suburban home one evening, he met a man who had just met another man, who on a capital of a few pounds had amassed a fortune by trading on the West Coast of Africa.

Jordon sought an introduction to the friend and they met in the splendour of a West End hotel, where the trader drank whiskey and talked of his "little place at Minehead."

"It's dead easy," he said, "especially if you get into a country which isn't overrun by traders, like Sanders' territory. But of course that's impossible. Sanders is a swine to traders—won't have them in his territory. He's a sort of little god. . . ."

He drew a picture of the wonderful possibilities of such a field, and the young man went home full of the prospect.

He and his pretty wife sat up till the early hours of the morning discussing the plan. They got a map of Africa showing the territory over which Mr. Commissioner Sanders had dominion. It seemed absurdly small, but it was a little map.

"I wonder what he is like?" asked the girl thoughtfully. She concealed her own agony of mind at the prospect of parting with him, because she was a woman, and women are very extraordinary in their unselfishness.

"Perhaps he would let you go in," she said wistfully. "I am sure he would if he knew what it meant to us."

Jordon shook his head a little ruefully.

"I don't suppose that our position will have much influence with him. Ammett says that he's a very strict man and unpleasant to deal with."

They went into the cost of the expedition. By selling up the furniture and moving into lodgings it could be done. He could leave her fifty or sixty pounds, sufficient to last her with economy for a year. The rest he would sink into goods—a list of which the successful trader had given him.

Some weeks later Jordon took the great step.

He sailed from Liverpool with a stock of gew-gaws and cloth, and, as the tiny figure of his weeping girl-wife grew more and more indistinct on the quay, he realised, as all men realise sooner or later, that death is not the most painful of humanity's trials.

He changed his ship at Grand Bassam for the accommodation of a small steamer.

He did not confide his plans to the men he met on board—hard-drinking men in white duck—but what he learnt of Sanders made his heart sink.

Sanders went down to the beach to meet the steamer, which usually brought the mails.

A tall young man in white sprang from the boat and a portmanteau followed. Sanders looked at the newcomer with suspicion. He did not love strangers —his regulation in this respect was known from Dacca to Mossamades and the phrase "Sanders' Welcome" had become idiomatic.

"Good morning," said Jordon, with his heart quaking.

"Good morning," said Sanders; "do you want to see me? I am afraid you will not have much time, the boat does not stay very long."

The newcomer bit his lip.

"I am not going on yet," he said, "I—I want to stay here."

"Oh!" said Sanders, without enthusiasm.

In the cool of the verandah over an iced drink the young man spoke without reserve.

"I've come out here to make a fortune, or at any rate a living," he said, and the thought of her he had left in her tiny lodging gave him courage.

"You've come to a very unlucky place," said Sanders, smiling in spite of his resentment at this intrusion on his privacy.

"That is why I came," said the other with surprising boldness; "all the likely places are used up, and I have got to justify my existence somehow."

And without attempting to hide his own poverty or his inexperience, he told his story.

The Commissioner was interested. This side of life, as the young man recited it, was new to him; it was a life which he himself did not know or understand, this struggle for existence in a great uncaring city.

"You seem to have had the average kind of bad luck," he said simply. "I can't advise you to go back because you have burned your boats, and in the second place because I am pretty sure that you would not go. Let me think."

He frowned at the police huts shimmering in the morning heat: he sought inspiration in the glimpse of yellow sands and thundering seas which was obtainable from whence he sat.

"I could find work for you," he said, "if you spoke any of the languages, which of course you do not, or if——" He was silent.

"I am supposed to have an assistant," he said at last, "I could appoint you——"

The young man shook his head.

"That's good of you, sir," he said, "but I'd be no use to you. Give me a trader's licence. I believe you've got authority to do so, in fact nobody else seems to have that authority."

Sanders grinned. There was a licence once issued by the Administrator's secretary to an Eurasian trader —but that story will keep.

"I'll give you the licence," he said after a pause, and the young man's heart leapt; "it will cost you a guinea to start with, all the money you've got eventually, and in course of time you will probably add to the bill of costs your health and your life."

He issued the licence that day.

For a couple of weeks the young man remained his guest whilst his stores came on from Sierra Leone.

Sanders found an interpreter and headman for him, and the young man started off in his new canoe to wrestle with fortune, after a letter to his wife in which he described Sanders as something between a Peabody and an angel.

Before he went Sanders gave him a few words of advice.

"I do not like traders," he said, "and I never issue a licence unless I can help it: do not upset my people, do not make any kind of trouble. Avoid the N'Gombi, who are thieves and the bush people, who are chronically homicidal. The Isisi will buy salt with rubber— there is plenty of rubber in the back country. The Ochori will buy cloth with gum—by the way, Bosambo, the chief, speaks English and will try to swindle you. Good-bye and good luck."

He watched the canoe till it disappeared round the bluff, and went back to his hut to record the departure in his diary.

After which he sat himself down to decipher a long despatch in Arabic from one of his intelligence men— a despatch which dealt minutely with three other strangers who had come to his land, and arriving mysteriously, had as mysteriously disappeared.

These were three men who dwelt by the River, being of no village, and of no defined race, for they were settled on the border-line between Akasava, Isisi, and Ochori, and though one had the lateral face-marks of a Bogindi man, yet there was little doubt that he was not of that people.

They lived in three huts set side by side and they fished and hunted. A strange fact was that none of these men had wives.

For some reason which the psychologist will understand, the circumstances isolated the three from their kind. Women avoided them, and when they came to the adjacent village to sell or to buy, the girls and the young matrons went into their huts and peered at them fearfully.

The chief of the three was named M'Karoka—or so

it sounded—and he was a broad, tall man, of surly countenance, sparing of speech, and unpleasant in dispute. He accounted himself outside of all the village laws, though he broke none, and as he acted and thought so did his fellows.

Their lives if strange were inoffensive, they did not steal nor abuse the privileges which were theirs. They were honest in their dealings and cleanly.

Sanders, who had made inquiries through channels which were familiar enough to those who understand the means by which a savage country is governed, received no ill-report, and left the three to their own devices. They fished, hunted, grew a little maize in a garden they won from the forest, sought for and prepared manioc for consumption, and behaved as honest husbandmen should do.

One day they disappeared.

They vanished as though the earth had opened and swallowed them up. None saw their going. Their huts were left untouched and unspoiled, their growing crops stood in the gardens they had cultivated, the dying fish hung on lines between poles just as they had placed them, and the solitary canoe they shared was left beached.

But the three had gone. The forest, impenetrable, unknown, had swallowed them, and no more was heard of them.

Sanders, who was never surprised and took it for granted that the most mysterious of happenings had a natural explanation, did no more than send word to the forest villages asking for news of the three men.

This was not forthcoming, and the matter ended so far as the Commissioner was concerned.

He heard of Jordon throughout the year. Letters addressed to his wife came to headquarters, and were forwarded. His progress from village to village was duly charted by Sanders' agents. Such accounts as reached Sanders were to the effect that the young man was finding it difficult to make both ends meet. The rubber that arrived at irregular intervals for shipment was not of the best quality, and one load of gum was lost in the river by the overturning of a canoe. Sanders, knowing the young man's story, was worried, and caused word to go up river that patronage of the trader would be pleasing to the Commissioner.

Then one day, a year after he had set forth, he unexpectedly turned up at headquarters, thinner, burnt black by the sun, and the possessor of a straggling beard.

He came in an old canoe with four paddlers, and he brought nothing with him save his rifle, his cooking pots and bedding.

His clothes were patched and soiled, he wore clumsy moccasins of skins, and a helmet which was no longer white and was considerably battered.

He had learnt something and greeted Sanders fluently in the Bomongo dialect.

"Chasi o!" he said, with a bitter little laugh, as he stepped from the canoe, and that word meant "finished" in a certain River dialect.

"As bad as that?" said Sanders.

"Pretty nearly," replied the other. "I'm no trader, Mr. Sanders, I'm a born philanthropist."

He laughed again and Sanders smiled in sympathy.

"I've seen a lot of life," he said, "but it doesn't pay dividends."

Sanders took him to the residency and found a suit that nearly fitted him.

"I'll have just one more try," Jordon went on, "then I light out for another field."

There were letters awaiting him—letters of infinite sweetness and patience. Letters filled with heroic lies —but too transparent to deceive anybody.

The young man read them and went old-looking.

There were remittances from his agent at Sierra

Leone—very small indeed these were, after commission and the like had been subtracted.

Still there was enough to lay in a fresh trading stock, and three weeks later the young man again disappeared into the unknown.

His departure from headquarters coincided with the return of one of the mysterious three.

*　　　*　　　*　　　*　　　*

He came back alone to the place by the River. The huts had disappeared, the garden was again forest, the canoe rotted on the beach—for none had dared disturb it.

He set to work to rebuild a hut. He cleared the garden unaided, and settled down in solitude to the routine of life. He was the chief of the three men, M'Karoka, and like the two men who had disappeared, a man of splendid physique.

Sanders heard of his return and the next time he passed that way he landed.

The man was squatting before his fire, stirring the contents of a steaming pot as Sanders came into sight round the hut which had screened his landing.

He leapt to his feet nimbly, looked for a moment as though he would run away, thought better of it, and raised his hand palm outward in salute.

"Inkoos," he said in a deep booming voice.

It was an unusual greeting, yet dimly familiar.

"I bring happiness," said Sanders, using a form of speech peculiar to the Ochori. "Yet since you are a stranger I would ask you what you do, and why do you dwell apart from your own people, for I am the King's eye and see for him?"

The man spoke slowly, and it was evident to Sanders that the Ochori was not his speech, for he would sometimes hesitate for a word and sometimes fill the deficiency with a word of Swaheli.

"I am from a far country, lord chief," he said, "and

my two cousins. Many moons we journeyed, and we
came to this place. Then for certain reasons we
returned to our land. And when we did that which
we had to do, we started to come back. And one
named Vellim was killed by a lion and another died of
sickness, and I came alone and here I sit till the appointed time."

There was a ring of truth in the man's speech.

Sanders had an instinct for such truth, and he knew
that he had not lied.

"What are your people?" he asked; "for it is plain
to me that your are a foreigner and like none that
I know save one race, the race of the great one
Ketchewayo."

"You have spoken, lord," said the man gravely;
"for though I eat fish, I am of the Zulu people, and I
have killed men."

Sanders eyed him in silence. It was an astounding
statement the man made, that he had walked four
thousand miles across desert and river and forest,
through a hundred hostile nations, had returned
thence four thousand miles with his companions and
again covered the distance.

Yet he was indisputably a Zulu—Sanders knew that
much from the moment he had raised his hand in
salute and greeted him as a "prince."

"Rest here," he said, "keep the law and do ill to
none, and you shall be as free as any man—it is
finished."

Sanders pursued a leisurely way down the river, for
no pressing matter called him, either to headquarters
or to any particular village.

He passed Jordon's canoe going up stream, and
megaphoned a cheery greeting.

The young man, though the reverse of cheerful,
responded, waving his hand to the white-clad figure
on the bridge of the *Zaire*.

It was with a heavy heart he went on. His stock was

dwindling, and he had little to show for his labours. Not even the most tempting and the most gaudy of Manchester goods had induced the lazy Isisi to collect rubber. They offered him dried fish, tiny chickens and service for his desirable cloth and beads, but rubber or gum they were disinclined to collect.

Night was coming on when he made the hut of the solitary stranger.

He directed his paddlers to the beach and landed for the night. Whilst his four men lit a fire he went on to the hut.

M'Karoka with folded arms watched his approach.

No other man on the river but would have hastened forward to pay tribute, for black is black and white is white, whether the white man be commissioner or trader.

Jordon had been long enough on the River to see in the attitude of indifference a hint of ungraciousness.

Yet the man was polite.

Together they sat and haggled over the price of a piece of cloth—M'Karoka had no use for beads—and when Jordon set his little tent up on the shore, the man was helpful and seemed used to the peculiar ways of tents.

But the most extraordinary circumstance was that M'Karoka had paid for his purchase in money. He had entered his hut when the bargain had been completed and reappeared with a golden sovereign.

He paid four times the value of the cloth, because the negotiations were conducted on a gum basis.

Jordon was thinking this matter out when he retired for the night. It puzzled him, because money, as he knew, was unknown on the River.

He went to sleep to dream of a suburban home and the pale face of his pretty wife.

He woke suddenly.

It was still night. Outside he could hear the swish-swish of the river and the faint murmur of trees.

But these had not awakened him.

There were voices outside the tent, voices that spoke in a language he could not understand.

He pulled on his mosquito boots and opened the fly of the tent.

There was a moon, and he saw M'Karoka standing before his hut and with him was another.

They were quarrelling and the fierce voice of the newcomer was raised in anger.

Then of a sudden, before Jordon could reach his revolver, the stranger stepped back a pace and struck twice at M'Karoka.

Jordon saw the gleam of steel in the moonlight, stooped and found his revolver, and dashed out of the tent. M'Karoka lay upon the ground, and his assailant had dashed for the river.

He leapt into Jordon's canoe. With a stroke he severed the native rope which moored the craft to the shore, and paddled frantically to midstream.

Three times Jordon fired at him. At the third shot he slid overboard like a man suddenly tired.

"Swim out and bring the canoe," ordered Jordon and turned his attention to M'Karoka.

The man was dying; it was not necessary to have an extensive knowledge of surgery to see that he was wounded beyond recovery.

Jordon attempted to plug the more terrible of the chest wounds and to arrest the bleeding. The Zulu opened his eyes.

"Baas," he said faintly, "what came of Vellim?"*

"I think he is dead," said Jordon.

M'Karoka closed his eyes.

"Listen, baas," he said after a while, "you will tell Sandi that I lied when I said Vellim was dead, though all else was true—we each took our share of the stones —then we went back because they were no use to us in this far land—and some we changed for money—

* This man's name was probably Wilhelm or William.

then we had to fly—and Vellim tried to kill us so that
he might have all—and we beat him, taking from him
his stones, and he ran into the forest——"

He paused, for he found difficulty in speaking.

When he spoke again it was in a language which
Jordon could not understand—the language the men
had spoken when they quarrelled.

He spoke vehemently, then seemed to realise that he
was not understood, for he changed his speech to the
Ochori dialect.

"Under the fire in my hut," he gasped, "are many
stones, master—they are for you, because you killed
Vellim——"

He died soon afterwards.

In the morning Jordon cleared away the ashes of the
fire, and dug through the baked earth. Two feet below
the surface he came upon a parcel wrapped in in-
numerable coverings of native cloth.

He opened it eagerly, his hands shaking.

There were twenty or thirty pebbles varying in size
from a marble to a pea. They were of irregular size
and mouse-coloured.

Jordon found his training as secretary to a South
African millionaire helpful, for he knew these to be
uncut diamonds.

*   *   *   *   *

Sanders listened to the story incoherently told.

Jordon was beside himself with joy.

"Think of it, Mr. Sanders," he said, "think of that
dear little wife of mine and that dear kiddie. They're
nearly starving, I know it—I can read between the
lines of her letter. And at a moment when everything
seems to be going wrong, this great fortune comes——"

Sanders let him rave on, not attempting to check
him. The homeward-bound steamer lay in the road-
stead, her launch bobbed and swayed in the swell by
the beach.

16

"You arrived in time," said Sanders grimly; "if I were you I should forget that you ever told me anything about this affair—and I shouldn't talk about it when you get home if I were you. Good-bye."

He held out his hand and Jordon gripped.

"You've been kindness itself," he began.

"Good-bye," said the Commissioner; "you'd better run or the launch will go without you."

He did not wait to see the last of the trader, but turned abruptly and went back to the residency.

He opened his desk and took out a printed document.

"To all Commissioners, Magistrates, Chiefs of Police, and Deputy Commissioners:

"Wanted on a warrant issued by the Chief Magistrate of Kimberley, Villim Dobomo, Joseph M'Karoka, Joseph Kama, Zulus, charged with illicit diamond buying, and believed to be making their way northward through Baroskeland, Angola and the Congo. Accused men disappeared from Kimberley two years ago, but have been seen recently in the neighbourhood of that town. It is now known that they have returned north."

At the foot of the communication was a written note from Sanders' chief:

"Please state if anything is known of these men."

Sanders sat staring at the document for a long time. It was of course his duty to report the matter and confiscate the diamonds in the possession of Jordon.

"A young wife and a baby," said Sanders thoughtfully; "how infernally improvident these people are!"

He took up his pen and wrote:

"Unknown: Sanders."

XVII

SPRING OF THE YEAR

THE life of one of His Britannic Majesty's Commissioners of Native Territories is necessarily a lonely one. He is shut off from communion with those things which men hold most dear. He is bound as by a steel wall to a life which has no part and no harmony with the life to which his instincts call him, and for which his early training, no less than the hereditary forces within him, have made no preparation. He lives and thinks with black people, who are children of thought, memory and action.

They love and hate like children; they are without the finesse and subtlety which is the possession of their civilised brethren, and in their elementary passions rather retrograde toward the common animal stock from whence we have all sprung, than progress to the nicenesses of refinement.

And white men who live with them and enter into their lives whole-heartedly become one of two things, clever children or clever beasts.

I make this bald statement; the reader must figure out the wherefore.

Sanders came down the river in the spring of the year, in a thoughtful mood. Under the striped awning which covered the bridge of his stern-wheeler he sat in a deep-seated lounge chair, his book on his knees, but he read little.

His eyes wandered idly over the broad, smooth surface of the big river: they followed the line of the dark N'Gombi forest to the left, and the flat rolling land of the Isisi to the right. They were attracted by the blue-grey smoke which arose from this village and that.

The little fishing canoes, anchored in likely places, the raucous call of the parrots overhead, the peering faces of the little monkeys of which he caught glimpses, when the *Zaire* moved to deep water in shore, all these things interested him and held him as they had not interested him since—oh, since quite a long time ago.

As he came abreast of a village he pulled the cord which controlled the siren, and the little steamer hooted a welcome to the waving figures on the beach.

With his fly whisk in his hand, and his unread book on his knee, he gazed by turns absently and interestedly at the landscape.

Bogindi, the steersman, who stood in the shadow of the awning with his hand on the wheel, called him by name.

"Lord, there is a man in a canoe ahead who desires to speak with your lordship."

Sanders shaded his eyes. Directly in the course of the steamer a canoe lay broadside on, and standing upright was a man whose outstretched arms spoke of desire for an urgent palaver.

Now only matters of great moment, such as rebellion and the like, justify holding up the King's ship on the river.

Sanders leapt forward in his chair and pulled over the handle of the telegraph to "Stop," then to "Astern Easy."

He rose and took a survey of the man through his glasses.

"This is a young man, Abiboo," he said, "and I think of the Isisi people; certainly he is no chief to bid me halt."

"He may be mad, lord," said Abiboo; "in the spring of the year the Isisi do strange things, as all men know."

The *Zaire* came slowly to the canoe, and its occupant, wielding his paddles scientifically, brought his little craft alongside and stepped aboard.

"Who are you?" asked Abiboo, "and what great matter have you in hand that you stop our lord on his splendid way?"

" I am Kobolo of the Isisi, of the village of Togo-bonobo," said the young man, "and I love a chief's daughter."

"May God send you to the bottom of the waters," swore the wrathful Abiboo, "that you bring your vile body to this ship; that you disturb our lord in his high meditations. Come thou, Kaffir, and whilst you speak with Sandi, I go to find the whip he will surely order for you."

Thus Kobolo came before Sanders and Abiboo introduced him in words which were not flattering.

"This is a strange palaver," said Sanders not un-kindly, "for it is not the practice for young men to stop the ship of the King's Commissioner because they love maidens."

The young man was tall, straight of back, and well made of shoulder, and he showed no remorse for his outrageous conduct. Rather there was an air about him of desperate earnestness.

"Lord," he said, "I love Nimimi, who is the daughter of my chief, the chief of the village of Togo-bonobo. And because she is a beautiful dancer, and men come from afar to see her, her father demands two thousand rods for her, and I am a poor man."

" 'The father is always right,' " quoted Sanders, "for it is said on the River, 'A thing is worth its price and that which you give away is worth nothing.' "

"This woman loves me," said the youth, "and be-cause of her I have saved a thousand matakos, which, as your lordship knows, is a great fortune."

"What can I do?" asked Sanders, with one of his rare smiles.

"Lord, you are all-powerful," said the agitated young man, "and if you say to the chief her father——"

Sanders shook his head.

"That may not be," he said.

There was something in the spring air, something responsive in his blood, that inclined him to act as he did, for after a moment's thought he turned to Abiboo.

"Take this man," he said, "and give him——"

"Lord, I have the whip ready," said Abiboo complacently. "For I knew that your lordship would be offended by this foolish one."

"Give him a thousand matakos from the store, that he may buy the woman of his desire."

Abiboo, a little dazed, went slowly to do his master's bidding.

"Lord," said Kobolo, and fell at the Commissioner's feet, "you are as my father and mother, and I will repay you with good words and thoughts."

"Repay me with matakos," said the practical Sanders. "Go, take your girl, and God help you!"

Yet he was in no cynical mood. Rather there was a gentleness, a mild stirring of emotions long repressed, a strange tenderness in heart, which harmonised with the tenderness of the young green trees, with the play of budding life about him.

He stood watching the native as he paddled to shore, singing a loud song, tuneless save for the tune of joy that ran through it. Wistfully Sanders watched. This man, little better than an animal, yet obedient to the inexorable laws which Sanders in his wisdom defied; hastening, with his brass rods, to a glorious life, to a hut and a wife, and the raising of young children to manhood. To toil and the dangers and vicissitudes of his peculiar lot; but to the fulfilment of his highest destiny.

The Commissioner stood watching him until he saw the canoe ground on the beach, and the man leap lightly ashore and make the boat fast.

Sanders shook his head and turned the handle of the telegraph to "full speed."

He made no pretence at reading; his gaze was abstracted. Presently he rose and walked into his cabin. He pulled the curtains across the door as though he desired none to witness his folly, then he took a key from his pocket and unlocked the little safe which was let into the wall over the head of his bunk. He opened a drawer and took out a fat brown book.

He laid it upon his desk and turned the leaves.

It was his bank book from the coast agent of Cox, and the balance to his credit ran into five figures, for Sanders had been a careful man all his life, and had bought land at Lagos in the days when you could secure a desirable building lot for the price of a dress suit.

He closed the book, and replacing it in the safe resumed his seat on the bridge.

In the course of the next day he arrived at headquarters.

It was late in the afternoon when the *Zaire* went slowly astern into the little dock, which Sanders with much labour had built.

It was a pretentious little dock, the pride of his days, for it had walls of concrete and a big sluice gate, and it had been erected at the time when the *Zaire* had undergone her repairs. Sanders never saw that dock without a feeling of intense gratification. It was the "child" which awaited his return; the creation of his mind which welcomed him back.

And there was a concrete footpath from the dock to the residency—this he had built. On each side Isisi palms had been planted—the work of his hands. They seemed pitiably insignificant.

He surveyed the residency without joy.

It stood on a little rise; from its corrugated roof to its distempered stoep, a model of neatness and order.

"God bless the place!" said Sanders irritably.

For its old charm had departed; the old pleasant home-coming had become a bleak and wearisome business. And the house was lonely and needed something.

It needed a touch which he could not supply.

He walked disconsolately through the rooms, lit a pipe, knocked it out again, and wandered vaguely in the direction of the Houssas lines.

Captain Hamilton, of the King's Houssas, in white shirt and riding breeches, leant over the rail of the stoep and watched him.

"Back again," he said conventionally.

"No," said Sanders disagreeably, "I'm on the top river catching flies."

Hamilton removed his pipe.

"You've been reading the American Sunday Supplements," he said calmly, "which is either a sign of mental decrepitude or the awakening of a much-needed sense of humour."

He called to his servant.

"Ali," he said solemnly, "prepare the lord Sandi such a cup of tea as the houris of paradise will prepare for the Khalifa on the great day."

"What rot you talk, Hamilton!" said Sanders irritably when the man had gone. "You know well enough the Khalifa would drink nothing but Turkish coffee on that occasion."

"Who knows?" asked the philosophical Hamilton. "Well, and how are all your good people?"

"They're all right," said Sanders, seating himself in a big chair.

"The usual murders, witchcraft and pillage," Hamilton grinned. "Bosambo the virtuous sitting on the foreshore of the Ochori, polishing his halo and singing comic songs!"

"Bosambo—oh, he's subdued just now!" said Sanders, stirring the tea which the man had brought, "he's the best chief on this river, Hamilton," the other nodded, "if I had my way—if I were the British Government—I'd make him paramount chief of all these territories."

"You'd have a war in ten minutes," said the Houssa skipper, "but he's a good man. Depressed, was he?"

"Horribly—I've never seen him so worried, and I'm blest if I know why!"

Hamilton smiled.

"Which shows that a poor devil of a soldier, who is not supposed to be au courant with the gossip of the River, may be wiser than a patent stamped-in-every-link Commissioner," he said. "Bosambo is very fond of that Kano wife of his."

"I know that, my good chap," said Sanders, "and a good wife is half the making of a man. Why, what is a man without——"

He saw the curious laughing eyes of the other watching him, and stopped, and under the tan his eyes went red.

"You're singularly enthusiastic, Sandi Labolo," he said, using the Commissioner's native name; "you're not thinking——"

"What about Bosambo's wife?" interrupted Sanders loudly.

The Houssa was eyeing him suspiciously.

"Bosambo's wife," he repeated, "oh—she goes the way of womankind! Bosambo hopes and fears—after the way of men. He has no child."

"Oh!—I didn't know that, who told you?"

"My men: they are singing a little song about it—I must introduce you to the regimental poet."

There was a long silence after this, neither men talking; then Hamilton asked carelessly:

"You went to Kosumkusu of course?"

"I went—yes," Sanders seemed reluctant to proceed.

"And Miss Glandynne, that medical missionary of ours?"

"She—oh, she was cheerful."

Hamilton smiled.

"I sent her a wad of letters which came by the last mail," he said; "you probably passed the mail canoe on your way down?"

Sanders nodded and there was another pause in the conversation.

"She's rather pretty, isn't she?" asked Hamilton.

"Very," responded Sanders with unnecessary emphasis.

"A very nice girl indeed," Hamilton continued absently.

Sanders made no response for a time—then:

"She is a charming lady, much too good for——"

He checked himself.

"For——?" enticed Hamilton.

"For—for that kind of life," stammered Sanders, hot all over.

He rose abruptly.

"I've got some letters to write," he said and took a hurried departure.

And Hamilton, watching the dapper figure stride along the path toward the residency, shook his head sorrowfully.

Sanders wrote no letters. He began many, tore them up and put the scraps in his pocket. He sat thinking till the servants came to put lights in the room. He hardly tasted his dinner, and the rest of the evening he spent on the stoep staring into the darkness, wondering, hoping, thinking. In the near-by village a wedding feast was in progress, and the mad tattoo of the drum was a fitting accompaniment to his thoughts.

Nor did the next day bring him nearer to a decision, nor the next, nor the next.

She was too good for him—he could not ask her to share his life in a country where none knew what the day would bring forth—a country filled with every known tropical disease, and populated by cannibal peoples who were never certain from day to day to retain their allegiance. It would not be fair to ask it—and yet she had said she loved the country; she was beginning to understand the people. And she could go home in the hot months—he would take his arrears of leave.

And a man ought to be married; he was getting on in years—nearly forty.

A panic seized him.

Perhaps he was too old? That was a terrible supposition. He discovered that he did not know how old he was, and spent two busy days collecting from his private documents authentic evidence. Thus three weeks passed before he wrote his final letter.

During all the period he saw little of the Houssa Captain. He thought once of telling him something of his plans, but funked it at the last.

He turned up at Hamilton's quarters one night.

"I am going up river to-morrow," he said awkwardly. "I leave as soon after the arrival of the homeward-bound mail as possible—I am expecting letters from the Administration."

Hamilton nodded.

"But why this outburst of confidence?" he asked. "You do not often favour me with your plans in advance."

"Well," began Sanders, "I think I was going to tell you something else, but I'll defer that."

He spent the rest of the evening playing picquet and made remarkable blunders.

In the morning he was up before daybreak, superintending the provisioning of the *Zaire*, and when this was completed he awaited impatiently the coming of the mail steamer. When it was only a smudge of black smoke on the horizon, he went down to the beach, though he knew, as a reasonable man, it could not arrive for at least an hour.

He was standing on the sand, his hands behind his back, fidgeting nervously, when he saw Abiboo running toward him.

"Master," said the orderly, "the God-woman is coming."

Sanders' heart gave a leap, and then he felt himself go cold.

"God-woman?" he said, "what—which God-woman?"

"Lord, she we left at the last moon at Kosumkusu."

Sanders ran back across the beach, through the Houssa barracks to the river dock. As he reached the stage he saw the girl's canoe come sweeping round the bend.

He went down to meet her and gave her his hand to assist her ashore.

She was, to Sanders' eyes, a radiant vision of loveliness. Snowy white from head to foot; a pair of grave grey eyes smiled at him from under the broad brim of her topee.

"I've brought you news which will please you," she said; "but tell me first, is the mail steamer gone?"

He found his tongue.

"If it had gone," he said, and his voice was a little husky, "I should not have been here."

Then his throat grew dry, for here was an opening did he but possess the courage to take it; and of courage he had none.

His brain was in a whirl. He could not muster two consecutive thoughts. He said something which was conventional and fairly trite.

"You will come up to breakfast," he managed to say at last, "and tell me—you said I should be pleased about some news."

She smiled at him as she had never smiled before—a mischievous, happy, human smile. Yes, that was what he saw for the first time, the human woman in her.

"I'm going home," she said.

He was making his way towards the residency, and she was walking by his side.

He stopped.

"Going home?" he said.

"I'm going home."

There was a sparkle in her eyes and a colour he had not seen before.

"Aren't you glad? I've been such a nuisance to you —and I am afraid I am rather a failure as a missionary."

It did not seem to depress her unduly, for he saw she was happy.

"Going home?" he repeated stupidly.

She nodded.

"I'll let you into a secret," she said, "for you have been so good a friend to me that I feel you ought to know—I'm going to be married."

"You're going to be married?" Sanders repeated.

His fingers were touching a letter he had written, and which lay in his pocket. He had intended sending it by canoe to her station and arriving himself a day later.

"You are going to be married?" he said again.

"Yes," she said, "I—I was very foolish, Mr. Sanders. I ought not to have come here—I quarrelled—you know the sort of thing that happens."

"I know," said Sanders.

She could not wait for breakfast. The mail steamer came in and sent its pinnace ashore. Sanders saw her baggage stored, took his mail from the second officer, then came to say good-bye to her.

"You haven't wished me—luck," she said.

At the back of her eyes was a hint of a troubled conscience, for she was a woman and she had been in his company for nearly an hour, and women learn things in an hour.

"I wish you every happiness," he said heartily and gripped her hand till she winced.

She was stepping in the boat when she turned back to him.

"I have often wondered——" she began, and hesitated.

"Yes?"

"It is an impertinence," she said hurriedly, "but I have wondered sometimes, and I wonder more now when my own happiness makes me take a greater interest—why you have never married?"

Sanders smiled, that crooked little smile of his.

"I nearly proposed once," he said. "Good-bye and good-luck!"

He left that morning for the Upper River, though the reason for his visit was gone and the ship that carried her to happiness below the western horizon.

Day by day the *Zaire* steamed northward, and there was in her commander's heart an aching emptiness, that made time and space of no account.

One day they came to a village and would have passed, but Abiboo at his side said:

"Lord, this is Togobonobo, where sits the man who your lordship gave a thousand matakos."

Sanders showed his teeth.

"Let us see this happy man," he said in Arabic, "for the Prophet hath said, 'The joy of my friend cleanseth my heart from sorrow.'"

When the *Zaire* reached the shore, Sanders would have sent for the bridegroom, but that young man was waiting, a woe-begone figure that shuffled to the bridge with dejected mien.

"I see," said Sanders, "that the father of your woman asked more than you could pay."

"Lord, I wish that he had," said the youth, "for, lord, I am a sorrowful man."

"Hath the woman died?"

"Lord," said the young man, "if the devils had taken her I should be happy: for this woman, though only a girl, has a great will and does that which she desires, taking no heed of me. And when I speak with her she has a bitter tongue, and, lord, this morning she gave me fish which was not cooked, and called me evil names when I corrected her. Also, lord!" said the youth with a catch in his voice, "the cooking-pot she threw at me before the whole village."

"That is a bad palaver," said Sanders hastily; "now you must give way to her, Tobolo, for she is your wife, and I cannot stay——"

"Lord," said the young man, catching his arm, "I am your debtor, owing you a thousand matakos—now if your lordship in justice will divorce me I will repay you with joy."

"Go in peace," said Sanders, and when the youth showed a reluctance to leave the ship, Abiboo threw him into the water.

The incident gave Sanders food for thought—and there was another matter.

Two days further up the River he came to the Ochori and found Bosambo's people in mourning.

The chief waited his master's coming in the dark of his hut and Sanders went in to see him.

"Bosambo," he said, soberly, "this is bad hearing."

"Lord," moaned the chief, "I wish I were dead— dead as my firstborn who lies in the hut of my wife."

He rocked to and fro in his grief, for Bosambo had the heart of a child, and in this little son, who had counted its existence by days, was centred all the ambition of his life.

"God be with you, Bosambo my brother," said Sanders gently, and laid his hand on the black man's heaving shoulder; "these things are ordained from the beginning of time."

"It is written," whispered Bosambo, between his sobs, and caught his lord's hand.

*   *   *   *   *

Sanders turned his steamer down-river, and that night, when he prepared for bed, the sorrow of his chief was fresh in his mind.

Before he turned in, he took a letter from his

pocket, tore it deliberately into a hundred scraps and threw it from the door of the cabin into the river.

Then he got into his bunk and switched out the light.

He thought of the young man of the Isisi, and he thought of Bosambo.

"Thank God I'm not married," he said, and went to sleep.

THE END